TH[illegible]

The [illegible]nty-first century.

THE PLACE—

A city called New York on the planet Earth.

THE INHABITANTS

are just normal human beings—but now there are too many of them. Far too many. For the raging population explosion has turned the world into a place where multitudes of men and women live in monstrous competition for the basic necessities of existence. The situation has long since gotten out of hand, and now there remains only one final solution—

THE PEOPLE TRAP

THE PEOPLE TRAP

and other Pitfalls,
Snares, Devices and Delusions,
as Well as Two
Sniggles and a Contrivance.

ROBERT SHECKLEY

A DELL BOOK

To Arthur Grunberger

Published by
DELL PUBLISHING CO., INC.
750 Third Avenue
New York, New York 10017

Dell ® TM 681510, Dell Publishing Co., Inc.
Printed in U.S.A.
First printing—December 1968

ACKNOWLEDGMENTS

THE LAST WEAPON and THE ODOR OF THOUGHT: Copyright 1953 by Ballantine Books, Inc.

RESTRICTED AREA originally appeared in *Amazing Stories*. Copyright 1953 by Ultimate Publishing Company.

THE VICTIM FROM SPACE, THE LAXIAN KEY, THE NECESSARY THING, DIPLOMATIC IMMUNITY, GHOST V, PROOF OF THE PUDDING and SHALL WE HAVE A LITTLE TALK? originally appeared in *Galaxy*. Copyright © 1952, 1953, 1954, 1955, 1957, 1965 by Galaxy Publishing Corporation.

FISHING SEASON originally appeared in *Thrilling Wonder Stories*. Copyright 1953 by Standard Magazines, Inc.

CONTENTS

THE PEOPLE TRAP

1

It was Land Race Day—a time of vaunting hope and un-relieved tragedy, a day which epitomized the unhappy twenty-first century. Steve Baxter had tried to reach the starting line early, like the other contestants, but had mis-calculated the amount of time he would require. Now he was in trouble. His Participant's Badge had gotten him through the outer, exocrowd without incident. But neither badge nor brawn could be relied upon to carry a man through the obdurate inner core of humanity which made up the endocrowd.

Baxter estimated this inner mass at 8.7 density—not far from the pandemic level. A flash-point might occur at any moment, despite the fact that the authorities had just aero-soled the endocrowd with tranquilizers. Given enough time, a man might circle around them; but Baxter had only six minutes before the race began.

Despite the risk, he pushed his way directly into their ranks. On his face he wore a fixed smile—absolutely essen-tial when dealing with a high-density human configuration. He could see the starting line now, a raised dais in Jersey City's Glebe Park. The other contestants were already there. Another 20 yards, Steve thought; if only the brutes don't stampede!

But deep within the corecrowd he still had to penetrate the final nuclear mob. This was composed of bulky, slack-jawed men with unfocused eyes—agglutinating hysterophil-iacs, in the jargon of the pandemiologists. Jammed togeth-er sardine fashion, reacting as a single organism, these men were incapable of anything but blind resistance and irra-tional fury toward anything that tried to penetrate their ranks.

Steve hesitated for a moment. The nuclear mob, more

dangerous than the fabled water buffaloes of antiquity, glared at him, their nostrils flared, their heavy feet shuffling ominously.

Without allowing himself time to think, Baxter plunged into their midst. He felt blows on his back and shoulders and heard the terrifying *urrr* of a maddened endomob. Shapeless bodies jammed against him, suffocating him, relentlessly pressing closer and closer.

Then, providentially, the authorities turned on the Muzak. This ancient and mysterious music, which for over a century had pacified the most intractable berserkers, did not fail now. The endomob was decibeled into a temporary immobility, and Steve Baxter clawed his way through to the starting line.

The chief judge had already begun to read the Prospectus. Every contestant and most of the spectators, knew this document by heart. Nevertheless, by law the terms had to be stated.

"Gentlemen," the judge read, "you are here assembled to take part in a race for the acquisition of public-domain lands. You 50 fortunate men have been chosen by public lottery from 50 million registrants in the South Westchester region. The race will proceed from this point to the registration line at the Land Office in Times Square, New York—an adjusted approximate mean distance of 5.7 statute miles. You contestants are permitted to take any route; to travel on the surface, above, or below ground. The only requirement is that you finish in person, substitutes not being permitted. The first ten finalists—"

The crowd became deathly still.

"—will each receive one acre of unencumbered land complete with house and farming implements. And each finalist will also be granted free government transportation to his freehold, for himself and for his immediate family. And this aforesaid acre shall be his to have and to hold, free and clear, perpetually unalienable, as long as the sun shines and water flows, for him and his heirs, even unto the third generation!"

The crowd sighed when they heard this. Not a man among them had ever seen an unencumbered acre, much less dreamed of possessing one. An acre of land entirely for yourself and your family, an acre which you didn't have to share with anyone—well, it was simply beyond the wildest fantasy.

"Be it further noted," the judge went on, "the government accepts no responsibility for deaths incurred during this contest. I am obliged to point out that the unweighted average mortality rate for Land Races is approximately 68.9 per cent. Any contestant who so wishes may withdraw now without prejudice."

The judge waited, and for a moment Steve Baxter considered dropping the whole suicidal idea. Surely he and Adele and the kids and Aunt Flo and Uncle George could continue to get by somehow in their cozy one-room apartment in Larchmont's Fred Allen Memorial Median Income Housing Cluster. After all, he was no man of action, no muscled bravo or hairy-fisted brawler. He was a systems-deformation consultant, and a good one. And he was also a mild-mannered ectomorph with stringy muscles and a distinct shortness of breath. Why in God's name should he thrust himself into the perils of darkest New York, most notorious of the Jungle Cities?

"Better give it up, Steve," a voice said, uncannily echoing his thoughts.

Baxter turned and saw Edward Freihoff St. John, his wealthy and obnoxious neighbor from Larchmont. St. John, tall and elegant and whipcord-strong from his days on the paddle-ball courts. St. John, with his smooth, saturnine good looks, whose hooded eyes were too frequently turned toward Adele's blonde loveliness.

"You'll never make it, Stevie baby," St. John said.

"That is possible," Baxter said evenly. "But you, I suppose, will make it?"

St. John winked and lay a forefinger alongside his nose in a knowing gesture. For weeks he had been hinting about the special information he had purchased from a venal Land Race comptroller. This information would vastly improve his chances of traversing Manhattan Borough—the densest and most dangerous urban concentration in the world.

"Stay out of it, Stevie baby," St. John said in his peculiar rasping voice. "Stay out, and I'll make it worth your while. Whaddaya say, sweetie pie?"

Baxter shook his head. He did not consider himself a

courageous man; but he would rather die than take a favor from St. John. And in any event, he could not go on as before. Under last month's Codicil to the Extended Families Domicile Act, Steve was now legally obliged to take in three unmarried cousins and a widowed aunt, whose one-room subbasement apartment in the Lake Placid industrial complex had been wiped out by the new Albany-Montreal Tunnel.

Even with antishock injections, ten persons in one room was too much. He simply had to win a piece of land!

"I'm staying," Baxter said quietly.

"OK, sucker," St. John said, a frown marring his hard, sardonic face. "But remember, I warned you."

The chief judge called out, "Gentlemen, on your marks!"

The contestants fell silent. They toed the starting line with slitted eyes and compressed mouths.

"Get ready!"

A hundred sets of leg muscles bunched as 50 determined men leaned forward.

"Go!"

And the race was on!

A blare of supersonics temporarily paralyzed the surrounding mob. The contestants squirmed through their immobile ranks and sprinted over and around the long lines of stalled automobiles. Then they fanned out, but tended mainly to the east, toward the Hudson River and the evil-visaged city that lay on its far shore, half-concealed in its sooty cloak of unburned hydrocarbons.

Only Steve Baxter had not turned to the east.

Alone among the contestants, he had swung north, toward the George Washington Bridge and Bear Mountain City. His mouth was tight, and he moved like a man in a dream.

In distant Larchmont, Adele Baxter was watching the race on television. Involuntarily, she gasped. Her eight-year-old son Tommy cried, "Mom, Mom, he's going north to the Bridge! But it's closed this month. He can't get through that way!"

"Don't worry, darling," Adele said. "Your father knows what he's doing."

She spoke with an assurance she did not feel. And, as the figure of her husband was lost in the crowds, she settled back to wait—and to pray. Did Steve know what he was doing? Or had he panicked under pressure?

2

The seeds of the problem had been sewn in the twentieth century; but the terrible harvest was reaped a hundred years later. After uncounted millenia of slow increase, the population of the world suddenly exploded, doubled, and doubled again. With disease checked and food supplies assured, death rates continued to fall as birthrates rose. Caught in a nightmare geometric progression, the ranks of humanity swelled like runaway cancers.

The four horsemen of the Apocalypse, those ancient policemen, could no longer be relied upon to maintain order. Pestilence and famine had been outlawed, and war was too luxurious for this subsistence age. Only death remained—much diminished, a mere shadow of his former self.

Science, with splendid irrationality, continued to work insensately toward the goal of more life for more people.

And *people* marched on, still increasing, crowding the earth with their numbers, stifling the air and poisoning the water, eating their processed algae between slices of fish-meal bread, dimly awaiting a catastrophe to thin out their unwieldy ranks, and waiting in vain.

The quantitative increase in numbers produced qualitative changes in human experience. In a more innocent age, adventure and danger had been properties of the waste places—the high mountains, bleak deserts, steaming jungles. But by the twenty-first century most of these places were being utilized in the accelerating search for living-space. Adventure and danger were now to be found in the monstrous, ungovernable cities.

In the cities one found the modern equivalent of savage tribes, fearsome beasts, and dread disease. An expedition into New York or Chicago required more resourcefulness and stamina, more ingenuity, than those lighthearted Victorian jaunts to Everest or the source of the Nile.

In this pressure-pot world, land was the most precious of commodities. The government parceled it out as it became available, by means of regional lotteries culminating in land races. These contests were patterned after those held in the 1890s for the opening of the Oklahoma Territory and the Cherokee Strip.

The land race was considered equitable and interesting —both sporty and sporting. Millions watched the races, and the tranquilizing effect of vicarious excitement upon the masses was duly noted and approved. This in itself was sufficient justification for the races.

Additionally, the high mortality rate among the contestants had to be considered an asset. It didn't amount to much in absolute numbers; but a stifled world was grateful for even the smallest alleviation.

The race was three hours old. Steve Baxter turned on his little transistor radio and listened to the latest reports. He heard how the first group of contestants had arrived at the Holland Tunnel and had been turned back by armored policemen. Others, more devious, had taken the long southern trek to Staten Island and were presently approaching the approaches of the Verrazzano Bridge. Freihoff St. John, all by himself, flashing a deputy mayor's badge, had been allowed past the Lincoln Tunnel barricades.

But now it was time for Steve Baxter's gamble. Grimfaced, with quiet courage, he entered the infamous Free Port of Hoboken.

3

It was dusk on the Hoboken foreshore. Before him, in a sweeping crescent, lay the trim, swift ships of the Hoboken smuggling fleet, each with its gleaming Coast Guard medallion. Some already had cargo lashed to their decks—cases of cigarettes from North Carolina, liquor from Kentucky, oranges from Florida, goof balls from California, guns from Texas. Each case bore the official marking, "CONTRABAND—TAX PAID." For in this unhappy day and age, the hard-pressed government was forced to tax even illegal enterprises, and thus to give them a quasi-legal status.

Choosing his moment carefully, Baxter stepped aboard a rakish marijuana runner and crouched down among the aromatic bales. The craft was ready for imminent departure; if he could only conceal himself during the short passage across the river . . .

"Har! What in hell have we here?"

A drunken second engineer, coming up unexpectedly from the fo'c'sle, had caught Baxter unawares. Responding to his shout, the rest of the crew swarmed onto the deck. They were a hard-bitten, swaggering lot, feared for their casually murderous ways. These were the same breed of Godless men who had sacked Weehawken some years ago, had put Fort Lee to the torch, had raided and pillaged all the way to the gates of Englewood. Steve Baxter knew that he could expect no mercy from them.

Nevertheless, with admirable coolness, he said, "Gentlemen, I am in need of transportation across the Hudson, if you please."

The ship's captain, a colossal mestizo with a scarred face and bulging muscles, leaned back and bellowed with laughter.

"Ye seek passage of *uns?*" he declared in the broad Hobokenese patois. "Think 'ee we be the Christopher Street ferry, hai?"

"Not at all, sir. But I had hoped—"

"To the boneyard wit' yer hopes!"

The crew roared at the witticism.

"I am willing to pay for my passage," Steve said with quiet dignity.

"*Pay* is it?" roared the captain. "Aye, we sometimes sell passages—nonstop to midstream, and thence straight down!"

The crew redoubled its laughter.

"If it is to be, then let it so be," Steve Baxter said. "I request only that you permit me to drop a postcard to my wife and children."

"Woife and tuckins?" the captain inquired. "Why didn't yer mention! Had that lot myself aforetime ago, until waunders did do marvain to the lot."

"I am sorry to hear that," Steve said with evident sincerity.

"Aye." The captain's iron visage softened. "I do remember how, in oftens colaim, the leetle blainsprites did leap giner on the saern; yes, and it was roses all till diggerdog."

"You must have been very happy," Steve said. He was following the man's statements with difficulty.

"I maun do," the captain said heavily.

A bowlegged little forebow deckman thrust himself forward. "Hi, Captain, let's do for him and get underway before the pot rots on the spot."

"Who you giving orders at, ye mangy, scut-faced hogifier!" the captain raved. "By Big Jesus, we'll let the pot rot till I say not! And as for doing him—nay, I'll do one deed for me blainsprites, shiver me if I won't!" Turning to Baxter, he said, "We'll carry ye, laddie, and for naught ought loot."

Thus, fortuitously, Steve Baxter had touched upon a bittersweet memory in the captain's recollection and had thereby won respite. The marijauna men pushed off, and soon the sleek craft was breasting the sallow gray-green waves of the Hudson.

But Steve Baxter's respite was short-lived. In midstream, just after they entered Federal waters, a powerful searchlight flashed out of the evening gloom and an officious voice ordered them to heave to. Evil luck had steered them straight into the path of a destroyer on the Hudson patrol.

"Damn them!" the captain raved. "Tax and kill, that's all they know! But we'll show them our mettle! To the guns, bullies!"

Swiftly the crew peeled the tarpaulins from the 50-calibre machine guns, and the boat's twin diesels roared defiance. Twisting and dodging, the pot runner raced for the sanctuary of the New York shore. But the destroyer, forereaching, had the legs of her, and machine guns were no match for four-inch cannon. Direct hits splintered the little ship's toe rail, exploded in the great cabin, smashed through the maintop forestays, and chopped down the starboard mizzen halyards.

Surrender or death seemed the only options. But, weatherwise, the captain sniffed the air. "Hang on, hearties!" he screamed. "There's a Wester do be coming!"

Shells rained around them. Then, out of the west, a vast and impenetrable smog bank rolled in, blanketing everything in its inky tentacles. The battered little kif ship slid away from the combat; and the crew, hastily donning respirators, gave thanks to the smoldering trashlands of Secaucus. As the captain remarked, it is an ill wind that blows no good.

Half an hour later they docked at the 79th Street Pier. The captain embraced Steve warmly and wished him good fortune. And Steve Baxter continued on his journey.

The broad Hudson was behind him. Ahead lay 30-odd downtown blocks and less than a dozen crosstown blocks. According to the latest radio report, he was well ahead of the other contestants, ahead even of Freihoff St. John, who still had not emerged from the labyrinth at the New York end of the Lincoln Tunnel. He seemed to be doing very nicely, all things considered.

But Baxter's optimism was premature. New York was not conquered so easily. Unknown to him, the most dangerous parts of his journey still lay before him.

4

After a few hours' sleep in the back of an abandoned car, Steve proceeded southward on West End Avenue. Soon it was dawn—a magical hour in the city, when no more than a few hundred early-risers were to be found at any given intersection. High overhead were the crenellated towers of Manhattan, and above them the clustered television antennae wove a faery tapestry against a dun and ocher sky. Seeing it like that, Baxter could imagine what New York had been like a hundred years ago, in the gracious, easygoing days before the population explosion.

He was abruptly shaken out of his musings. Appearing as if from nowhere, a party of armed men suddenly barred his path. They wore masks, wide-brimmed black hats and bandoliers of ammunition. Their aspect was both villainous and picturesque.

One of them, evidently the leader, stepped forward. He was a craggy-featured, balding old man with a heavy black moustache and mournful red-rimmed eyes. "Stranger," he said, "let's see yore pass."

"I don't believe I have one," Baxter said.

"Damned right you don't," the old man said. "I'm Pablo Steinmetz, and I issue all the passes around here and I don't recollect ever seeing you afore in these parts."

"I'm a stranger here," Baxter said. "I'm just passing through."

The black-hatted men grinned and nudged each other.

Pablo Steinmetz rubbed his unshaven jaw and said, "Well, sonny, it just so happens that you're trying to pass through a private toll road without permission of the owner, who happens to be me; so I reckon that means you're illegally trespassing."

"But how could anyone have a private toll road in the heart of New York City?" Baxter asked.

"It's mine 'cause I say it's mine," Pablo Steinmetz said, fingering the notches on the stock of his Winchester 78. "That's just the way it is, stranger, so I reckon you'd better pay or play."

Baxter reached for his wallet and found it was missing. Evidently the pot-boat captain, upon parting, had yielded to his baser instincts and picked his pocket.

"I have no money," Baxter said. He laughed uneasily. "Perhaps I should turn back."

Steinmetz shook his head. "Going back's the same as going forward. It's toll road either way. You still gotta pay or play."

"Then I guess I'll have to play," Baxter said. "What do I do?"

"You run," Old Pablo said, "and we take turns shooting at you, aiming only at the upper part of your head. First man to bring you down wins a turkey."

"That is infamous!" Baxter declared.

"It *is* kinda tough on you," Steinmetz said mildly. "But that's the way the mortar crumbles. Rules is rules, even in an anarchy. So, therefore, if you will be good enough to break into a wild sprint for freedom . . ."

The bandits grinned and nudged each other and loosened their guns in their holsters and pushed back their wide-brimmed black hats. Baxter readied himself for the death run—

And at that moment, a voice cried, "Stop!"

A woman had spoken. Baxter turned and saw that a tall, red-headed girl was striding through the bandit ranks. She was dressed in toreador pants, plastic galoshes and Hawaiian blouse. The exotic clothing served to enhance her bold beauty. There was a paper rose in her hair, and a string of cultured pearls set off the slender line of her neck. Never had Baxter seen a more flamboyant loveliness.

Pablo Steinmetz frowned and tugged at his moustache. "Flame!" he roared. "What in tarnation are you up to?"

"I've come to stop your little game, Father," the girl said coolly. "I want a chance to talk to this tanglefoot."

"This is man's business," Steinmetz said. "Stranger, git set to run!"

"Stranger, don't move a muscle!" Flame cried, and a deadly little derringer appeared in her hand.

Father and daughter glared at each other. Old Pablo was the first to break the tableau.

"Damn it all, Flame, you can't do this," he said. "Rules is rules, even for you. This here illegal trespasser can't pay, so he's gotta play."

"That's no problem," Flame announced. Reaching inside her blouse she extracted a shiny silver double eagle. "There!" she said, throwing it at Pablo's feet. "I've done the paying, and just maybe I'll do the playing, too. Come along, stranger."

She took Baxter by the hand and led him away. The bandits watched them go and grinned and nudged each other until Steinmetz scowled at them. Old Pablo shook his head, scratched his ear, blew his nose, and said, "Consarn that girl!"

The words were harsh, but the tone was unmistakably tender.

5

Night came to the city, and the bandits pitched camp on the corner of 69th Street and West End Avenue. The black-hatted men lounged in attitudes of ease before a roaring fire. A juicy brisket of beef was set out on a spit, and packages of flash-frozen green vegetables were thrown into a capacious black cauldron. Old Pablo Steinmetz, easing the imaginary pain in his wooden leg, drank deep from a jerry can of premixed Martinis. In the darkness beyond the campfire you could hear a lonely poodle howling for his mate.

Steve and Flame sat a little apart from the others. The night, silent except for the distant roar of garbage trucks, worked its enchantment upon them both. Their fingers met, touched and clung.

Flame said at last, "Steve, you—you do like me, don't you?"

"Why, of course I do," Baxter replied, and slipped his arm around her shoulders in a brotherly gesture not incapable of misinterpretation.

"Well, I've been thinking," the bandit girl said. "I've thought . . ." She paused, suddenly shy, then went on. "Oh, Steve, why don't you give up this suicidal race? Why don't you stay here with me! I've got land, Steve, real land —a hundred square yards in the New York Central Switchyard! You and I, Steve, we could farm it together!"

Baxter was tempted—what man would not be? He had not been unaware of the feelings which the beautiful bandit girl entertained for him, nor was he entirely unresponsive to them. Flame Steinmetz's haunting beauty and proud spirit, even without the added attraction of land, might easily have won any man's heart. For a heartbeat he wavered, and his arm tightened around the girl's slim shoulders.

But then, fundamental loyalties reasserted themselves. Flame was the essence of romance, the flash of ecstacy about which a man dreams throughout his life. Yet Adele was his childhood sweetheart, his wife, the mother of his children, the patient helpmate of the long years together. For a man of Steve Baxter's character, there could be no other choice.

The imperious girl was unused to refusal. Angry as a scalded puma, she threatened to tear out Baxter's heart with her fingernails and serve it up lightly dusted in flour and toasted over a medium fire. Her great flashing eyes and trembling bosom showed that this was no mere idle imagery.

Despite this, quietly and implacably, Steve Baxter stuck to his convictions. And Flame realized sadly that she would never have loved this man were he not replete with the very high principles which rendered her desires unattainable.

So in the morning, she offered no resistance when the quiet stranger insisted upon leaving. She even silenced her irate father, who swore that Steve was an irresponsible fool who should be restrained for his own good.

"It's no use, Dad—can't you see that?" she asked. "He

must lead his own life, even if it means the end of his life."

Pablo Steinmetz desisted, grumbling. And Steve Baxter set out again upon his desperate Odyssey.

6

Downtown he travelled, jostled and crowded to the point of hysteria, blinded by the flash of neon against chrome, deafened by the incessant city noises. He came at last into a region of proliferating signs:

ONE WAY

DO NOT ENTER

KEEP OFF THE MEDIAN

CLOSED SUNDAYS AND HOLIDAYS

CLOSED WEEKDAYS

LEFT LANE *MUST* TURN LEFT!

Winding through this maze of conflicting commands, he stumbled accidentally into that vast stretch of misery known as Central Park. Before him, as far as the eye could see, every square foot of land was occupied by squalid lean-tos, mean teepees, disreputable shacks, and noisome stews. His sudden appearance among the brutalized park inhabitants excited comment, none of it favorable. They got it into their heads that he was a health inspector, come to close down their malarial wells, slaughter their trichinoidal hogs, and vaccinate their scabrous children. A mob gathered around him, waving their crutches and mouthing threats.

Luckily, a malfunctioning toaster in central Ontario triggered off a sudden blackout. In the ensuing panic, Steve made good his escape.

But now he found himself in an area where the street signs had long ago been torn down to confuse the tax assessors. The sun was hidden behind a glaring white overcast. Not even a compass could be used because of the proximity of vast quantities of scrap iron—all that remained of the city's legendary subway system.

Steve Baxter realized that he was utterly and hopelessly lost.

Yet he persevered, with a courage surpassed only by his ignorance. For uncounted days he wandered through the nondescript streets, past endless brownstones, mounds of plate glass, automobile cairns, and the like. The superstitious inhabitants refused to answer his questions, fearing he might be an FBI man. He staggered on, unable to obtain food or drink, unable even to rest for fear of being trampled by the crowds.

A kindly social worker stopped him just as Baxter was about to drink from a hepatitic fountain. This wise gray-haired old man nursed him back to health in his own home —a hut built entirely of rolled newspapers near the moss-covered ruins of Lincoln Center. He advised Baxter to give up his impetuous quest and to devote his life to assisting the wretched, brutalized, superfluous masses of humanity that pullulated on all sides of him.

It was a noble ideal, and Steve came near to wavering; but then, as luck would have it, he heard the latest race results on the social worker's venerable Hallicrafter.

Many of the contestants had met their fates in urban-idiosyncratic ways. Freihoff St. John had been imprisoned for second-degree litterbugging. And the party that crossed the Verrazzano Bridge had subsequently disappeared into the snow-capped fastnesses of Brooklyn Heights and had not been heard from again.

Baxter realized that he was still in the running.

7

His spirits were considerably lifted when he started forth once again. But now he fell into an overconfidence more dangerous than the most profound depression. Journeying rapidly to the south, he took advantage of a traffic lull to step onto an express walkaway. He did this carelessly, without a proper examination of the consequences.

Irrevocably committed, he found to his horror that he was on a one-way route, no turns permitted. This walkaway, he now saw, led nonstop to the *terra incognita* of Jones Beach, Fire Island, Patchogue, and East Hampton.

The situation called for immediate action. To his left

was a blank concrete wall. To his right there was a waist-high partition marked "NO VAULTING ALLOWED BE-TWEEN 12:00 NOON AND 12:00 MIDNIGHT, TUES-DAYS, THURSDAYS AND SATURDAYS."

Today was Tuesday afternoon—a time of interdiction. Nevertheless, without hesitation, Steve vaulted over the barrier.

Retribution was swift and terrible. A camouflaged police car emerged from one of the city's notorious ambushes. It bore down upon him, firing wildly into the crowd. (In this unhappy age, the police were required by law to fire wildly into the crowd when in pursuit of a suspect.)

Baxter took refuge in a nearby candy store. There, recognizing the inevitable, he tried to give himself up. But this was not permitted because of the overcrowded state of the prisons. A hail of bullets kept him pinned down while the stern-faced policemen set up mortars and portable flame-throwers.

It looked like the end, not only of Steve Baxter's hopes, but of his very life. Lying on the floor among gaudy jaw-breakers and brittle licorice whips, he commended his soul to God and prepared to meet his end with dignity.

But his despair was as premature as his earlier optimism had been. He heard sounds of a disturbance and, raising his head, saw that a group of armed men had attacked the police car from the rear. Turning to meet this threat, the men in blue were enfiladed from the flank and wiped out to the last man.

Baxter came out to thank his rescuers and found Flame O'Rourke Steinmetz at their head. The beautiful bandit girl had been unable to forget the soft-spoken stranger. Despite the mumbled objections of her drunken father, she had shadowed Steve's movements and come to his rescue.

The black-hatted men plundered the area with noisy abandon. Flame and Steve retired to the shadowy solitude of an abandoned Howard Johnson's restaurant. There, beneath the peeling orange gables of a gentler, more courteous age, a tremulous love scene was enacted between them. It was no more than a brief, bittersweet interlude, however. Soon, Steve Baxter plunged once again into the ravening maelstrom of the city.

8

Advancing relentlessly, his eyes closed to slits against the driving smog storm and his mouth a grim white line in the lower third of his face, Baxter won through to 49th Street and 8th Avenue. There, in an instant, conditions changed with that disastrous suddenness typical of a Jungle City.

While crossing the street, Baxter heard a deep, ominous roar. He realized that the traffic light had changed. The drivers, frenzied by days of waiting and oblivious to minor obstacles, had simultaneously floored their accelerators. Steve Baxter was directly in the path of a vehicular stampede.

Advance or retreat across the broad boulevard was clearly impossible. Thinking fast, Baxter flung aside a manhole cover and plunged underground. He made it with perhaps a half second to spare. Overhead, he heard the shrieks of tortured metal and the heavy impact of colliding vehicles.

He continued to press ahead by way of the sewer system. This network of tunnels was densely populated, but was marginally safer than the surface roads. Steve encountered trouble only once, when a jackroller attacked him along the margin of a sediment tank.

Toughened by his experiences, Baxter subdued the bravo and took his canoe—an absolute necessity in some of the lower passageways. Then he pushed on, paddling all the way to 42nd Street and 8th Avenue before a flash flood drove him to the surface.

Now, indeed, his long-desired goal was near to hand. Only one more block remained; one block, and he would be at the Times Square Land Office!

But at this moment he encountered the final, shattering obstacle that wrote *finis* to all his dreams.

9

In the middle of 42nd Street, extending without visible limit to the north and south, there was a wall. It was a cyclopean structure, and it had sprung up overnight in the quasi-sentient manner of New York architecture. This,

Baxter learned, was one side of a gigantic new upper middle-income housing project. During its construction, all traffic for Times Square was being rerouted via the Queens-Battery tunnel and the East 37th Street Shunpike.

Steve estimated that the new route would take him no less than three weeks and would lead him through the uncharted Garment District. His race, he realized, was over.

Courage, tenacity and righteousness had failed; and, were he not a religious man, Steve Baxter might have contemplated suicide. With undisguised bitterness, he turned on his little transistor radio and listened to the latest reports.

Four contestants had already reached the Land Office. Five others were within a few hundred yards of the goal, coming in by the open southern approaches. And, to compound Steve's misery, he heard that Freihoff St. John, having received a plenary pardon from the governor, was on his way once more, approaching Times Square from the east.

At this blackest of all possible moments, Steve felt a hand on his shoulder. He turned and saw that Flame had come to him again. Although the spirited girl had sworn to have nothing further to do with him, she had relented. This mild, even-tempered man meant more to her than pride; more, perhaps, than life itself.

What to do about the wall? A simple matter for the daughter of a bandit chief! If one could not go around it or through it or under it, why, one must then go over it! And to this purpose she had brought ropes, boots, pitons, crampons, hammers, axes—a full complement of climbing equipment. She was determined that Baxter should have one final chance at his heart's desire—and that Flame O'-Rourke Steinmetz should accompany him, and not accept no for an answer!

They climbed, side by side, up the building's glass-smooth expanse. There were countless dangers—birds, aircraft, snipers, wise guys—all the risks of the unpredictable city. And, far below, old Pablo Steinmetz watched, his face like corrugated granite.

After an eternity of peril, they reached the top and started down the other side—

And Flame slipped!

In horror Baxter watched the slender girl fall to her doom in Times Square, to die impaled upon the needle-sharp point of a car's aerial. Baxter scrambled down and knelt beside her, almost out of his head with grief.

And, on the other side of the wall, old Pablo sensed that something irrevocable had happened. He shuddered, his mouth writhed in anticipation of grief, and he reached blindly for a bottle.

Strong hands lifted Baxter to his feet. Uncomprehendingly, he looked up into the kindly red face of the Federal Land Clerk.

It was difficult for him to realize that he had completed the race. With curiously deadened emotions, he heard how St. John's pushiness and hauteur had caused a riot in the explosive Burmese Quarter of East 42nd Street, and how St. John had been forced to claim sanctuary in the labyrinthine ruins of the Public Library, from which refuge he still had not been able to extricate himself.

But it was not in Steve Baxter's nature to gloat, even when gloating was the only conceivable response. All that mattered to him was that he had won, had reached the Land Office in time to claim the last remaining acre of land.

All it had cost was effort and pain, and the life of a young bandit girl.

10

Time was merciful; and some weeks later, Steve Baxter was not thinking of the tragic events of the race. A government jet had transported him and his family to the town of Cormorant in the Sierra Nevada mountains. From Cormorant, a helicopter brought them to their prize. A leathery Land Office marshall was on hand to greet them and to point out their new freehold.

Their land lay before them, sketchily fenced, on an almost vertical mountainside. Surrounding it were other similarly fenced acres, stretching as far as the eye could see. The land had recently been strip-mined; it existed now as a series of gigantic raw slashes across a dusty, dun-colored earth. Not a tree or a blade of grass could be seen. There was a house, as promised; more precisely, there was a shack. It looked as if it might last until the next hard rain.

For a few minutes the Baxters stared in silence. Then Adele said, "Oh, Steve."

Steve said, "I know."

"It's our new land," Adele said.

Steve nodded. "It's not very—pretty," he said hesitantly.

"Pretty? What do we care about that?" Adele declared. "It's *ours*, Steve, and there's a whole acre of it! We can *grow* things here, Steve!"

"Well, maybe not at first—"

"I know, I know! But we'll put this land back into shape, and then we'll plant it and harvest it! We'll *live* here, Steve! Won't we?"

Steve Baxter was silent, gazing over his dearly won land. His children—Tommy and blonde little Amelia—were playing with a clod of earth. The U.S. marshall cleared his throat and said, "You can still change your mind, you know."

"What?" Steve asked.

"You can still change your mind, go back to your apartment in the city. I mean, some folks think it's sorta crude out here, sorta not what they was expecting."

"Oh, Steve, no!" his wife moaned.

"No, Daddy, no!" his children cried.

"Go *back?*" Baxter asked. "I wasn't thinking of going *back*. I was just *looking* at it all. Mister, I never saw so much land all in one place in my whole life!"

"I know," the marshall said softly. "I been 20 years out here and the sight of it still gets to me."

Baxter and his wife looked at each other ecstatically. The marshall rubbed his nose and said, "Well, I reckon you folks won't be needin' me no more." He exited inobtrusively.

Steve and Adele gazed out over their land. Then Adele said, "Oh, Steve, Steve! It's all ours! And you won it for us —you did it all by yourself!"

Baxter's mouth tightened. He said very quietly, "No, honey, I didn't do it all alone. I had some help."

"Who, Steve? Who helped you?"

"Someday I'll tell you about it," Baxter said. "But right now—let's go into our house."

Hand in hand they entered the shack. Behind them, the sun was setting in the opaque Los Angeles smog. It was as happy an ending as could be found in the latter half of the twenty-first century.

THE VICTIM FROM SPACE

Hadwell stared at the planet below. A tremor of excitement ran through him, for it was a beautiful world of green plains and red mountains and restless blue-gray seas. His ship's instruments quickly gathered their information and decided that the planet was eminently suited for human life. Hadwell punched a deceleration orbit and opened his notebook.

He was a writer, the author of *White Shadows in the Asteroid Belt*, *The Saga of Deepest Space*, *Wanderings of an Interplanetary Vagabond*, and *Terira—Planet of Mystery!*

He wrote in his notebook, "A new planet looms below me, inviting and mysterious, a challenge to the imagination. What will I find here, I, the vagabond from beyond the stars? What strange mysteries lie beneath the verdant green cover? Will there be danger? Love? Fulfillment? Will there be a resting place for a weary wanderer?"

Richard Hadwell was a tall, thin, redheaded young man. He had inherited a sizable fortune from his father and had invested it in a CC-Class Space Schooner. In this elderly craft, he had voyaged for the past six years and had written ecstatic books about the places he had seen. But most of the ecstacy had been counterfeit, for alien planets were disappointing places.

Aliens, Hadwell had found, were remarkably stupid and amazingly ugly. Their foods were impossible and their manners deplorable. Nevertheless, Hadwell wrote romances and hoped some day to live one.

The planet below was cityless, tropical, beautiful. His ship was already homing on a small thatch-hut village.

"Perhaps I'll find it here," Hadwell said to himself as the spaceship began braking sharply.

Early that morning, Kataga and his daughter, Mele, crossed the bridge of vines to Ragged Mountain, to gather frag blossoms. Nowhere on Igathi did the frag bloom so lustily as it did on Ragged Mountain. And this was as it should be, for the mountain was sacred to Thangookari, the smiling god.

Later in the day they were joined by Brog, a dull-faced youth of no importance whatsoever, except possibly to himself.

Mele had the feeling that something very important was about to happen. She was a tall, slender girl, and she worked as though in a trance, moving slowly and dreamily, her long black hair tossed by the wind. Familiar objects seemed imbued with unusual clarity and significance. She gazed at the village, a tiny cluster of huts across the river, and with wonder looked behind her at the Pinnacle, where all Igathian marriages were performed, and beyond that, to the delicately tinted sea.

She was the prettiest girl in Igathi; even the old priest admitted it. She longed for a dramatic role in life. But day after day passed monotonously in the village, and here she was, picking frag blossoms under two hot suns. It seemed unfair.

Her father gathered energetically, humming as he worked. He knew that the blossoms would soon be fermenting in the village vat. Lag, the priest, would mumble suitable words over the brew, and a libation would be poured in front of Thangookari's image. When these formalities were concluded, the entire village, dogs included, would go on a splendid drunk.

These thoughts made the work go faster. Also, Kataga had evolved a subtle and dangerous scheme to increase his prestige. It made for pleasant speculation.

Brog straightened up, mopped his face with the end of his loincloth, and glanced overhead for signs of rain.

"Hey!" he shouted.

Kataga and Mele looked up.

"There!" Brog screamed. "There, up there!"

High overhead, a silver speck surrounded by red and green flames was descending slowly, growing larger as they watched, and resolving itself into a shiny sphere.

"The prophecy!" Kataga murmured reverently. "At last —after all the centuries of waiting!"

"Let's tell the village!" Mele cried.

"Wait," Brog said. He flushed a fiery red and dug his toe into the ground. "I saw it first, you know."

"Of course you did," Mele said impatiently.

"And *since* I saw it first," Brog continued, "thereby rendering an important service to the village, don't you think —wouldn't it be proper—"

Brog wanted what every Igathian desired, worked and prayed for, and what intelligent men like Kataga cast subtle schemes for. But it was unseemly to call the desired thing by name. Mele and her father understood, however.

"What do you think?" Kataga asked.

"I suppose he *does* deserve something," Mele said.

Brog rubbed his hands together. "Would you, Mele? Would you do it yourself?"

"However," Mele said, "the whole thing is up to the priest."

"Please!" Brog cried. "Lag might not feel I'm ready. Please, Kataga! Do it yourself!"

Kataga studied his daughter's inflexible expression and sighed. "Sorry, Brog. If it was just between us. . . . But Mele is scrupulously orthodox. Let the priest decide."

Brog nodded, completely defeated. Overhead, the shiny sphere dropped lower, toward the level plain near the village. The three Igathians gathered their sacks of frag blossoms and began the trek home.

They reached the bridge of vines which spanned a raging river. Kataga sent Brog first and Mele next. Then he followed, drawing a small knife he had concealed in his loincloth.

As he expected, Mele and Brog didn't look back. They were too busy keeping their balance on the flimsy, swaying structure. When Kataga reached the center of the bridge he ran his fingers beneath the main supporting vine. In a moment had touched the worn spot he had located days earlier. Quickly he sawed with his knife and felt the fibers part. Another slash or two and the vine would part under a man's weight.

But this was enough for now. Well satisfied with himself,

Kataga replaced the knife in his loincloth and hurried after Brog and Mele.

The village came alive at the news of the visitor. Men and women could talk of nothing but the great event, and an impromptu dance began in front of the Shrine of the Instrument. But it stopped when the old priest hobbled out of the Temple of Thangookari.

Lag, the priest, was a tall, emaciated old man. After years of service, his face had grown to resemble the smiling, benevolent countenance of the god he worshipped. On his bald head was the feathered crown of the priestly caste, and he leaned heavily on a sacred black mace.

The people gathered in front of him. Brog stood near the priest, rubbing his hands together hopefully, but afraid to press for his reward.

"My people," Lag said, "the ancient prophecy of the Igathi is now to be fulfilled. A great gleaming sphere has dropped from the heavens, as the old legends predicted. Within the sphere will be a being such as ourselves, and he will be an emissary of Thangookari."

The people nodded, faces rapt.

"The emissary will be a doer of great things. He will perform acts of good such as no man has ever before seen. And when he has completed his work and claimed his rest, he will expect his reward." Lag's voice fell to an impressive whisper.

"This reward is what every Igathian desires, dreams about, prays for. It is the final gift which Thangookari grants to those who serve him and the village well."

The priest turned to Brog.

"You, Brog," he said, "have been the first to witness the coming of the emissary. You have served the village well." The priest raised his arms. "Friends! Do you feel that Brog should receive the reward he craves?"

Most of the people felt he should. But Vassi, a wealthy merchant, stepped forward, frowning.

"It isn't fair," he said. "The rest of us work toward this for years and give expensive gifts to the temple. Brog hasn't done enough to merit even the most basic reward. Besides, he's humbly born."

"You have a point," the priest admitted, and Brog

groaned audibly. *"But,"* he continued, "the bounty of Thangookari is not only for the highborn. The humblest citizen may aspire to it. If Brog were not suitably rewarded, would not others lose hope?"

The people roared their assent, and Brog's eyes grew wet with thankfulness.

"Kneel, Brog," said the priest, and his face seemed to radiate with kindliness and love.

Brog knelt. The villagers held their breath.

Lag lifted his heavy mace and brought it down with all his strength on Brog's skull. It was a good blow, squarely struck. Brog collapsed, squirmed once, and expired. The expression of joy on his face was beautiful to behold.

"How lovely it was," Kataga murmured enviously.

Mele grasped his arm. "Don't worry, Father. Some day you will have your reward."

"I hope so," Kataga said. "But how can I be sure? Look at Rii. A nicer, more pious fellow never lived. That poor old man worked and prayed all his life for a violent death. *Any* kind of a violent death! And what happened? He passed away in his sleep! What kind of a death is that for a man?"

"There are always one or two exceptions."

"I could name a dozen others," Kataga said.

"Try not to worry about it, Father," Mele said. "I know you'll die beautifully, like Brog."

"Yes, yes. . . . But if you think about it, Brog's was such a *simple* ending." His eyes lighted up. "I would like something really big, something painful and complicated and wonderful, like the emissary will have."

Mele looked away. "That is presuming above your station, Father."

"True, true," Kataga said. "Oh well, some day . . ." He smiled to himself. Some day indeed! An intelligent and courageous man took matters into his own hands and arranged for his own violent death, instead of meekly waiting for the priest to make up his feeble mind. Call it heresy or anything else; something deep within him told Kataga that a man had the right to die as painfully and violently as he pleased—if he could get away with it.

The thought of the half-severed vine filled him with satisfaction. How fortunate that he had never learned to swim!

"Come," Mele said. "Let's welcome the emissary."

They followed the villagers to the level plain where the sphere had landed.

Richard Hadwell leaned back in his padded pilot's chair and wiped perspiration from his forehead. The last natives had just left his ship, and he could hear them singing and laughing as they returned to their village in the evening twilight. The pilot's compartment smelled of flowers and honey and wine, and throbbing drums seemed to echo still from the gray metal walls.

He smiled reminiscently and took down his notebook. Selecting a pen, he wrote:

> Beautiful to behold is Igathi, a place of stately mountains and raging mountain streams, beaches of black sand, verdant vegetation in the jungles, great flowering trees in the forests.

Not bad, Hadwell told himself. He pursed his lips and continued.

> "The people here are a comely humanoid race, a light tan in coloration, supple to behold. They greeted me with flowers and dancing, and many signs of joy and affection. I had no trouble hypnopeding their language, and soon felt as though this had always been my home. They are a lighthearted, laughter-loving people, gentle and courteous, living serenely in a state of near-nature. What a lesson there is here for Civilized Man!
>
> One's heart goes out to them, and to Thangookari, their benevolent deity. One hopes that Civilized Man, with his genius for destruction and frenetic behavior, does not come here, to turn these folk from their path of joyous moderation.

Hadwell selected a pen with a finer point, and wrote, "There is a girl named Mele who—" He crossed out the line, and wrote, "A black-haired girl named Mele, beautiful beyond compare, came close to me and gazed deep into my eyes—" He crossed that out, too.

Frowning deeply, he tried several possible lines:

"Her limpid brown eyes gave promise of joys beyond—"

"Her small red mouth quivered ever so slightly when I—"

"Though her small hand rested on my arm for but a moment—"

He crumpled the page. Five months of enforced celibacy in space was having its effect, he decided. He had better return to the main issue and leave Mele for later.

He wrote:

> There are many ways in which a sympathetic observer could help these people. But the temptation is strong to do *absolutely nothing,* for fear of disrupting their culture.

Closing his notebook, Hadwell looked out a port at the distant village, now lighted by torches. Then he opened the notebook again.

> However their culture appears to be strong and flexible. Certain kinds of aid can do nothing but profit them. And these I will freely give.

He closed the notebook with a snap and put away his pens.

The following day, Hadwell began his good works. He found many Igathians suffering from mosquito-transmitted diseases. By judicious selection of antibiotics, he was able to arrest all except the most advanced cases. Then he directed work teams to drain the pools of stagnant water where the mosquitos bred.

As he went on his healing rounds, Mele accompanied him. The beautiful Igathian girl quickly learned the rudiments of nursing, and Hadwell found her assistance invaluable.

Soon, all significant disease was cleared up in the village. Hadwell then began to spend his days in a sunny grove not far from Igathi, where he rested and worked on his book.

A town meeting was called at once by Lag, to discuss the import of this.

"Friends," said the old priest, "our friend, Hadwell, has done wonderful things for the village. He has cured our sick, so they too may live to partake of Thangookari's gift.

Now Hadwell is tired and rests in the sun. Now Hadwell expects the reward he came here for."

"It is fitting," said the merchant, Vassi, "that the emissary receive his reward. I suggest that the priest take his mace and go forth—"

"Why so stingy?" asked Juele, a priest in training. "Is Thangookari's messenger deserving of no finer death? Hadwell deserves more than the mace! Much more!"

"You are right," Vassi admitted slowly. "In that case, I suggest that we drive poisonous legenberry quills under his fingernails."

"Maybe that's good enough for a merchant," said Tgara, the stonecutter, "but not for Hadwell. He deserves a chief's death! I move that we tie him down and kindle a small fire beneath his toes, gradually—"

"Wait," said Lag. "The emissary has earned the Death of an Adept. Therefore, let him be taken, tenderly and firmly, to the nearest giant anthill, and there buried to his neck."

There were shouts of approval. Tgara said, "And as long as he screams, the ancient ceremonial drums will pound."

"And there will be dances for him," said Vassi.

"And a glorious drunk," said Kataga.

Everyone agreed that it would be a beautiful death.

So the final details were decided, and a time was set. The village throbbed with religious ecstacy. All the huts were decorated with flowers, except the Shrine of the Instrument, which had to remain bare. The women laughed and sang as they prepared the death feast. Only Mele, for some unaccountable reason, was forlorn. With lowered head she walked through the village and climbed slowly to the hills beyond, to Hadwell.

Hadwell was stripped to the waist and basking under the two suns. "Hi, Mele," he said. "I heard the drums. Is something up?"

"There will be a celebration," Mele said, sitting down beside him.

"That's nice. OK if I attend?"

Mele stared at him, nodding slowly. Her heart melted at the sight of such courage. The emissary was showing a true observance of the ancient punctilio, by which a man pretended that his own death feast was something that really didn't concern him. Men in this day and age were not able to maintain the necessary aplomb. But of course, an emissary of Thangookari would follow the rules better than anyone.

"How soon does it start?"

"In an hour," Mele said. Formerly she had been straightforward and free with him. Now her heart was heavy, oppressed. She didn't know why. Shyly she glanced at his bright alien garments, his red hair.

"Oughta be nice," Hadwell said. "Yessir, it oughta be nice . . ." His voice trailed away. From under lowered eyelids he looked at the comely Igathian girl, observed the pure line of neck and shoulder, her straight dark hair, and sensed rather than smelt her faint sachet. Nervously he plucked a blade of grass.

"Mele," he said, "I . . ."

The words died on his lips. Suddenly, startlingly, she was in his arms.

"Oh, Mele!"

"Hadwell!" she cried, and strained close to him. Abruptly she pulled free, looking at him with worried eyes.

"What's the matter, honey?" Hadwell asked.

"Hadwell, is there anything more you could do for the village? Anything? My people would appreciate it so."

"Sure there is," Hadwell said. "But I thought I'd rest up first, take it easy."

"No! Please!" she begged. "Those irrigation ditches you spoke of. Could you start them now?"

"If you want me to," Hadwell said. "But—"

"Oh darling!" She sprang to her feet. Hadwell reached for her, but she stepped back.

"There is no time! I must hurry back and tell the village!"

She ran from him. And Hadwell was left to ponder the strange ways of aliens, and particularly of alien women.

Mele ran back to the village and found the priest in the temple, praying for wisdom and guidance. Quickly she told him about the emissary's new plans for aiding the village.

The old priest nodded slowly. "Then the ceremony shall be deferred. But tell me, daughter. Why are *you* involved in this?"

Mele blushed and could not answer.

The old priest smiled. But then his face became stern. "I understand. But listen to me, girl. Do not allow love to sway you from the proper worship of Thangookari and from the observances of the ancient ways of our village."

"Of course not!" Mele said. "I simply felt that an Adept's death was not good enough for Hadwell. He deserves more! He deserves—The Ultimate!"

"No man has been worthy of the Ultimate for 600 years," Lag said. "Not since the hero and demigod, V'ktat, saved the Igathian race from the dread Huelva Beasts."

"But Hadwell has the stuff of heroes in him," Mele cried. "Give him time, let him strive! He will prove worthy!"

"Perhaps so," the priest mused. "It would be a great thing for the village. . . . But consider, Mele! It might take a lifetime for Hadwell to prove himself."

"Wouldn't it be worth waiting for?" she asked.

The old priest fingered his mace, and his forehead wrinkled in thought. "You may be right," he said slowly, "yes, you may be right." Suddenly he straightened and glanced sharply at her.

"But tell me the truth, Mele. Are you really trying to preserve him for the Ultimate Death? Or do you merely want to keep him for yourself?"

"He must have the death he deserves," Mele said serenely. But she was unable to meet the priest's eye.

"I wonder," the old man said. "I wonder what lies in your heart. I think you tread dangerously close to heresy, Mele. You, who were among the most orthodox."

Mele was about to answer when the merchant, Vassi, rushed into the temple.

"Come quickly!" he cried. "It is the farmer, Iglai! *He has evaded the taboo!*"

The fat, jolly farmer had died a terrible death. He had been walking his usual route from his hut to the village center, past an old thorn tree. Without warning, the tree had toppled on him. Thorns had impaled him through and through. Eyewitnesses said the farmer had writhed and moaned for over an hour before expiring.

But he had died with a smile on his face.

The priest looked at the crowd surrounding Iglai's body.

Several of the villagers were hiding grins behind their hands. Lag walked over to the thorn tree and examined it. There were faint marks of a saw blade, which had been roughened over and concealed with clay. The priest turned to the crowd.

"Was Iglai near this tree often?" he asked.

"He sure was," another farmer said. "Always ate his lunch under this tree."

The crowd was grinning openly now, proud of Iglai's achievement. Remarks began to fly back and forth.

"I *wondered* why he always ate here."

"Never wanted company. Said he liked to eat alone."

"Hah!"

"He must have been sawing all the time."

"For months, probably. That's tough wood."

"Very clever of Iglai."

"I'll say! He was only a farmer, and no one would call him religious. But he got himself a damned fine death."

"Listen, good people!" cried Lag. "Iglai did a sacrilegious thing! Only a priest can grant violent death!"

"What the priests don't see can't hurt them," someone muttered.

"So it was sacrilege," another man said. "Iglai got himself a beautiful death. *That's* the important thing."

The old priest turned sadly away. There was nothing he could do. If he had caught Iglai in time, he would have applied strict sanctions. Iglai would never have dared arrange another death and would probably have died quietly and forlornly in bed, at a ripe old age. But now it was too late. The farmer had achieved his death and on the wings of it had already gone to Rookechangi. Asking the god to punish Iglai in the afterlife was useless, for the farmer was right there on the spot to plead his own case.

Lag asked, "Didn't any of you see him sawing that tree?"

If anyone had, he wouldn't admit it. They stuck together, Lag knew. In spite of the religious training he had instilled in them from earliest childhood, they persisted in trying to outwit the priests.

When would they realize that an unauthorized death could never be so satisfying as a death one worked for, deserved, and had performed with all ceremonial observations?

He sighed. Life was sometimes a burden.

A week later, Hadwell wrote in his diary:

There has never been a race like these Igathians. I have lived among them now, eaten and drunk with them, and observed their ceremonies. I know and understand them. And the truth about them is startling, to say the least.

The fact is, *the Igathians do not know the meaning of war!* Consider that, Civilized Man! Never in all their recorded and oral history have they had one. They simply cannot conceive of it. I give the following illustration.

I tried to explain war to Kataga, father of the incomparable Mele. The man scratched his head, and asked, "You say that many kill many? That is war?"

"That's a part of it," I said. "Thousands, killing thousands."

"In that case," Kataga said, "many are dead at the same time, in the same way?"

"Correct," said I.

He pondered this for a long time, then turned to me and said, "It is not good for many to die at the same time in the same way. Not satisfactory. Every man should die his own individual death."

Consider, Civilized Man, the incredible naïveté of that reply. And yet, think of the considerable truth which resides beneath the naïveté; a truth which all might do well to learn.

Moreover, these people do not engage in quarrels among themselves, have no blood feuds, no crimes of passion, no murder.

The conclusion I come to is this: Violent death is *unknown* among these people—except, of course, for accidents.

It is a shame that accidents occur so often here and are so often fatal. But this I ascribe to the wildness of the surroundings and to the lighthearted, devil-may-care nature of the people. And as a matter of fact, even accidents do not go unnoticed and unchecked. The priest, with whom I have formed a considerable friendship, deplores the high accident rate, and is constantly proclaiming against it. Always he urges the people to take more caution.

He is a good man.

And now I write the final, most wonderful news of all. [Hadwell smiled sheepishly, hesitated for a moment, then returned to his notebook.]

Mele has consented to become my wife! As soon as I complete this, the ceremony begins. Already the festivities have started, the feast prepared. I consider myself the most fortunate of men, for Mele is a beautiful woman. And a most unusual woman, as well.

She has great social consciousness. A little *too* much, perhaps. She has been urging me constantly to do work for the village. And I have done much. I have completed an irrigation system for them, introduced several fast-growing food crops, started the profession of metal-working, and other things too numerous to mention. And she wants me to do more, much more.

But here I have put my foot down. I have a right to rest. I want a long, languorous honeymoon, and then a year or so of basking in the sun and finishing my book.

Mele finds this difficult to understand. She keeps on trying to tell me that I *must* continue working. And she speaks of some ceremony involving the "Ultimate" (if my translation is correct).

But I have done enough work. I refused to do more, for a year or two, at least.

This "Ultimate" ceremony is to take place directly after our wedding. I suppose it will be some high honor or other that these simple people wish to bestow on me. I have signified my willingness to accept it.

It should be interesting.

For the wedding the entire village, led by the old priest, marched to the Pinnacle, where all Igathian marriages were performed. The men wore ceremonial feathers, and the women were decked in shell jewelry and iridescent stones. Four husky villagers in the middle of the procession bore a strange-looking apparatus. Hadwell caught only a glimpse of it, but he knew it had been taken, with solemn ceremony, from a plain black-thatched hut which seemed to be a shrine of some sort.

In single file they proceeded over the shaky bridge of vines. Kataga, bringing up the rear, grinned to himself as he secretively slashed again at the worn spot.

The Pinnacle was a narrow spur of black rock thrust out over the sea. Hadwell and Mele stood on the end of it, faced by the priest. The people fell silent as Lag raised his arms.

"Oh great Thangookari!" the priest cried. "Cherish this man Hadwell, your emissary, who has come to us from out of the sky in a shining vehicle, and who has done service for the Igathi such as no man has ever done. And cherish your daughter, Mele. Teach her to love the memory of her husband—*and to remain strong in her tribal beliefs.*"

The priest stared hard at Mele as he said that. And Mele, her head held high, gave him look for look.

"I now pronounce you," said the priest, "man and wife!"

Hadwell clasped his wife in his arms and kissed her. The people cheered. Kataga grinned his sly grin.

"And now," said the priest in his warmest voice, "I have good news for you, Hadwell. Great news!"

"Oh?" Hadwell said, reluctantly releasing his bride.

"We have judged you," said Lag, "and we have found you worthy—of the Ultimate!"

"Why, thanks," Hadwell said.

The priest motioned. Four men came up lugging the strange apparatus which Hadwell had glimpsed earlier. Now he saw that it was a platform the size of a large bed, made of some ancient-looking black wood. Lashed to the frame were various barbs, hooks, sharpened shells and needle-shaped thorns. There were cups, which contained no liquid as yet. And there were other things, strange in shape, whose purpose Hadwell could not guess.

"Not for 600 years," said Lag, "has the Instrument been removed from the Shrine of the Instrument. Not since the days of V'ktat, the hero-god who single-handed saved the Igathian people from destruction. But it has been removed for you, Hadwell!"

"Really, I'm not worthy," Hadwell said.

A murmur rose from the crowd at such modesty.

"Believe me," Lag said earnestly, "you *are* worthy. Do you accept the Ultimate, Hadwell?"

Hadwell looked at Mele. He could not read the expression on her beautiful face. He looked at the priest. Lag's face was impassive. The crowd was deathly still. Hadwell looked at the Instrument. He didn't like its appearance. A doubt began to creep into his mind.

Had he misjudged these people? That Instrument must have been used for torture at some ancient time. Those barbs and hooks. . . . But what were the other things for? Thinking hard, Hadwell conceived some of their possible usages, and shuddered. The crowd was closely packed in front of him. Behind him was the narrow point of rock and a sheer thousand-foot drop below it. Hadwell looked again at Mele.

The love and devotion in her face was unmistakable.

Glancing at the villagers, he saw their concern for him. What was he worried about? They would never do anything to harm him, not after all he had done for the village.

The Instrument undoubtedly had some symbolic use.

"I accept the Ultimate," Hadwell said to the priest.

The villagers shouted, a deep-throated roar that echoed from the mountains. They formed closely around him, smiling, shaking his hands.

"The ceremony will take place at once," said the priest. "In the village, in front of the statue of Thangookari."

Immediately they started back, the priest leading. Hadwell and his bride were in the center now. Mele still had not spoken since the ceremony.

Silently they crossed the swaying bridge of vines. Once across, the villagers pressed more closely around Hadwell than before, giving him a slightly claustrophobic feeling. If he had not been convinced of their essential goodness, he told himself, he might have felt apprehensive.

Ahead lay the village and the altar of Thangookari. The priest hurried toward it.

Suddenly there was a shriek. Everyone turned and rushed back to the bridge.

At the brink of the river, Hadwell saw what had happened. Kataga, Mele's father, had brought up the rear of the procession. As he had reached the midpoint, the central supporting vine had inexplicably snapped. Kataga had managed to clutch a secondary vine, but only for a moment. As the villagers watched, his hold weakened, released, and he dropped into the river.

Hadwell watched, frozen into shock. With dreamlike clarity he saw it all: Kataga falling, a smile of magnificent courage on his face, the raging white water, the jagged rocks below.

It was a certain, terrible death.

"Can he swim?" Hadwell asked Mele.

"No," the girl said. "He refused to learn. . . . Oh, Father! How could you!"

The raging white water frightened Hadwell more than anything he had ever seen, more than the emptiness of space. But the father of his wife was in danger. A man had to act.

He plunged headlong into the icy water.

Kataga was almost unconscious when Hadwell reached him, which was fortunate, for the Igathian did not struggle when Hadwell seized him by the hair and started to swim vigorously for the nearest shore. But he couldn't make it. Currents swept the men along, pulling them under and throwing them to the surface again. By a strenuous effort, Hadwell was able to avoid the first rocks. But more loomed ahead.

The villagers ran along the bank, shouting at him.

With his strength ebbing rapidly, Hadwell fought again for the shore. A submerged rock scraped his side and his grip on Kataga's hair began to weaken. The Igathian was starting to recover and struggle.

"Don't give up, old man," Hadwell gasped. The bank sped past. Hadwell came within ten feet of it, then the current began to carry him out again.

With his last surge of strength, he managed to grab an overhead branch and to hold on while the current wrenched and tore at his body. Moments later, guided by the priest, the villagers pulled the two men in to the safety of the shore.

They were carried to the village. When Hadwell was able to breathe normally again, he turned and grinned feebly at Kataga.

"Close call, old man," he said.

"Meddler!" Kataga said. He spat at Hadwell and stalked off.

Hadwell stared after him, scratching his head. "Must

have affected his brain," he said. "Well, shall we get on with the Ultimate?"

The villagers drew close to him, their faces menacing.

"Hah! The Ultimate he wants!"

"A man like that."

"After dragging poor Kataga out of the river, he has the nerve . . ."

"His own father-in-law and he saves his life!"

"A man like that doesn't deserve the Ultimate!"

"A man like that," Vassi, the merchant, summed up, "damned well doesn't even deserve to die!"

Hadwell wondered if they had all gone temporarily insane. He stood up, a bit shakily, and appealed to the priest.

"What *is* all this?" Hadwell asked.

Lag, with mournful eyes and pale, set lips, stared at him and did not answer.

"Can't I have the Ultimate ceremony?" Hadwell asked, a plaintive note in his voice.

"You *do* deserve it," the priest said. "If any man has ever deserved the Ultimate, you do, Hadwell. I feel you should have it, as a matter of abstract justice. But there is more involved here than abstract justice. There are principles of mercy and human pity which are dear to Thangookari. By these principles, Hadwell, you did a terrible and inhuman thing when you rescued poor Kataga from the river. I am afraid the action is unforgivable."

Hadwell didn't know what to say. Apparently there was some taboo against rescuing men who had fallen into the river. But how could they expect him to know about it? How could they let this one little thing outweigh all he had done for them?

"Isn't there *some* ceremony you can give me?" he begged. "I like you people, I want to live here. Surely there's something you can do."

The old priest's eyes misted with compassion. He gripped his mace, started to lift it.

He was stopped by an ominous roar from the crowd.

"There is nothing I can do," he said. "Leave us, false emissary. Leave us, oh Hadwell—who does not deserve to die!"

"All right!" Hadwell shouted, his temper suddenly snapping. "To hell with you bunch of dirty savages. I wouldn't stay here if you begged me. I'm going. Are you with me, Mele?"

The girl blinked convulsively, looked at Hadwell, then at the priest. There was a long moment of silence. Then the priest murmured, "Remember your father, Mele. Remember the beliefs of your people."

Mele's proud little chin came up. "I know where my duty lies," she said. "Let's go, Richard dear."

"Right," said Hadwell. He stalked off to his spaceship, followed by Mele.

In despair, the old priest watched. He cried, "Mele!" once, in a heartbroken voice. But Mele did not turn back. He saw her enter the ship, and the port slide shut.

Within minutes, red and blue flames bathed the silver sphere. The sphere lifted, gained speed, dwindled to a speck, and vanished.

Tears rolled down the old priest's cheeks as he watched it go.

Hours later, Hadwell said, "Darling, I'm taking you to Earth, the planet I come from. You'll like it there."

"I know I will," Mele murmured, staring out a porthole at the brilliant spear points of the stars.

Somewhere among them was her home, lost to her forever. She was homesick already. But there had been no other choice. Not for her. A woman goes with the man she loves. And a woman who loves truly and well never loses faith in her man.

Mele hadn't lost faith in Hadwell.

She fingered a tiny sheathed dagger concealed in her clothing. The dagger was tipped with a peculiarly painful and slow-acting poison. It was a family heirloom, to be used when there was no priest around, and only on those one loved most dearly.

"I'm through wasting my time," Hadwell said. "With your help I'm going to do great things. You'll be proud of me, sweetheart."

Mele knew he meant it. Someday, she thought, Hadwell would atone for the sin against her father. He would do something, some fine deed, perhaps today, perhaps tomorrow, perhaps next year. And then she would give him the most precious thing a woman can give to a man.

A painful death.

SHALL WE HAVE A LITTLE TALK?

The landing was a piece of cake despite gravitational vagaries produced by two suns and six moons. Low-level cloud cover could have given him some trouble if Jackson had been coming in visually. But he considered that to be kid stuff. It was better and safer to plug in the computer and lean back and enjoy the ride.

The cloud cover broke up at 2,000 feet. Jackson was able to confirm his earlier sighting: there was a city down there, just as sure as sure.

He was in one of the world's loneliest jobs; but his line of work, paradoxically enough, required an extremely gregarious man. Because of this built-in contradiction, Jackson was in the habit of talking to himself. Most of the men in his line of work did. Jackson would talk to anyone, human or alien, no matter what their size or shape or color.

It was what he was paid to do, and what he had to do anyhow. He talked when he was alone on the long interstellar runs, and he talked even more when he was with someone or something that would talk back. He figured he was lucky to be paid for his compulsions.

"And not just *paid,* either," he reminded himself. *"Well* paid, and with a bonus arrangement on top of that. And furthermore, this feels like my lucky planet. I feel like I could get rich on this one—unless they kill me down there, of course."

The lonely flights between the planets and the imminence of death were the only disadvantages of this job; but if the work weren't hazardous and difficult, the pay wouldn't be so good.

Would they kill him? You could never tell. Alien life

forms were unpredictable—just like humans, only more so.

"But I don't think they'll kill me," Jackson said. "I just feel downright lucky today."

This simple philosophy had sustained him for years, across the endless lonely miles of space, and in and out of ten, 12, 20 planets. He saw no reason to change his outlook now.

The ship landed. Jackson switched the status controls to standby.

He checked the analyzer for oxygen and trace-element content in the atmosphere, and took a quick survey of the local microorganisms. The place was viable. He leaned back in his chair and waited. It didn't take long, of course. They—the locals, indigenes, autochthons, whatever you wanted to call them—came out of their city to look at the spaceship. And Jackson looked through the port at them.

"Well now," he said. "Seems like the alien life forms in this neck of the woods are honest-to-Joe humanoids. That means a five-thousand-dollar bonus for old Uncle Jackson."

The inhabitants of the city were bipedal monocephaloids. They had the appropriate number of fingers, noses, eyes, ears and mouths. Their skin was a flesh-colored beige, their lips were a faded red, their hair was black, brown, or red.

"Shucks, they're just like home folks!" Jackson said. "Hell, I ought to get an extra bonus for that. Humanoid-issimus, eh?"

The aliens wore clothes. Some of them carried elaborately carved lengths of wood like swagger sticks. The women decorated themselves with carved and enameled ornaments. At a flying guess, Jackson ranked them about equivalent to Late Bronze Age on Earth.

They talked and gestured among themselves. Their language was, of course, incomprehensible to Jackson; but that didn't matter. The important thing was that they *had* a language and that their speech sounds could be produced by his vocal apparatus.

"Not like on that heavy planet last year," Jackson said. "Those supersonic sons of bitches! I had to wear special earphones and mike, and it was 110 in the shade."

The aliens were waiting for him, and Jackson knew it. That first moment of actual contact—it always was a nervous business.

That's when they were most apt to let you have it.

Reluctantly he moved to the hatch, undogged it, rubbed his eyes, and cleared his throat. He managed to produce a smile. He told himself, "Don't get sweaty; 'member, you're just a little old interstellar wanderer—kind of galactic vagabond—to extend the hand of friendship and all that jazz. You've just dropped in for a little talk, nothing more. Keep on believing that, sweety, and the extraterrestrial Johns will believe right along with you. Remember Jackson's Law: All intelligent life forms share the divine faculty of gullibility; which means that the triple-tongued Thung of Orangus V can be conned out of his skin just as Joe Doakes of St. Paul."

And so, wearing a brave, artificial little smile, Jackson swung the port open and stepped out to have a little talk.

"Well now, how y'all?" Jackson asked at once, just to hear the sound of his own voice.

The nearest aliens shrank away from him. Nearly all of them were frowning. Several of the younger ones carried bronze knives in a forearm scabbard. These were clumsy weapons, but as effective as anything ever invented. The aliens started to draw.

"Now take it easy," Jackson said, keeping his voice light and unalarmed.

They drew their knives and began to edge forward. Jackson stood his ground, waiting, ready to bolt through the hatch like a jet-propelled jackrabbit, hoping he could make it.

Then a third man (might as well call them "men," Jackson decided) stepped in front of the belligerent two. This one was older. He spoke rapidly. He gestured. The two with the knives looked.

"That's right," Jackson said encouragingly. "Take a good look. Heap big spaceship. Plenty strong medicine. Vehicle of great power, fabricated by a real advanced technology. Sort of makes you stop and think, doesn't it?"

It did.

The aliens had stopped; and if not thinking, they were at

least doing a great deal of talking. They pointed at the ship, then back at their city.

"You're getting the idea," Jackson told them. "Power speaks a universal language, eh, cousins?"

He had been witness to many of these scenes on many different planets. He could nearly write their dialogue for them. It usually went like this:

Intruder lands in outlandish space vehicle, thereby eliciting (1) curiosity, (2), fear and (3) hostility. After some minutes of awed contemplation, one autochthon usually says to his friend: "Hey, that damned metal thing packs one hell of a lot of power."

"You're right, Herbie," his friend Fred, the second autochthon, replies.

"You bet I'm right," Herbie says. "And hell, with that much power and technology and stuff, this son of a gun could like *enslave* us. I mean he really could."

"You've hit it, Herbie, that's just exactly what could happen."

"So what I say," Herbie continues, "I say, let's not take any risks. I mean, *sure,* he *looks* friendly enough, but he's just got too damned much *power,* and that's not right. And right now is the best chance we'll ever get to take him on account of he's just standing there waiting for like an ovation or something. So let's put this bastard out of his misery, and then we can talk the whole thing over and see how it stacks up situationwise."

"By Jesus, I'm with you!" cries Fred. Others signify their assent.

"Good for you, lads," cries Herbie. "Let's wade in and take this alien joker like *now!*"

So they start to make their move; but suddenly, at the last second, Old Doc, (the third autochthon) intervenes, saying, "Hold it a minute, boys, we can't do it like that. For one thing, we got laws around here—"

"To hell with that," says Fred (a born troublemaker and somewhat simple to boot).

"—and aside from the laws, it would be just too damned dangerous for *us.*"

"Me 'n' Fred here ain't scared," says valiant Herb. "Maybe you getter go take in a movie or something, Doc. Us guys'll handle this."

"I was not referring to a short-range personal danger," Old Doc says scornfully. "What I fear is the destruction of our city, the slaughter of our loved ones, and the annihilation of our culture."

Herb and Fred stop. "What you talking about, Doc? He's just one stinking alien; you push a knife in his guts, he'll bleed like anyone else."

"Fools! *Schlemiels!*" thunders wise Old Doc. "Of course, you can kill him! But what happens after that?"

"Huh?" says Fred, squinting his china-blue pop eyes.

"Idiots! *Cochons!* You think this is the only spaceship these aliens got? You think they don't even know whereabouts this guy has gone? Man, you gotta assume they got *plenty* more ships where this one came from, and you gotta also assume that they'll be damned mad if this ship doesn't show up when it's supposed to, and you gotta assume that when these aliens learn the score, they're gonna be damned sore and buzz back here and stomp on everything and everybody."

"How come I gotta assume that?" asks feeble-witted Fred.

" 'Cause it's what *you'd* do in a deal like that, right?"

"I guess maybe I would at that," says Fred with a sheepish grin. "Yeah, I just might do that little thing. But look, maybe *they* wouldn't."

"Maybe, maybe," mimics wise Old Doc. "Well, baby, we can't risk the whole ball game on a goddamned *maybe*. We can't afford to kill this alien joker on the chance that *maybe* his people wouldn't do what any reasonable-minded guy would do, which is, namely, to blow us all to hell."

"Well, I suppose we maybe can't," Herbie says. "But Doc, what *can* we do?"

"Just wait and see what he wants."

2

A scene very much like that, according to reliable reconstruction, had been enacted at least 30 or 40 times. It usually resulted in a policy of wait and see. Occasionally, the contactor from Earth was killed before wise counsel could prevail; but Jackson was paid to take risks like that.

Whenever the contactor was killed, retribution followed with swift and terrible inevitability. Also with regret, of course, because Earth was an extremely civilized place and accustomed to living within the law. No civilized, law-abiding race likes to commit genocide. In fact, the folks on Earth consider genocide a very unpleasant matter, and they don't like to read about it or anything like it in their morning papers. Envoys must be protected, of course, and murder must be punished; everybody knows that. But it still doesn't feel nice to read about a genocide over your morning coffee. News like that can spoil a man's entire day. Three or four genocides and a man just might get angry enough to switch his vote.

Fortunately, there was never much occasion for that sort of mess. Aliens usually caught on pretty fast. Despite the language barrier, aliens learned that you simply *don't* kill Earthmen.

And then, later, bit by bit, they learned all the rest.

The hotheads had sheathed their knives. Everybody was smiling except Jackson, who was grinning like a hyena. The aliens were making graceful arm and leg motions, probably of welcome.

"Well, that's real nice," Jackson said, making a few graceful gestures of his own. "Makes me feel real to-home. And now, suppose you take me to your leader, show me the town, and all that jazz. Then I'll set myself down and figure out that lingo of yours, and we'll have a little talk. And after that, everything will proceed splendidly. *En avant!*"

So saying, Jackson stepped out at a brisk pace in the direction of the city. After a brief hesitation, his new found friends fell into step behind him.

Everything was moving according to plan.

Jackson, like all the other contactors, was a polyglot of singular capabilities. As basic equipment, he had an eidetic memory and an extremely discriminating ear. More important, he possessed a startling aptitude for language and an uncanny intuition for meaning. When Jackson came up against an incomprehensible tongue, he picked out, quickly and unerringly, the significant units, the fundamental building blocks of the language. Quite without effort he sorted vocalizations into cognitive, volitional, and emotional aspects of speech. Grammatical elements presented themselves at once to his practiced ear. Prefixes and suffixes were no trouble; word sequence, pitch, and reduplication were no sweat. He didn't know much about the science of linguistics, but he didn't need to know. Jackson was a natural. Linguistics had been developed to describe and explain things which he knew intuitively.

He had not yet encountered the language which he could not learn. He never really expected to find one. As he often told his friends in the Forked Tongue Club in New York, "Waal, shukins, there just really ain't nuthin *tough* about them alien tongues. Leastwise, not the ones I've run across. I mean that sincerely. I mean to tell you, boys, that the man who can express hisself in Sioux or Khmer ain't going to encounter too much trouble out there amongst the stars."

And so it had been, to date. . . .

Once in the city, there were many tedious ceremonies which Jackson had to endure. They stretched on for three days—about par for the course; it wasn't every day that a traveler from space came in for a visit. So naturally enough every mayor, governor, president, and alderman, *and* their wives, wanted to shake his hand. It was all very understandable, but Jackson resented the waste of his time. He had work to do, some of it not very pleasant, and the sooner he got started, the quicker it would be over.

On the fourth day he was able to reduce the official nonsense to a minimum. That was the day on which he began in earnest to learn the local language.

A language, as any linguist will tell you, is undoubtedly the most beautiful creation one is ever likely to encounter. But with that beauty goes a certain element of danger.

Language might aptly be compared to the sparkling, everchanging face of the sea. Like the sea, you never know what reefs may be concealed in its pellucid depths. The brightest water hides the most treacherous shoals.

Jackson, well prepared for trouble, encountered none at first. The main language (Hon) of this planet (Na) was spoken by the overwhelming majority of its inhabitants (Ena-To-Na—literally, men of the Na, or Naians, as Jackson preferred to think of them). Hon seemed quite a straightforward affair. It used one term for one concept, and allowed no fusions, juxtapositions, or agglutinations. Concepts were built up by sequences of simple words ("spaceship" was *ho-pa-aie-an*—boat-flying-outer-sky). Thus, Hon was very much like Chinese and Annamite on Earth. Pitch differences were employed not only intentionally to differentiate between homonyms, but also positionally, to denote gradations of "perceived realism," bodily discomfort, and three classes of pleasurable expectation. All of which was mildly interesting but of no particular difficulty to a competent linguist.

To be sure, a language like Hon was rather a bore because of the long word-lists one had to memorize. But pitch and position could be fun, as well as being absolutely essential if one wanted to make any sense out of the sentence units. So, taken all in all, Jackson was not dissatisfied, and he absorbed the language as quickly as it could be given to him.

It was a proud day for Jackson, about a week later, when he could say to his tutor: "A very nice and pleasant good morning to you, most estimable and honored tutor, and how is your blessed health upon this glorious day?"

"Felicitations most *ird wunk!*" the tutor replied with a smile of deep warmth. "Your accent, dear pupil, is superb! Positively *gor nak*, in fact, and your grasp of my dear mother tongue is little short of *ur nak tai.*"

Jackson glowed all over from the gentle old tutor's compliments. He felt quite pleased with himself. Of course, he hadn't recognized several words; *ird wunk* and *ur nak tai* sounded faintly familiar, but *gor nak* was completely unknown. Still, lapses were expected of a beginner in any language. He did know enough to understand the Naians and to make himself understood by them. And that was what his job required.

He returned to his spaceship that afternoon. The hatch had been standing open during his entire stay on Na but he found that not a single article had been stolen. He shook his head ruefully at this, but refused to let it upset him. He loaded his pockets with a variety of objects and sauntered back to the city. He was ready to perform the final and most important part of his job.

3

In the heart of the business district, at the intersection of Um and Alhretto, he found what he was looking for: a real-estate office. He entered and was taken to the office of Mr. Erum, a junior partner of the firm.

"Well, well, well, well!" Erum said, shaking hands heartily. "This is a real honor, sir, a very considerable and genuine privilege. Are you thinking of acquiring a piece of property?"

"That was my intention," Jackson said. "Unless, of course, you have discriminatory laws that forbid your selling to a foreigner."

"No difficulty there," Erum said. "In fact, it'll be a veritable *orai* of a pleasure to have a man from your distant and glorious civilization in our midst."

Jackson restrained a snicker. "The only other difficulty I can imagine is the question of legal tender. I don't have any of your currency, of course; but I have certain quantities of gold, platinum, diamonds, and other objects which are considered valuable on Earth."

"They are considered valuable here, too," Erum said. "Quantities, did you say? My dear sir, we will have no difficulties; not even a *blaggle* shall *mit* or *ows,* as the poet said."

"Quite so," Jackson replied. Erum was using some words he didn't know, but that didn't matter. The main drift was clear enough. "Now, suppose we begin with a nice industrial site. After all, I'll have to do something with my time. And after that, we can pick out a house."

"Most decidedly *prominex,*" Erum said gaily. "Suppose I just *raish* through my listings here. . . . Yes, what do you say to a *bromicaine* factory? It's in a first-class condition and could easily be converted to *vor* manufacture or used as it is."

"Is there any real market for *bromicaine?*" Jackson asked.

"Well, bless my *muergentan,* of course there is! *Bromicaine* is indispensable, though its sales are seasonable. You see, refined *bromicaine,* or *ariisi,* is used by the *protigash* devolvers, who of course harvest by the soltice season, except in those branches of the industry that have switched over to *ticothene revature*. Those from a steadily—"

"Fine, fine," Jackson said. He didn't care what a *bromicaine* was and never expected to see one. As long as it was a gainful employment of some kind, it filled his specifications.

"I'll buy it," he said.

"You won't regret it," Erum told him. "A good *bromicaine* factory is a *garveldis hagatis,* and *menifoy* as well."

"Sure," Jackson said, wishing that he had a more extensive Hon vocabulary. "How much?"

"Well, sir, the price is no difficulty. But first you'll have to fill out the *ollanbrit* form. It is just a few *sken* questions which *ny naga* of everyone."

Erum handed Jackson the form. The first question read: "Have you, now or at any past time, *elikated mushkies forsically?* State date of all occurrences. If no occurrences, state the reason for *transgrishal reduct* as found."

Jackson read no farther. "What does it mean," he asked Erum, "to *elikate mushkies forsically?*"

"Mean?" Erum smiled uncertainly. "Why, it means exactly what it says. Or so I would imagine."

"I meant," Jackson said, "that I do not understand the words. Could you explain them to me?"

"Nothing simpler," Erum replied. "To *elikate mushkies* is almost the same as a *bifur probishkai.*"

"I beg your pardon?" Jackson said.

"It means—well, to *elikate* is really rather simple, though perhaps not in the eyes of the law. *Scorbadising* is a form of *elikation*, and so is *manruv garing*. Some say that when we breathe *drorsically* in the evening *subsis*, we are actually *elikating*. Personally, I consider that a bit fanciful."

"Let's try *mushkies*," Jackson suggested.

"By all means, let's!" Erum replied, with a coarse boom of laughter. "If only one could—eh!" He dug Jackson in the ribs with a sly elbow.

"Hm, yes," Jackson replied coldly. "Perhaps you could tell me what, exactly, a *mushkie* is?"

"Of course. As it happens, there is no such thing," Erum replied. "Not in the singular, at any rate. One mushkie would be a logical fallacy, don't you see?"

"I'll take your word for it. What *are mushkies*?"

"Well, primarily, they're the object of *elikation*. Secondarily, they are half-sized wooden sandals which are used to stimulate erotic fantasies among the Kutor religionists."

"Now we're getting someplace!" Jackson cried.

"Only if your tastes happen to run that way," Erum answered with discernable coldness.

"I meant in terms of understanding the question on the form—"

"Of course, excuse me," Erum said. "But you see, the question asks if you have ever *elikated mushkies forsically*. And that makes all the difference."

"Does it really?"

"Of course! The modification changes the entire meaning."

"I was afraid that it would," Jackson said. "I don't suppose you could explain what *forsically* means?"

"I certainly can!" Erum said. "Our conversation now could—with a slight assist from the *deme* imagination—be termed a '*forsically designed* talk.'"

"Ah," said Jackson.

"Quite so," said Erum. "*Forsically* is a mode, a manner. It means 'spiritually-forward-leading-by-way-of-fortuitous-friendship.'"

"That's a little more like it," Jackson said. "In that case, when one *elikates mushkies forsically*—"

"I'm terribly afraid you're on the wrong track," Erum said. "The definition I gave you applies only to conversations. It is something rather different when one speaks of *mushkies*."

"What does it mean then?"

"Well, it means—or rather it *expresses*—an advanced and intensified case of *mushkie elikidation,* but with a definite *nmogmetic* bias. I consider it a rather unfortunate phraseology, personally."

"How would you put it?"

"I'd lay it on the line and to hell with the fancy talk," Erum said toughly. "I'd come right out and say: 'Have you now or at any other time *dunfiglers voc* in illegal, immoral, or *insirtis* circumstances, with or without the aid and/or consent of a *brachniian?* If so, state when and why. If not, state *neugris kris* and why not.'"

"That's how you'd put it, huh?" Jackson said.

"Sure, I would," Erum said defiantly. "These forms are

for adults, aren't they? So why not come right out and call a *spigler* a *spigler* a *spey*? Everybody *dunfiglers voc* some of the time, and so what? No one's feelings are ever hurt by it, for heaven's sake. I mean, after all, it simply involves oneself and a twisted old piece of wood, so why should anyone care?"

"Wood?" Jackson echoed.

"Yes, *wood*. A commonplace, dirty old piece of wood. Or at least that's all it would be if people didn't get their feelings so ridiculously involved."

"What do they do with the wood?" Jackson asked quickly.

"*Do* with it? Nothing much, when you come right down to it. But the religious aura is simply too much for our so-called intellectuals. They are unable, in my opinion, to isolate the simple primordial fact—*wood*—from the cultural *volturneiss* which surrounds it at *festerhiss*, and to some extent at *uuis*, too."

"That's how intellectuals are," Jackson said. "But *you* can isolate it, and you find—"

"I find it's really nothing to get excited about. I really mean that. I mean to say that a cathedral, viewed correctly, is no more than a pile of rocks and a forest is just an assembly of atoms. Why should we see this case differently? I mean, really, you could *elikate mushkies forsically* without even *using* wood! What do you think of that?"

"I'm impressed," Jackson said.

"Don't get me wrong! I'm not saying it would be *easy*, or natural, or even *right*. But still, you damned well could! Why, you could substitute *cormed grayti* and still come out all right!" Erum paused and chuckled. "You'd look foolish, but you'd still come out all right."

"Very interesting," Jackson said.

"I'm afraid I became a bit vehement," Erum said, wiping his forehead. "Was I talking very loudly? Do you think perhaps I was overheard?"

"Of course not. I found it all very interesting. I must leave just now, Mr. Erum, but I'll be back tomorrow to fill out that form and buy the property."

"I'll hold it for you," Erum said, rising and shaking Jackson's hand warmly. "And I want to thank you. It isn't often that I have the opportunity for this kind of frank, no-holds-barred conversation."

"I found it very instructive," Jackson said. He left Erum's office and walked slowly back to his ship. He was disturbed, upset, and annoyed. Linguistic incomprehension irked him, no matter how comprehensible it might be. He *should* have been able to figure out, somehow, how one went about *elikating mushkies forsically*.

Never mind, he told himself. You'll work it out tonight, Jackson baby, and then you'll go back in there and cannon-ball through them forms. So don't get het up over it, man.

He'd work it out. He damned well had to work it out, as he had to own a piece of property.

That was the second part of his job.

Earth had come a long way since the bad old days of naked, aggressive warfare. According to the history books, a ruler back in those ancient times could simply send out his troops to seize whatever the ruler wanted. And if any of the folks at home had the temerity to ask why he wanted it, the ruler could have them beheaded or locked up in a dungeon or sewn up in a sack and thrown into the sea. And he wouldn't even feel guilty about doing any of those things because he invariably believed that he was right and they were wrong.

This policy, technically called the *droit de seigneur* was one of the most remarkable features of the *laisser-faire capitalism* which the ancients knew.

But, down the slow passage of centuries, cultural processes were inexorably at work. A new ethic came into the world; and slowly but surely, a sense of fair play and justice was bred into the human race. Rulers came to be chosen by ballot and were responsive to the desires of the electorate. Conceptions of Justice, Mercy, and Pity came to the forefront of men's minds, ameliorating the old law of tooth and talon and amending the savage bestiality of the ancient time of unreconstruction.

The old days were gone forever. Today, no ruler could simply *take;* the voters would never stand for it.

Nowadays one had to have an excuse for taking.

Like for example a Terran citizen who happened to own property all legal and aboveboard on an alien planet, and who urgently needed and requested Terran military assistance in order to protect himself, his home, his means of a legitimate livelihood. . . .

But first he had to own that property. He had to *really* own it, to protect himself from the bleeding-hearts Congressmen and the soft-on-aliens newsmen who always started an investigation whenever Earth took charge of another planet.

To provide a legal basis for conquest—that was what the contactors were for.

"Jackson," Jackson said to himself, "you gonna git yourself that li'l' ole *bromicaine* factory tomorrow and you gonna own it without let or hindrance. You heah me, boy? I mean it sincerely."

On the morrow, shortly before noon, Jackson was back in the city. Several hours of intensive study and a long consultation with his tutor had sufficed to show him where he had gone wrong.

It was simple enough. He had merely been a trifle hasty in assuming an extreme and invariant isolating technique in the Hon use of radicals. He had thought, on the basis of his early studies, that word meaning and word order were the only significant factors required for an understanding of the language. But that wasn't so. Upon further examination, Jackson found that the Hon language had some unexpected resources: affixation, for example, and an elementary form of reduplication. Yesterday he hadn't even been prepared for any morphological inconsistencies; when they had occurred, he had found himself in semantic difficulties.

The new forms were easy enough to learn. The trouble was, they were thoroughly illogical and contrary to the entire spirit of Hon.

One word produced by one sound and bearing one meaning—that was the rule he had previously deduced. But now he discovered 18 important exceptions—compounds produced by a variety of techniques, each of them with a list of modifying suffixes. For Jackson, this was as odd as stumbling across a grove of palm trees in Antarctica.

He learned the 18 exceptions, and thought about the article he would write when he finally got home.

And the next day, wiser and warier, Jackson strode meaningfully back to the city.

4

In Erum's office, he filled out the government forms with ease. That first question—"Have you, now or at any past time, *elikated mushkies forsically?*"—he could now answer with an honest no. The plural *"mushkies"* in its primary meaning, represented in this context the singular "woman." (The singular *"mushkies"* used similarly would denote an uncorporeal state of femininity.)

Elikation was, of course, the role of sexual termination, unless one employed the modifier *"forsically."* If one did, this quiet term took on a charged meaning in this particular context, tantamount to edematous polysexual advocation.

Thus, Jackson could honestly write that, as he was not a Naian, he had never had that particular urge.

It was as simple as that. Jackson was annoyed at himself for not having figured it out on his own.

He filled in the rest of the questions without difficulty, and handed the paper back to Erum.

"That's really quite *skoe,*" Erum said. "Now, there are just a few more simple items for us to complete. The first we can do immediately. After that, I will arrange a brief official ceremony for the Property Transferral Act, and that will be followed by several other small bits of business. All of it should take no more than a day or so, and then the property will be all yours."

"Sure, kid, that's great," Jackson said. He wasn't bothered by the delays. Quite the contrary, he had expected many more of them. On most planets, the locals caught on quickly to what was happening. It took no great reasoning power to figure out that Earth wanted what she wanted, but wanted it in a legalistic manner.

As for why she wanted it that way—that wasn't too hard to fathom, either. A great majority of Terrans were idealists, and they believed fervently in concepts such as truth, justice, mercy, and the like. And not only did they believe, they also let those noble concepts guide their actions—except when it would be inconvenient or unprofitable. When that happened, they acted expediently, but continued to talk moralistically. This meant that they were "hypocrites"—a term which every race has its counterpart of.

Terrans wanted what they wanted, but they also wanted that what they wanted should look nice. This was a lot to expect sometimes, especially when what they wanted was ownership of someone else's planet. But in one way or another, they usually got it.

Most alien races realized that overt resistance was impossible and so resorted to various stalling tactics.

Sometimes they refused to sell, or they required an infinite multiplicity of forms or the approval of some local official who was always absent. But for each ploy the contactor always had a suitable counterploy.

Did they refuse to sell property on racial grounds? The laws of Earth specifically forbade such practices, and the Declaration of Sentient Rights stated the freedom of all sentients to live and work wherever they pleased. This was a freedom that Terra would fight for, if anyone forced her to.

Were they stalling? The Terran Doctrine of Temporal Propriety would not allow it.

Was the necessary official absent? The Uniform Earth Code Against Implicit Sequestration in Acts of Omission expressly forbade such a practice. And so on and so on. It was a game of wits Earth invariably won, for the strongest is usually judged the cleverest.

But the Naians weren't even *trying* to fight back. Jackson considered that downright despicable.

The exchange of Naian currency for Terran platinum was completed and Jackson was given his change in crisp 50-Vrso bills. Erum beamed with pleasure and said, "Now, Mr. Jackson, we can complete today's business if you will kindly *trombramcthulanchierir* in the usual manner."

Jackson turned, his eyes narrowed and his mouth compressed into a bloodless downward-curving line.

"What did you say?"

"I merely asked you to—"

"I know what you asked! But what does it *mean?*"

"Well, it means—it means—" Erum laughed weakly. "It means exactly what it says. That is to say—*ethybolically* speaking—"

Jackson said in a low, dangerous voice, "Give me a synonym."

"There is no synonym," Erum said.

"Baby, you better come up with one anyhow," Jackson said, his hand closing over Erum's throat.

"Stop! Wait! Ulp!" Erum cried. "Mr. Jackson, I beg of you! How can there be a synonym when there is one and only one term for the thing expressed—if I may so express it?"

"You're putting me on!" Jackson howled. "And you better quit it, on account of we got laws against willful obfuscation, intentional obstructionism, implicit superimposition, and other stuff like you're doing. You hear me?"

"I hear you," Erum trembled.

"Then hear this: *stop agglutinating,* you devious dog! You've got a perfectly ordinary run-of-the-mill analytical-type language, distinguished only by its extreme isolating tendency. And when you got a language like that, man, then you simply don't agglutinate a lot of big messy compounds. Get me?"

"Yes, yes," Erum cried. "But believe me, I don't intend to *numniscaterate* in the slightest! Not *noniskakkekaki,* and you really must *debruchili* that!"

Jackson drew back his fist, but got himself under control in time. It was unwise to hit aliens if there was any possibility that they were telling the truth. Folks on Terra didn't like it. His pay could be docked; and if, by some unlucky chance, he killed Erum, he could be slapped with a six-month jail sentence.

But still. . . .

"I'll find out if you're lying or not!" Jackson screamed, and stormed out of the office.

He walked for nearly an hour, mingling with the crowds in the slum quarters of Grath-Eth, below the gray, evil-smelling Ungperdis. No one paid any attention to him. To all outward appearances, he could have been a Naian, just as any Naian could have been a Terran.

Jackson located a cheerful saloon on the corner of Niis and Da Streets and went in.

It was quiet and masculine inside. Jackson ordered a local variety of beer. When it was served, he said to the bartender, "Funny thing happened to me the other day."

"Yeah?" said the bartender.

"Yeah, really," Jackson said. "I had this big business deal on, see, and then at the last minute they asked to *trombramcthulanchierir* in the usual manner."

He watched the bartender's face carefully. A faint expression of puzzlement crossed the man's stolid features.

"So why didn't you?" the bartender asked.

"You mean *you* would have?"

"Sure I would have. Hell, it's the standard *cathanpriptiaia*, ain't it?"

"Course it is," one of the loungers at the bar said. "Unless, of course, you suspected they was trying to *numniscaterate*."

"No, I don't think they were trying anything like that," Jackson said in a flat low, lifeless voice. He paid for his drink and started to leave.

"Hey," the bartender called after him, "You sure they wasn't *noniskakkekaki?*"

"You never know," Jackson said, walking slump-shouldered into the street.

Jackson trusted his instincts, both with languages and with people. His instincts told him now that the Naians were straight and were not practicing an elaborate deception on him. Erum had not been inventing new words for the sake of willful confusion. He had been really speaking the Hon language as he knew it.

But if that were true, then Na was a very strange language. In fact, it was downright eccentric. And its implications were not merely curious. They were disastrous.

5

That evening Jackson went back to work. He discovered a further class of exceptions which he had not known or even suspected. That was a group of 29 multivalued potentiators. These words, meaningless in themselves, acted to elicit a complicated and discordant series of shadings from other words. Their particular type of potentiation varied according to their position in the sentence.

Thus, when Erum had asked him "to *trombramcthulanchierir* in the usual manner," he had merely wanted Jackson to make an obligatory ritual obeisance. This consisted of clasping his hands behind his neck and rocking back on his heels. He was required to perform this action with an expression of definite yet modest pleasure, in accordance with the totality of the situation, and also in accord with the state of his stomach and nerves and with his religion and ethical code, and bearing in mind minor temperamental differences due to fluctuations in heat and humidity, and not forgetting the virtues of patience, similitude, and forgiveness.

It was all quite understandable. And all completely contradictory to everything Jackson had previously learned about Hon.

It was more than contradictory; it was unthinkable, impossible, and entirely out of order. It was as if, having discovered palm trees in frigid Antarctica, he had further found that the fruit of these trees was not coconuts, but muscatel grapes.

It couldn't be—but it was.

Jackson did what was required of him. When he had finished *trombramcthulanchieriring* in the usual manner, he had only to get through the official ceremony and the several small requirements after it.

Erum assured him that it was all quite simple, but Jackson suspected that he might somehow have difficulties.

So, in preparation, he put in three days of hard work acquiring a real mastery of the 29 exceptional potentiators, together with their most common positions and their potentiating effect in each of these positions. He finished, bone-weary and with his irritability index risen to 97.3620 on the Grafheimer scale. An impartial observer might have noticed an ominous gleam in his china-blue eyes.

Jackson had had it. He was sick of the Hon language and of all things Naian. He had the vertiginous feeling that the more he learned, the less he knew. It was downright perverse.

"Hokay," Jackson said, to himself and to the universe at large. "I have learned the Naian language, and I have learned a set of completely inexplicable exceptions, *and* I have *also* learned a further and even more contradictory set of exceptions to the exceptions."

Jackson paused and in a very low voice said: "I have learned an *exceptional* number of exceptions. Indeed, an impartial observer might think that this language is composed of nothing *but* exceptions.

"But *that*," he continued, "is damned well impossible, unthinkable, and unacceptable. A language is by God and by definition *systematic,* which means it's gotta follow some kind of *rules.* Otherwise, nobody can't understand *nobody.* That's the way it works and that's the way it's gotta be. And if anyone thinks they can horse around linguisticwise with Fred C. Jackson—"

Here Jackson paused and drew the blaster from his holster. He checked the charge, snapped off the safety, and replaced the weapon.

"Just better no one give old Jackson no more double-talking," old Jackson muttered. "Because the next alien who tries it is going to get a three-inch circle drilled through his lousy cheating guts."

So saying, Jackson marched back to the city. He was feeling decidedly lightheaded, but absolutely determined. His job was to steal this planet out from under its inhabitants in a legal manner, and in order to do that he had to make sense out of their language. Therefore, in one way or another, he was going to *make* sense. Either that, or he was going to make some corpses.

At this point, he didn't much care which.

Erum was in his office, waiting for him. With him were the mayor, the president of the City Council, the borough president, two aldermen and the director of the Board of Estimates. All of them were smiling—affably, albeit nervously. Strong spirits were present on a sideboard, and there was a subdued air of fellowship in the room.

All in all, it looked as if Jackson were being welcomed as a new and highly respected property owner, an adornment to Fakka. Aliens took it that way sometimes: made the best of a bad bargain by trying to ingratiate themselves with the Inevitable Earthman.

"Mun," said Erum, shaking his hand enthusiastically.

"Same to you, kid," Jackson said. He had no idea what the word meant. Nor did he care. He had plenty of other Naian words to choose among, and he had the determination to force matters to a conclusion.

"Mun!" said the mayor.

"Thanks, pop," said Jackson.

"Mun!" declared the other officials.

"Glad you boys feel that way," said Jackson. He turned to Erum. "Well, let's get it over with, okay?"

"Mun-mun-mun," Erum replied. *"Mun, mun-mun."*

Jackson stared at him for several seconds. Then he said, in a low, controlled voice, "Erum, baby, just exactly *what* are you trying to say to me?"

"Mun, mun, mun," Erum stated firmly. *"Mun, mun mun mun. Mun mun."* He paused, and in a somewhat nervous voice asked the mayor: *"Mun, mun?"*

"Mun . . . mun mun," the mayor replied firmly, and the other officials nodded. They all turned to Jackson.

"Mun, mun-mun?" Erum asked him, tremulously, but with dignity.

Jackson was numbed speechless. His face turned a choleric red and a large blue vein started to pulse in his neck. But he managed to speak slowly, calmly, and with infinite menace.

"Just *what*," he said, "do you lousy third-rate yokels think you're pulling?"

"Mun-mun?" the mayor asked Erum.

"Mun-mun, mun-mun-mun," Erum replied quickly, making a gesture of incomprehension.

"You better talk sense," Jackson said. His voice was still low, but the vein in his neck writhed like a firehose under pressure.

"Mun!" one of the alderman said quickly to the borough president.

"Mun mun-mun mun?" the borough president answered piteously, his voice breaking on the last word.

"So you won't talk sense, huh?"

"Mun! Mun-mun!" the mayor cried, his face gone ashen with fright.

The others looked and saw Jackson's hand clearing the blaster and taking aim at Erum's chest.

"Quit horsing around!" Jackson commanded. The vein in his neck pulsed like a python in travail.

"Mun-mun-mun!" Erum pleaded, dropping to his knees.

"Mun-mun-mun!" the mayor shrieked, rolling his eyes and fainting.

"You get it now," Jackson said to Erum. His finger whitened on the trigger.

Erum, his teeth chattering, managed to gasp out a strangled *"Mun-mun, mun?"* But then his nerves gave way and he waited for death with jaw agape and eyes unfocused.

Jackson took up the last fraction of slack in the trigger. Then, abruptly, he let up and shoved the blaster back in its holster.

"Mun, mun!" Erum managed to say.

"Shaddap," Jackson said. He stepped back and glared at the cringing Naian officials.

He would have dearly loved to blast them all. But he couldn't do it. Jackson had to come to a belated acknowledgement of an unacceptable reality.

His impeccable linguist's ear had heard, and his polyglot brain had analyzed. Dismayingly, he had realized that the Naians were not trying to put anything over on him. They were speaking not nonsense, but a true language.

This language was made up at present of the single sound *"mun."* This sound could carry an extensive repertoire of meanings through variations in pitch and pattern, changes in stress and quantity, alteration of rhythm and repetition, and through accompanying gestures and facial expressions.

A language consisting of infinite variations on a single word! Jackson didn't want to believe it, but he was too good a linguist to doubt the evidence of his own trained senses.

He could learn this language, of course.

But by the time he had learned it, what would it have changed into?

Jackson sighed and rubbed his face wearily. In a sense it was inevitable. All languages change. But on Earth and the few dozen worlds she had contacted, the languages changed with relative slowness.

On Na, the rate of change was faster. Quite a bit faster.

The Na language changed as fashions change on Earth, only faster. It changed as prices change or as the weather changes. It changed endlessly and incessantly, in accordance with unknown rules and invisible principles. It changed its form as an avalanche changes its shape. Compared with it, English was like a glacier.

The Na language was, truly and monstrously, a simulacrum of Heraclitus's river. You cannot step into the same river twice, said Heraclitus; for other waters are forever flowing on.

Concerning the language of Na, this was simply and literally true.

That made it bad enough. But even worse was the fact that an observer like Jackson could never hope to fix or isolate even one term out of the dynamic shifting network of terms that composed the Na language. For the observer's action would be gross enough by itself to disrupt and alter the system, causing it to change unpredictably. And so, if the term were isolated, its relationship to the other terms in the system would necessarily be destroyed, and the term itself, by definition, would be false.

By the fact of its change, the language was rendered impervious to codification and control. Through indeterminacy, the Na tongue resisted all attempts to conquer it. And Jackson had gone from Heraclitus to Heisenberg without touching second base. He was dazed and dazzled, and he looked upon the officials with something approaching awe.

"You've done it, boys," he told them. "You've beaten the system. Old Earth could swallow you and never notice the difference; you couldn't do a damned thing about it. But the folks back home like their legalism, and our law says that we must be in a state of communication as a prior condition to any transaction."

"Mun?" Erum asked politely.

"So I guess that means I leave you folks alone," Jackson said. "At least, I do as long as they keep that law on the books. But what the hell, a reprieve is the best anyone can ask for. Eh?"

"Mun mun," the mayor said hesitantly.

"I'll be getting along now," Jackson said. "Fair's fair. . . . But if I ever find out that you Naians were putting one over on me—"

He left the sentence unfinished. Without another word, Jackson turned and went back to his ship.

In half an hour he was spaceworthy, and fifteen minutes after that he was underway.

6

In Erum's office, the officials watched while Jackson's

spaceship glowed like a comet in the dark afternoon sky. It dwindled to a brilliant needlepoint, and then vanished into the vastness of space.

The officials were silent for a moment; then they turned and looked at each other. Suddenly, spontaneously, they burst into laughter. Harder and harder they laughed, clutching their sides while tears rolled down their cheeks.

The mayor was the first to check the hysteria. Getting a grip on himself he said, *"Mun, mun, mun-mun."*

This thought instantly sobered the others. Their mirth died away. Uneasily they contemplated the distant unfriendly sky, and they thought back over their recent adventures.

At last young Erum asked, *"Mun-mun? Mun-mun?"*

Several of the officials smiled at the naïveté of the question. And yet, none could answer that simple yet crucial demand. Why indeed? Did anyone dare hazard even a guess?

It was a perplexity leaving in doubt not only the future but the past as well. And, if a real answer were unthinkable, then no answer at all was surely insupportable.

The silence grew, and Erum's young mouth twisted downward in premature cynicism. He said quite harshly, *"Mun! Mun-mun! Mun?"*

His shocking words were no more than the hasty cruelty of the young; but such a statement could not go unchallenged. And the venerable first alderman stepped forward to essay a reply.

"Mun mun, mun-mun," the old man said, with disarming simplicity. *"Mun mun mun-mun? Mun mun-mun-mun. Mun mun mun; mun mun mun; mun mun. Mun, mun mun mun—mun mun mun. Mun-mun? Mun mun mun mun!"*

This straightforward declaration of faith pierced Erum to the core of his being. Tears sprang unanticipated to his eyes. All postures forgotten, he turned to the sky, clenched his fist and shouted, *"Mun! Mun! Mun-mun!"*

Smiling serenely, the old alderman murmured, *"Mun-mun-mun; mun, mun-mun."*

This was, ironically enough, the marvelous and frightening truth of the situation. Perhaps it was just as well that the others did not hear.

RESTRICTED AREA

"Nice-looking place, isn't it, Captain?" Simmons asked with elaborate casualness, looking through the port. "Rather a paradise." He yawned.

"You can't go out yet," Captain Kilpepper said, noting the biologist's immediate disappointed expression.

"But, Captain—"

"No." Kilpepper looked out the port at the rolling meadow of grass. Sprinkled with red flowers, it appeared as luscious as it had two days ago when they had landed. To the right of the meadow was a brown forest shot through with yellow and orange blossoms. To the left was a row of hills, colored in contrasting shades of blue-green. A waterfall tumbled down one of the hills.

Trees, flowers, all that sort of thing. The place was undeniably pretty, and it was for that reason that Kilpepper distrusted it. Experience with two wives and five new ships had taught him that a lovely exterior can conceal almost anything. And 15 years in space had added lines to his forehead and gray to his hair, but hadn't given him any reason for altering his conviction.

"Here are the reports, sir," Mate Morena said, handing him a sheaf of papers. Morena had a petulant expression on his broad, rugged face. Behind the door, Kilpepper could hear shuffling feet and whispering voices. He knew it was the crew, assembled to hear what he would say this time.

They wanted outside, but bad.

Kilpepper skimmed the reports. They were the same as the last four groups. Atmosphere breathable and free of dangerous microorganisms, bacteria count nil, radargraph all clear. Some form of animal life in the nearby forest, but no energy manifestations. Detection of a large metallic mass, possibly an iron-rich mountain, several miles south. Noted for further investigation.

"That's fine," Kilpepper said unhappily. The reports vaguely annoyed him. He knew from past experience that there was usually something wrong with every planet. It paid to find it at the start, before costly accidents resulted.

"Can we go out, sir?" Morena asked, his short body stiffly erect. Kilpepper could almost feel the crewmen behind the door holding their breath.

"I don't know," Kilpepper said. He scratched his head, trying to think of some good reason for refusing again. There *must* be something wrong.

"All right," he said at last. "Post a full guard for the time being. Let four men out. No one goes beyond 25 feet of the ship." He had to let them go. After 16 months in the hot, cramped spaceship, he'd have a mutiny on his hands if he didn't.

"Yes sir!" Mate Morena said, and dashed out the door.

"I suppose that means the scientific team can go out," Simmons said, his hands jammed in his pockets.

"Sure," Kilpepper said wearily. "I'll go with you. After all, this expedition is expendable."

The air of the unnamed planet was fragrant after the musty, recirculated air of the ship. The breeze from the mountains was light and steady and refreshing.

Captain Kilpepper sniffed appreciatively, arms folded across his chest. The four crewmen were walking around, stretching their legs and breathing in great lungfuls of fresh air. The scientific team was standing together, wondering where to begin. Simmons bent down and plucked a spear of grass.

"Funny-looking stuff," he said, holding it up to the sunlight.

"Why?" Captain Kilpepper asked, walking over.

"Look at it." The thin biologist held it higher. "Perfectly smooth. Doesn't show any sign of cell formation. Let me see—" He bent over a red blossom.

"Hey! We got visitors!" A crewman named Flynn was the first to spot the natives. They came out of the forest and trotted across the meadow to the ship.

Captain Kilpepper glanced at the ship. The gunners were ready and alert. He touched his sidearm for reassurance, and waited.

"Oh, brother," Aramic murmured. As the ship's linguist, he eyed the advancing natives with intense professional interest. The rest of the men just stared.

In the lead was a creature with a neck at least eight feet long, like a giraffe's, and thick, stubby legs, like a hippopotamus'. It had a cheerful expression on its face. Its hide was purple, sprinkled with large white dots.

Next in line came five little beasts with pure white fur. They were about the size of terriers, and they had an owlishly solemn expression. A fat, red little creature with a green tail at least 16 feet long brought up the rear.

They stopped in front of the men and bowed. There was a long moment of silence, then everyone burst into laughter.

The laughter seemed to be a signal. The five little ones leaped to the back of the hippo-giraffe. They scrambled for a moment, then climbed on each other's shoulders. In a moment they were balanced, five high, like a team of acrobats.

The men applauded wildly.

The fat animal immediately started balancing on his tail.

"Bravo!" shouted Simmons.

The five furry animals jumped off the giraffe's back and started to dance around the pig.

"Hurray!" Morrison, the bacteriologist, called.

The hippo-giraffe turned a clumsy somersault, landed on one ear, scrambled to his feet and bowed deeply.

Captain Kilpepper frowned and rubbed one hand against another. He was trying to figure out some reason for this behavior.

The natives burst into song. The melody was strange, but recognizable as a tune. They harmonized for a few seconds, then bowed and began to roll on the grass.

The crewmen were still applauding. Aramic had taken out his notebook and was jotting down the sounds.

"All right," Kilpepper said. "Crew, back inside."

They gave him reproachful looks.

"Let some of the other men have a chance," the captain said. Regretfully, the men filed back inside.

"I suppose you want to examine them some more," Kilpepper said to the scientists.

"We sure do," Simmons stated. "Never saw anything like it."

Kilpepper nodded and went back into the ship. Four more crewmen filed past him.

"Morena!" Kilpepper shouted. The mate came bounding into the bridge. "I want you to find that metal mass. Take a man and keep in radio contact with the ship at all times."

"Yes sir," Morena said, grinning broadly. "Friendly, aren't they, sir?"

"Yes," Kilpepper said.

"Nice little world," the mate said.

"Yes."

Mate Morena went off to collect his equipment.

Captain Kilpepper sat down and tried to figure out what was wrong with the planet.

Kilpepper spent most of the next day filling out progress reports. In the late afternoon he put down his pencil and went out for a walk.

"Have you got a moment, Captain?" Simmons asked. "There's something I'd like to show you in the forest." Kilpepper grumbled out of habit, but followed the biologist. He had been curious about the forest himself.

On the way, they were accompanied by three natives. These particular three looked like dogs, except for their coloring—red and white, like peppermint candy.

"Now then," Simmons said with ill-concealed eagerness once they were in the forest. "Look around. What do you see that strikes you as odd?"

Kilpepper looked. The trees were thick-trunked and spaced wide apart. So wide apart, in fact, that it was possible to see the next clearing through them.

"Well," he said, "you couldn't get lost here."

"It's not that," Simmons said. "Come on, look again."

Kilpepper smiled. Simmons had brought him here because he made a better audience than any of his preoccupied colleagues.

Behind them, the three natives leaped and played.

"There's no underbrush," Kilpepper stated, after walking a few yards farther. There were vines twisting up the sides of the trees, covered with multicolored flowers. Glancing around, Kilpepper saw a bird dart down, flutter around the head of one of the peppermint-colored dogs, and fly away again.

The bird was colored silver and gold:

"Don't you see anything wrong yet?" Simmons asked impatiently.

"Only the color scheme," Kilpepper said. "Is there something else?"

"Look at the trees."

The boughs were laden with fruit. It hung in clumps, all on the lower branches, of a bewildering variety of colors, sizes, and shapes. There were things that looked like grapes, and things that looked like bananas, and things that looked like watermelons, and—

"Lots of different species, I guess," Kilpepper hazarded, not sure what it was Simmons wanted him to see.

"Different species! Look, man. There are as many as ten different kinds of fruit growing on one branch!"

Examining closer, Kilpepper saw it was true. Each tree had an amazing multiplicity of fruit.

"And that's just impossible," Simmons said. "It's not my field, of course, but I can state with fair certainty that each fruit is a separate and distinct entity. They're not stages of each other."

"How do you account for it?" Kilpepper asked.

"I don't have to," the biologist grinned. "But some poor botanist is going to have his hands full."

They turned and started to walk back. "What were you here for?" Kilpepper asked.

"Me? I was doing a little anthropological work on the side. Wanted to find out where our friends lived. No luck. There are no paths, implements, clearings, anything. Not even caves."

Kilpepper didn't think it unusual that a biologist should be making a quick anthropological survey. It was impossible to represent all the sciences on an expedition of this sort. Survival was the first consideration—biology and bacteriology. Then language. After that, any botanical, ecological, psychological, sociological, or any other knowledge was appreciated.

Eight or nine birds had joined the animals—or natives—

around the ship when they got back. The birds were brilliant-
ly colored also: polka dots, stripes, piebalds. There wasn't a
dun or gray in the lot.

Mate Morena and Crewman Flynn trudged through an
outcropping of the forest. They stopped at the foot of a
little hill.

"Do we have to climb it?" Flynn asked, sighing. The large
camera on his back was weighing him down.

"The little hand says we gotta." Morena pointed to his
dial. The indicator showed the presence of metallic mass
just over the rise.

"Spaceships ought to carry cars," Flynn said, leaning
forward to balance himself against the gentle slope of the
hill.

"Yeh, or camels."

Above them red and gold birds dipped and sailed, cheep-
ing merrily. The breeze fanned the tall grass and hummed
melodiously through the leaves and branches of the nearby
forest. Behind them, two of the natives followed. They
were horse-shaped, except for their hides of green and white
dots.

"Like a bloody circus," Flynn observed as one of the
horses capered a circle around him.

"Yeh," Morena said. They reached the top of the hill
and started down. Then Flynn stopped.

"Look at that!"

At the base of the hill, rising slim and erect, was a
metal pillar. They followed it up with their eyes. It climbed
and climbed—and its top was lost in the clouds.

They hurried down and examined it. Closer, the pillar
was more massy than they had thought. Almost twenty
feet through, Morena estimated. At a guess he placed the
metal as an alloy of steel, by its gray-blue color. But what
steel, he asked himself, could support a shaft that size?

"How high would you say those clouds are?" Morena
asked.

Flynn craned back his neck. "Lord, they must be half a
mile up. Maybe a mile." The pillar had been hidden from
the ship by the clouds, and by its gray-blue color, which
blended into the background.

"I don't believe it," Morena said. "I wonder what the

compression strain on this thing is." They stared in awe at the tremendous shaft.

"Well," Flynn said, "I'd better get some pictures." He unloaded his camera and snapped three shots of the shaft from 20 feet, then a shot with Morena for size comparison. For the next three pictures he sighted up the shaft.

"What do you figure it is?" Morena asked.

"Let the big brains figure it out," Flynn said. "It ought to drive them nuts." He strapped the camera back together. "Now I suppose we have to walk all the way back." He looked at the green and white horses. "Wonder if I could hitch a ride."

"Go ahead and break your stupid neck," Morena said.

"Here, boy, come on here," Flynn called. One of the horses came over and knelt beside him. Flynn climbed on his back gingerly. Once he was astride, he grinned at Morena.

"Just don't smash that camera," Morena said. "It's government property."

"Nice boy," Flynn said to the horse. "Good fellow." The horse got to his feet—and smiled.

"See you back in camp," Flynn said, guiding the horse toward the hill.

"Hold it a second," Morena said. He looked glumly at Flynn, then beckoned to the other horse. "Come on, boy." The horse knelt and he climbed on.

They rode in circles for a few moments, experimenting. The horses could be guided by a touch. Their broad backs were amazingly comfortable. One of the red and gold birds came down and perched on Flynn's shoulder.

"Hey, hey, this is the life," Flynn said, patting the glossy hide of his mount. "Race you back to camp, Mate."

"You're on," Morena said. But their horses would move no faster than a slow walk, in spite of all their urging.

At the ship, Kilpepper was squatting in the grass, watching Aramic at work. The linguist was a patient man. His sisters had always remarked on his patience. His colleagues had praised him for it, and his students, during his years of teaching, had appreciated it. Now, the backlog of 16 years of self-containment was being called to the front.

"We'll try it again," Aramic said in his calmest voice. He

flipped through the pages of *Language Approach for Alien Grade-Two Intelligences*—a text written by himself—and found the diagram he wanted. He opened to the page and pointed.

The animal beside him looked like an inconceivable cross between a chipmunk and a giant panda. It cocked one eye at the diagram, the other eye wandering ludicrously around its socket.

"Planet," Aramic said, pointing. "Planet."

"Excuse me, Skipper," Simmons said. "I'd like to set up this X-ray gadget here."

"Certainly," Kilpepper said, moving to let the biologist drag the machine into place.

"Planet," Aramic said again.

"Elam vessel holam cram," the chipmunk-panda said pleasantly.

Damn it, they had a language. The sounds they made were certainly representational. It was just a question of finding a common meeting ground. Had they mastered simple abstractions? Aramic put down his book and pointed to the chipmunk-panda.

"Animal," he said, and waited.

"Get him to hold still," Simmons said, focusing the X-ray. "That's good. Now a few more."

"Animal," Aramic repeated hopefully.

"Eeful beeful box," the animal said. *"Hoful toful lox, ramadan, Samduran, eeful beeful box."*

Patience, Aramic reminded himself. Positive attitude. Be cheerful. Faint heart never.

He picked up another of his manuals. This one was called *Language Approach to Alien Grade-One Intelligences*.

He found what he wanted and put it down again. Smiling, he held up a finger.

"One," he said.

The animal leaned forward and sniffed his finger.

Smiling grimly, Aramic held up another finger. "Two." A third. "Three."

"Hoogelex," the animal said suddenly.

A diphthong? Their word for "one"? "One," he said again, waving the same finger.

"Vereserevef," the animal replied, beaming.

Could that be an alternate "one"? "One," he said again.

The animal burst into song.

"*Sevef hevef ulud cram, aragan, biligan, homus dram—*"

It stopped and looked at the *Language Approach* manual, fluttering in the air, and at the back of the linguist, who, with remarkable patience, had refrained from throttling him.

After Morena and Flynn returned, Kilpepper puzzled over their report. He had the photographs rushed through and studied them with care.

The shaft was round and smooth and obviously manufactured. Any race that could put up a thing like that could give them trouble. Big trouble.

But who had put the shaft up? Not the happy, stupid animals around the ship, certainly.

"You say the top is hidden in the clouds?" Kilpepper asked.

"Yes sir," Morena said. "That damn thing must be all of a mile high."

"Go back," Kilpepper said. "Take a radarscope. Take infrared equipment. Get me a picture of the top of that shaft. I want to know how high it goes and what's on top of it. Quick."

Flynn and Morena left the bridge.

Kilpepper looked at the still-wet photographs for a minute longer, then put them down. He wandered into the ship's lab, vague worries nagging at him. The planet didn't make sense, and that bothered him. Kilpepper had discovered the hard way that there's a pattern to everything. If you can't find it in time, that's just too bad for you.

Morrison, the bacteriologist, was a small, sad man. Right now he looked like an extension of the microscope he was peering into.

"Find anything?" Kilpepper asked.

"I've found the absence of something," Morrison said, looking up and blinking. "I've found the absence of a hell of a lot of something."

"What's that?" Kilpepper asked.

"I've run tests on the flowers," Morrison said, "and I've run tests on the earth, and tests on water samples. Nothing definitive yet, but brace yourself."

"I'm braced. What is it?"

"There isn't an ounce of bacteria on this planet!"

"Oh?" Kilpepper said, because he couldn't think of any-thing else to say. He didn't consider it a particularly shock-ing announcement. But the bacteriologist was acting as if he had announced that the subsoil of the planet was 100 percent pure green cheese.

"That's it. The water in the stream is purer than distilled alcohol. The dirt on this planet is cleaner than a boiled scal-pel. The only bacteria are the ones we brought. And they're being killed off."

"How?"

"The air of this place has about three disinfecting agents I've detected, and probably a dozen more I haven't. Same with the dirt and water. This place is sterile!"

"Well, now," Kilpepper said. He couldn't appreciate the full force of the statement. He was still worried about the steel shaft. "What does that mean?"

"I'm glad you asked me that," Morrison said. "Yes, I'm really glad you asked me. It means simply that this place doesn't exist."

"Oh, come now."

"I mean it. There can't be life without microorganisms. One whole section of the life cycle is missing here."

"Unfortunately, it does exist," Kilpepper pointed out gently. "Have you any other theories?"

"Yes, but I want to finish these tests first. But I'll tell you one thing, and maybe you can work it out for yourself."

"Go on."

"I haven't been able to detect a piece of rock on this planet. That's not strictly my field, of course—but we're all jacks-of-all-trades on this expedition. Anyhow, I'm inter-ested in geology. There's no loose rock or stone anywhere around. The smallest stone is about seven tons, I'd estimate."

"What does that mean?"

"Ah! You were wondering also?" Morrison smiled. "Ex-cuse me. I want to complete these tests before supper."

Just before sunset, the X rays of the animals were finished. Kilpepper had another surprise. Morrison had told him that the planet couldn't exist. Then Simmons in-sisted the animals couldn't exist.

"Just look at these pictures," he said to Kilpepper. "Look. Do you see any organs?"

"I don't know much about X rays."

"You don't have to. Just look." The X ray showed a few bones and one or two organs. There were traces of a nervous system on some of the pictures but, mostly, the animals seemed homogeneous throughout.

"There isn't enough internal structure to keep a tapeworm going," Simmons said. "This simplification is impossible. There's nothing that corresponds to lungs or heart. No bloodstream. No brain. Damn little nervous system. What organs they have just don't make sense."

"And your conclusion—"

"That these animals don't exist," Simmons said in high good humor. He liked the idea. It would be fun to do a paper on a nonexistent animal. Aramic passed them, swearing softly.

"Any luck on that lingo?" Simmons asked him.

"No!" Aramic shouted, then blushed. "Sorry. I tested them right down to intelligence grade C3BB. That's amoeba class. No response."

"Perhaps they're just completely brainless," Kilpepper suggested.

"No. The ability to do tricks shows a certain level of intelligence. They have a language of sorts, also, and a definite response pattern. But they won't pay any attention. All they do is sing songs."

"I think we all need supper," Kilpepper said. "And perhaps a slug or two of the old standby."

The old standby was much in evidence at supper. After a fifth or two had been consumed, the scientists mellowed sufficiently to consider some possibilities. They put together their facts.

Item, the natives—or animals—showed no sign of internal organs, no reproductive or excretive equipment. There seemed to be at least three dozen species, not counting birds, and more appearing every day.

The same with the plants.

Item, the planet was amazingly sterile and acted to keep itself so.

Item, the natives had a language but evidently couldn't

impart it to others. Nor could they learn another language.

Item, there were no small rocks or stones around.

Item, there was a tremendous steel shaft, rising to a height of at least half a mile, exact height to be determined when the new pictures were developed. Although there was no sign of a machine culture, the shaft was obviously the product of one. Someone must have built it and put it there.

"Throw it all together and what have you got?" Kilpepper asked.

"I have a theory," Morrison said. "It's a beautiful theory. Would you care to hear it?"

Everyone said yes except Aramic, who was still brooding over his inability to learn the native language.

"The way I see it, this planet is man-made. It must be. No race would evolve without bacteria. It was made by a super race, the race who put that steel spire there. They built it for these animals."

"Why?" Kilpepper asked.

"This is the beautiful part," Morrison said dreamily. "Pure altruism. Look at the natives. Happy, playful. Completely devoid of violence, rid of all nasty habits. Don't they deserve a world to themselves? A world where they can romp and play in an eternal summer?"

"That *is* beautiful," Kilpepper said, stifling a grin. "But—"

"These people are here as a reminder," Morrison continued. "A message to all passing races that man can live in peace."

"There's only one flaw in that," Simmons said. "The animals could never have evolved naturally. You saw the X rays."

"That's true." The dreamer struggled briefly with the biologist, and the dreamer lost. "Perhaps they're robots."

"That's the explanation I favor," Simmons said. "The way I see it, the race that built the steel spire built these animals, also. They're servants, slaves. Why, they might even think *we're* their masters."

"Where would the real masters have gone?" Morrison asked.

"How the hell should I know?" Simmons said.

"And where would these masters live?" Kilpepper asked. "We haven't spotted anything that looks like a habitation."

"They're so far advanced they don't need machines or houses. They live directly with nature."

"Then why do they need servants?" Morrison asked mercilessly. "And why did they build the spire?"

That evening the new pictures of the steel pillar were completed and the scientists examined them eagerly. The top of the pillar was almost a mile high, hidden in thick clouds. There was a projection on either side of the top, jutting out at right angles to a distance of 85 feet.

"Looks like it might be a watchtower," Simmons said.

"What could they watch that high up?" Morrison asked. "All they'd see would be clouds."

"Perhaps they like looking at clouds," Simmons said.

"I'm going to bed," Kilpepper stated in utter disgust.

When Kilpepper woke up the next morning, something didn't feel right. He dressed and went outside. There seemed to be something intangible in the wind. Or was it just his nerves?

Kilpepper shook his head. He had faith in his premonitions. They usually meant that, unconsciously, he had completed some process in reasoning.

Everything seemed to be in order around the ship. The animals were outside, wandering lazily around.

Kilpepper glared at them and walked around the ship. The scientists were back at work trying to solve the mysteries of the planet. Aramic was trying to learn the language from a mournful-eyed green and silver beast. The beast seemed unusually apathetic this morning. It barely muttered its songs and paid no attention to Aramic.

Kilpepper thought of Circe. Could the animals be people, changed into beasts by some wicked sorcerer? He rejected the fanciful idea and walked on.

The crew hadn't noticed anything different. They had headed, en masse, for the waterfall, to get in some swimming. Kilpepper assigned two men to make a microscopic inspection of the steel shaft.

That worried him more than anything else. It didn't seem to bother the other scientists, but Kilpepper figured that was natural. Every cobbler to his last. A linguist would be bound to attach primary importance to the language of the people, while a botanist would think the key to the planet lay in the multifruit-bearing trees.

And what did he think? Captain Kilpepper examined his ideas. What he needed, he decided, was a field theory. Something that would unify all the observed phenomena.

What theory would do that? Why weren't there any germs? Why weren't there any rocks? Why, why, why. Kilpepper felt sure that the explanation was relatively simple. He could almost see it—but not quite.

He sat down in the shade, leaning against the ship, and tried to think.

Around midday Aramic, the linguist, walked over. He threw his books, one by one, against the side of the ship.

"Temper," Kilpepper said.

"I give up," Aramic said. "Those beasts won't pay any attention now. They're barely talking. And they've stopped doing tricks."

Kilpepper got to his feet and walked over to the animals. Sure enough, they didn't seem at all lively. They crept around as though they were in the last stages of malnutrition.

Simmons was standing beside them, jotting down notes on a little pad.

"What's wrong with your little friends?" Kilpepper asked.

"I don't know," Simmons said. "Perhaps they were so excited they didn't sleep last night."

The giraffe-like animal sat down suddenly. Slowly he rolled over on his side and lay still.

"That's strange," Simmons said. "First time I saw one of them do that." He bent over the fallen animal and searched for a heartbeat. After a few seconds he straightened.

"No sign of life," he said.

Two of the smaller ones with glossy black fur toppled over.

"Oh lord," Simmons said, hurrying over to them. "What's happening now?"

"I'm afraid I know," Morrison said, coming out of the ship, his face ashen. "Germs."

"What are you talking about?"

"Captain, I feel like a murderer. I think we've killed

these poor beasts. You remember, I told you there was no sign of any microorganism on this planet? Think of how many we've introduced! Bacteria streaming off our bodies onto these hosts. Hosts with no resistance, remember."

"I thought you said the air had several disinfecting agents?" Kilpepper asked.

"Evidently they didn't work fast enough." Morrison bent over and examined one of the little animals. "I'm sure of it."

The rest of the animals around the ship were falling now and lying quite still. Captain Kilpepper looked around anxiously.

One of the crewmen dashed up, panting. He was still wet from his swim by the waterfall.

"Sir," he gasped. "Over by the falls—the animals—"

"I know," he said. "Get all the men down here."

"That's not all, sir," the man said. "The waterfall—you know, the waterfall—"

"Well, spit it out, man."

"It's stopped, sir. It's stopped running."

"Get those men down here!" The crewman sprinted back to the falls. Kilpepper looked around, not sure what he was looking for. The brown forest was quiet. Too quiet.

He almost had the answer. . . .

Kilpepper realized that the gentle, steady breeze that had been blowing ever since they landed had stopped.

"What in hell is going on here?" Simmons said uneasily. They started backing toward the ship.

"Is the sun getting darker?" Morrison whispered. They weren't sure. It was midafternoon, but the sun did seem less bright.

The crewmen hurried back from the waterfall, glistening wet. At Kilpepper's order they piled back into the ship. The scientists remained standing, looking over the silent land.

"What could we have done?" Aramic asked. He shuddered at the sight of the fallen animals.

The men who had been examining the shaft came running down the hill, bounding through the long grass as though the devil himself were after them.

"What now?" Kilpepper asked.

"It's that damned shaft, sir!" Morena said. "It's turning!"
The shaft—that mile-high mass of incredibly strong metal
—was being turned!

"What are we going to do?" Simmons asked.

"Get back in the ship," Kilpepper muttered. He could
feel the answer taking shape now. There was just one more
bit of evidence he needed. One thing more—

The animals sprang to their feet! The red and silver
birds started flying again, winging high into the air. The
giraffe-hippo reared to his feet, snorted, and raced off. The
rest of the animals followed him. From the forest an avalanche of strange beasts poured onto the meadow.

At full speed they headed west, away from the ship.

"Get back in the ship!" Kilpepper shouted suddenly.
That did it. He knew now, and he only hoped he could get
the ship into deep space in time.

"Hurry the hell up! Get those engines going!" he shouted to the gawking crewmen.

"But we've still got equipment scattered around," Simmons said. "I don't see any need for this—"

"Man the guns!" Captain Kilpepper roared, pushing the
scientists toward the bay of the ship.

Suddenly there were long shadows in the west.

"Captain. We haven't completed our investigation yet—"

"You'll be lucky if you live through this," Kilpepper
said as they entered the bay. "Haven't you put it together
yet? Close that bay! Get everything tight!"

"You mean the turning shaft?" Simmons said, stumbling
over Morrison in the corridor of the ship. "All right, I suppose there's some 'super race—"

"That turning shaft is a key in the side of the planet,"
Kilpepper said, racing toward the bridge. "It winds the
place up. The whole world is like that. Animals, rivers,
wind—everything runs down."

He punched a quick orbit on the ship's tape.

"Strap down," he said. "Figure it out. A place where all
kinds of wonderful food hangs from the trees. Where
there's no bacteria to hurt you, not even a sharp rock to
stub your toes. A place filled with marvelous, amusing,
gentle animals. Where everything's designed to delight
you.

"A playground!"

The scientists stared at him.

"The shaft is a key. The place ran down while we made our unauthorized visit. Now someone's winding the planet up again."

Outside the port the shadows were stretching for thousands of feet across the green meadow.

"Hang on," Kilpepper said as he punched the takeoff stud. "Unlike the toy animals, I don't want to meet the children who play here. And I especially don't want to meet their parents."

THE ODOR OF THOUGHT

Leroy Cleevy's real trouble started when he was taking Mailship 243 through the uncolonized Seergon Cluster. Before this, he had the usual problems of an interstellar mailman; an old ship, scored tubes, and faulty astrogation. But now, while he was taking line-of-direction readings, he noticed that his ship was growing uncomfortably warm.

He sighed unhappily, switched on the refrigeration, and contacted the postmaster at Base. He was at the extreme limit of radio contact, and the postmaster's voice floated in on a sea of static.

"More trouble, Cleevy?" the postmaster asked, in the ominous tones of a man who writes schedules and believes in them.

"Oh, I don't know," Cleevy said brightly. "Aside from the tubes and astrogation and wiring, everything's fine except for the insulation and refrigeration."

"It's a damned shame," the postmaster said, suddenly sympathetic. "I know how you feel."

Cleevy switched the refrigeration to FULL, wiped perspiration from his eyes, and decided that the postmaster only *thought* he knew how he felt.

"Haven't I asked the government for new ships over and over again?" The postmaster laughed ruefully. "They seem to feel that I can get the mail through in any old crate."

As the moment Cleevy wasn't interested in the postmaster's troubles. Even with the refrigeration laboring at FULL, the ship was overheating.

"Hang on a moment," he said. He went to the rear of the ship, where the heat seemed to be emanating, and found that three of his tanks were filled not with fuel, but with a bubbling white-hot slag. The fourth tank was rapidly undergoing the same change.

Cleevy stared for a moment, turned, and sprinted to the radio.

"No more fuel," he said. "Catalytic actions, I think. I told you we needed new tanks. I'm putting down on the first oxygen planet I can find."

He pulled down the *Emergency Manual* and looked up the Seergon Cluster. There were no colonies in the group, but the oxygen worlds had been charted for future reference. What was on them, aside from oxygen, no one knew. Cleevy expected to find out, if his ship stayed together long enough.

"I'll try 3-M-22!" he shouted over the mounting static.

"Take good care of the mail," the postmaster howled back. "I'm sending a ship right out."

Cleevy told him what he could do with the mail, all 20 pounds of it. But the postmaster had signed off by then.

Cleevy made a good landing on 3-M-22, exceptionally good, taking into consideration the fact that his instruments were too hot to touch, his tubes were warped by heat, and the mail sack strapped to his back hampered his movements. Mailship 243 sailed in like a swan. Twenty feet above the planet's surface it gave up and dropped like a stone.

Cleevy held on to consciousness, although he was certain every bone in his body was broken. The sides of the ship were turning a dull red when he stumbled through the escape hatch, the mail sack still firmly strapped to his back.

He staggered 100 yards, eyes closed. Then the ship exploded and knocked him flat on his face. He stood up, took two more steps, and passed out completely.

When he recovered consciousness, he was lying on a little hillside, face down in tall grass. He was in a beautiful state of shock. He felt that he was detached from his body, a pure intellect floating in the air. All worries, emotions, fears remained with his body; *he* was free.

He looked around and saw that a small animal was passing near him. It was about the size of a squirrel, but with dull green fur.

As it came close, he saw that it had no eyes or ears. This didn't surprise him. On the contrary, it seemed quite fitting. Why in hell *should* a squirrel have eyes or ears? Squirrels were better off not seeing the pain and torture of the world, not hearing the anguished screams of . . .

Another animal approached, and this one was the size and shape of a timber wolf, but also colored green. Parallel evolution? It didn't matter in the total scheme of things, he decided. This one, too, was eyeless and earless. But it had a magnificent set of teeth.

Cleevy watched with only faint interest. What does a pure intellect care for wolves and squirrels, eyeless or otherwise? He observed that the squirrel had frozen, not more than five feet from the wolf. The wolf approached slowly. Then, not three feet away, he seemed to lose the scent. He shook his head and turned a slow circle. When he moved forward again, he wasn't going in the right direction.

The blind hunt the blind, Cleevy told himself, and it seemed a deep and eternal truth. As he watched, the squirrel quivered; the wolf whirled, pounced, and devoured it in three gulps.

What large teeth wolves have, Cleevy thought. Instantly the eyeless wolf whirled and faced him.

Now he's going to eat me, Cleevy thought. It amused him to realize that he was the first human to be eaten on this planet.

The wolf was snarling in his face when Cleevy passed out again.

It was evening when he recovered. Long shadows had formed over the land, and the sun was low in the sky. Cleevy sat up and flexed his arms and legs experimentally. Nothing was broken.

He got on one knee, groggy, but in possession of his senses. What had happened? He remembered the crash as though it were a thousand years ago. The ship had burned, he had walked away and fainted. After that he had met a wolf and a squirrel.

He climbed unsteadily to his feet and looked around. He must have dreamed that last part. If there had been a wolf, he would have been killed.

Glancing down at his feet, he saw the squirrel's green tail and, a little farther away, its head.

He tried desperately to think. So there *had* been a wolf, and a hungry one. If he expected to survive until the rescue ship came, he had to find out exactly what had happened, and why.

Neither animal had eyes or ears. How did they track each other? Smell? If so, why did the wolf have so much trouble finding the squirrel?

He heard a low growl and turned. There, not 50 feet away, was something that looked like a panther. A yellow-brown, eyeless, earless panther.

Damned menagerie, Cleevy thought, and crouched down in the tall grass. This planet was rushing him along too fast. He needed time to think. How did these animals operate? Instead of sight, did they have a sense of location?

The panther began to move away.

Cleevy breathed a little easier. Perhaps, if he stayed out of sight, the panther . . .

As soon as he thought the word "panther," the beast turned in his direction.

What have I done? Cleevy asked himself, burrowing deeper into the grass. He can't smell me or see me or hear me. All I did was decide to stay out of his way. . . .

Head high, the panther began to pace toward him.

That did it. Without eyes or ears, there was only one way the beast could have detected him.

It had to be telepathic!

To test his theory, he thought the word "panther," identifying it automatically with the animal that was approaching him. The panther roared furiously and shortened the distance between them.

In a fraction of a second, Cleevy understood a lot of things. The wolf had been tracking the squirrel by telepathy. The squirrel had frozen—perhaps it had even stopped thinking! The wolf had been thrown off the scent—until the squirrel wasn't able to keep from thinking any longer.

In that case, why hadn't the wolf attacked him while he was unconscious? Perhaps he had stopped thinking—or at least, stopped thinking on a wavelength that the wolf could receive. Probably there was more to it than that.

Right now, his problem was the *panther*.

The beast roared again. It was only 30 feet away and closing the distance rapidly.

All he had to do, Cleevy thought, was not to think of—was to think of something else. In that way, perhaps the—well, perhaps it would lose the scent. He started to think about all the girls he had ever known, in painstaking detail.

The panther stopped and pawed the ground doubtfully.

Cleevy went on thinking; about girls, and ships, and planets, and girls, and ships, and everything but panthers. . . .

The panther advanced another five feet.

Damn it, he thought, how do you *not* think of something? You think furiously about stones and rocks and people and places and things, but your mind always returns to—but you ignore that and concentrate on your sainted grandmother, your drunken old father, the bruises on your right leg. (Count them. Eight. Count them again. Still eight.) And now you glance up, casually, seeing, but not really recognizing the—anyhow, it's still advancing.

Cleevy found that trying *not* to think of something is like trying to stop an avalanche with your bare hands. He realized that the human mind couldn't be inhibited so directly and consciously as all that. It takes time and practice.

He had about 15 feet left in which to learn how not to think of a . . .

Well, there are also card games to think about, and parties, and dogs, cats, horses, mice, sheep, wolves (move away!), and bruises, battleships, caves, lairs, dens, cubs (watch out), *p-paramounts,* and tantamounts and gadabouts and roundabouts and roustabouts and ins-and-outs (about eight feet), meals, food, fire, fox, fur, pigs, pokes, prams, and p-p-p-p- . . .

The panther was about five feet away now and crouching for the spring. Cleevy couldn't hold back the thought any longer. Then, in a burst of inspiration, he thought:

Pantheress!

The panther, still crouching, faced him doubtfully.

Cleevy concentrated on the idea of a pantheress. *He* was a pantheress, and what did this panther mean by frightening her that way? He thought about his (her, damn it!)

cubs, a warm cave, the pleasure of tracking down squirrels. . . .

The panther advanced slowly and rubbed against Cleevy. Cleevy thought desperately, What fine weather we've been having, and what a fine panther this chap really is, so big, so strong, and with such enormous teeth.

The panther purred!

Cleevy lay down and curled an imaginary tail around him and decided he was going to sleep. The panther stood by indecisively. He seemed to feel that something was wrong. He growled once, deep in his throat, then turned and loped away.

The sun had just set, and the entire land was a deep blue. Cleevy found that he was shaking uncontrollably, and on the verge of hysterical laughter. If the panther had stayed another moment . . .

He controlled himself with an effort. It was time for some serious thinking.

Probably every animal had its characteristic thought-smell. A squirrel emitted one kind, a wolf another, and a human still another. The all-important question was, could he be traced only when he thought of some animal? Or could his thought patterns, like an odor, be detected even when he was not thinking of anything in particular?

Apparently, the panther had scented him only when he thought, specifically of it. But that could be due to unfamiliarity. His alien thought-smell might have confused the panther—this time.

He'd just have to wait and see. The panther probably wasn't stupid. It was just the first time that trick had been played on him.

Any trick will work—once.

Cleevy lay back and stared at the sky. He was too tired to move, and his bruised body ached. What would happen now, at night? Did the beasts continue to hunt? Or was there a truce of some sort? He didn't give a damn.

To hell with squirrels, wolves, panthers, lions, tigers, and reindeer.

He slept.

The next morning, he was surprised to find himself still alive. So far, so good. It might be a good day after all. Cheerfully he walked to his ship.

All that was left of Mailship 243 was a pile of twisted metal strewn across the scorched earth. Cleevy found a bar of metal, hefted it, and slid it into his belt below the mail sack. It wasn't much of a weapon, but it gave him a certain confidence.

The ship was a total loss. He left and began to look for food. In the surrounding countryside there were several fruit-bearing shrubs. He sampled one warily and found it tart, but not unpleasant. He gorged himself on fruit and washed it down with water from a nearby stream.

He hadn't seen any animals so far. Of course, for all he knew, they could be closing in on him now.

He avoided the thought and started looking for a place to hide. His best bet was to stay out of sight until the rescue ship came. He tramped over the gentle rolling hills, looking for a cliff, a tree, a cave. But the amiable landscape presented nothing larger than a six-foot shrub.

By afternoon he was tired and irritated, and scanning the skies anxiously. Why wasn't the ship here? It should take no longer than a day or two, he estimated, for a fast emergency ship to reach him.

If the postmaster was looking on the right planet.

There was a movement in the sky. He looked up, his heart racing furiously. There was something there!

It was a bird. It sailed slowly over him, balancing easily on its gigantic wings. It dipped once, then flew on.

It looked amazingly like a vulture.

He continued walking. In another moment, he found himself face to face with four blind wolves.

That took care of one question. He *could* be traced by his characteristic thought-smell. Evidently the beasts of this planet had decided he wasn't too alien to eat.

The wolves moved cautiously toward him. Cleevy tried the trick he had used the other day. Lifting the metal bar out of his belt, he thought of himself as a female wolf searching for her cubs. Won't one of you gentlemen help me find them? They were here only a few minutes ago. One was green, one was spotted, and the other . . .

Perhaps these wolves didn't have spotted cubs. One of them leaped at Cleevy. Cleevy struck him in midair with his bar, and the wolf staggered back.

Shoulder to shoulder, the four closed in.

Desperately, Cleevy tried to think himself out of existence. No use. The wolves kept on coming.

Cleevy thought of a panther. *He* was a panther, a big one, and he was looking forward to a meal of wolf.

That stopped them. They switched their tails anxiously, but held their ground.

Cleevy growled, pawed the earth, and stalked forward. The wolves retreated, but one started to slip in back of him.

He moved sideways, trying to keep from being circled. It seemed that they really didn't believe him. Perhaps he didn't make a good panther. They had stopped retreating. One was in back of him, and the others stood firm, their tongues lolling out on their wet, open jaws. Cleevy growled ferociously and swung his club. A wolf darted back, but the one behind him sprang, landed on the mail sack, and knocked him over.

As they piled on, Cleevy had another inspiration. He imagined himself to be a snake, very fast, deadly, with poison fangs that could take a wolf's life in an instant.

They were off him at once. Cleevy hissed and arched his boneless neck. The wolves howled angrily, but showed no inclination to attack.

Then Cleevy made a mistake. He knew that he should stand firm and brazen it out. But his body had its own ideas. Involuntarily he turned and sprinted away.

The wolves loped after him, and glancing up, Cleevy could see the vultures gathering for the remains. He controlled himself and tried to become a snake again, but the wolves kept coming.

The vultures overhead gave him an idea. As a spaceman, he knew what the land looked like from the air. Cleevy decided to become a bird. He imagined himself soaring, balanced easily on an updraft, looking down on the green, rolling land.

The wolves were confused. They ran in circles and leaped into the air. Cleevy continued soaring, higher and higher, backing away slowly as he did so.

Finally he was out of sight of the wolves, and it was evening. He was exhausted. He had lived through another day. But evidently his gambits were good only once. What was he going to do tomorrow, if the rescue ship didn't come?

After it grew dark, he lay awake for a long time, watching the sky. But all he saw were stars. And all he heard was the occasional growl of a wolf, or the roar of a panther dreaming of his breakfast.

Morning came too soon. Cleevy awoke still tired and unrefreshed. He lay back and waited for something to happen.

Where was the rescue ship? They had had plenty of time, he decided. Why weren't they here? If they waited too long, the panther . . .

He shouldn't have thought it. In answer, he heard a roar on his right.

He stood up and moved away from the sound. He decided he'd be better off facing the wolves. . . .

He shouldn't have thought that either, because now the roar of the panther was joined by the howl of a wolf pack.

Cleevy met them simultaneously. A green-yellow panther stepped daintily out of the underbrush in front of him. On the other side, he could make out the shapes of several wolves. For a moment, he thought they might fight it out. If the wolves jumped the panther, he could get away. . . .

But they were interested only in him. Why should they fight each other, he realized, when he was around, broadcasting his fears and helplessness for all to hear?

The panther moved toward him. The wolves stayed back, evidently content to take the remains. Cleevy tried the bird routine, but the panther, after hesitating a moment, kept on coming.

Cheevy backed toward the wolves, wishing he had something to climb. What he needed was a cliff, or even a decent-sized tree. . . .

But there were shrubs! With inventiveness born of desperation, Cleevy became a six-foot shrub. He didn't really know how a shrub would think, but he did his best.

He was blossoming now. And one of his roots felt a little wobbly—the result of that last storm. Still, he was a pretty good shrub, taking everything into consideration.

Out of the corner of his branches, he saw the wolves

stop moving. The panther circled him, sniffed, and cocked his head to one side.

Really now, he thought, who would want to take a bite out of a shrub? You might have thought I was something else, but actually, I'm just a shrub. You wouldn't want a mouthful of leaves, would you? And you might break a tooth on my branches. Who ever heard of panthers eating shrubs? And I *am* a shrub. Ask my mother. She was a shrub, too. We've all been shrubs, ever since the Carboniferous Age.

The panther showed no signs of attacking. But he showed no signs of leaving, either. Cleevy wondered if he could keep it up. What should he think about next? The beauties of spring? A nest of robins in his hair?

A little bird landed on his shoulder.

Isn't that nice, Cleevy thought. He thinks I'm a shrub, too. He's going to build a nest in my branches. That's perfectly lovely. All the other shrubs will be jealous of me.

The bird tapped lightly at Cleevy's neck.

Easy, Cleevy thought. Wouldn't want to kill the tree that feeds you. . . .

The bird tapped again, experimentally. Then, setting its webbed feet firmly, proceeded to tap at Cleevy's neck with the speed of a pneumatic hammer.

A damned woodpecker, Cleevy thought, trying to stay shrublike. He noticed that the panther was suddenly restive. But after the bird had punctured his neck for the fifteenth time, Cleevy couldn't help himself. He picked up the bird and threw it at the panther.

The panther snapped, but not in time. Outraged, the bird flew around Cleevy's head, scouting. Then it streaked away for the quieter shrubs.

Instantly, Cleevy became a shrub again, but that game was over. The panther cuffed at him. Cleevy tried to run, stumbled over a wolf, and fell. With the panther growling in his ear, he knew that he was a corpse already.

The panther hesitated.

Cleevy now became a corpse to his melting fingertips. He had been dead for days, weeks. His blood had long since drained away. His flesh stank. All that was left was rot and decay. No sane animal would touch him, no matter how hungry it was.

The panther seemed to agree. He backed away. The wolves howled hungrily, but they, too, were in retreat.

Cleevy advanced his putrefaction several days. He concentrated on how horribly indigestible he was, how genuinely unsavory. And there was conviction in back of his thought. He honestly didn't believe he would make a good meal for anyone.

The panther continued to move away, followed by the wolves. He was saved! He could go on being a corpse for the rest of his life, if necessary. . . .

And then he smelled *truly* rotten flesh. Looking around, he saw that an enormous bird had landed beside him.

On Earth, it would have been called a vulture.

Cleevy could have cried at that moment. Wouldn't anything work? The vulture waddled toward him, and Cleevy jumped to his feet and kicked it away. If he had to be eaten, it wasn't going to be by a vulture.

The panther came back like a lightning bolt, and there seemed to be anger and frustration on that blank, furry face. Cleevy raised his metal bar, wishing he had a tree to climb, a gun to shoot, or even a torch to wave. . . .

A torch!

He knew at once that he had found the answer. He blazed in the panther's face, and the panther backed away, squealing. Quickly Cleevy began to burn in all directions, devouring the dry grass, setting fire to the shrubs.

The panther and the wolves darted away.

Now it was his turn! He should have remembered that all animals have a deep, instinctive dread of fire. By God, he was going to be the greatest fire that ever hit this place!

A light breeze came up and fanned him across the rolling land. Squirrels fled from the underbrush and streaked away from him. Families of birds took flight, and panthers, wolves, and other animals ran side by side, all thought of food driven from their minds, wishing only to escape from the fire—to escape from him!

Dimly, Cleevy realized that he had now become truly telepathic himself. Eyes closed, he could see on all sides of him and sense what was going on. As a roaring fire he advanced, sweeping everything before him. And he could *feel* the fear in their minds as they raced away.

It was fitting. Hadn't man always been the master, because of his adaptability, his superior intelligence? The same results obtained here, too. Proudly he jumped a narrow stream three miles away, ignited a clump of bushes, flamed, spurted. . . .

And then he felt the first drop of water.

He burned on, but the one drop became five, then 15, then 500. He was drenched, and his fuel, the grass and shrubs, were soon dripping with water.

He was being put out.

It just wasn't fair, Cleevy thought. By rights he should have won. He had met this planet on its own terms and beaten it—only to have an act of nature ruin everything.

Cautiously, the animals were starting to return.

The water poured down. The last of Cleevy's flames went out. Cleevy sighed, and fainted.

". . . a damned fine job. You held onto your mail, and that's the mark of a good postman. Perhaps we can arrange a medal."

Cleevy opened his eyes. The postmaster was standing over him, beaming proudly. He was lying on a bunk, and overhead he could see curving metal walls.

He was on the rescue ship.

"What happened?" he croaked.

"We got you just in time," the postmaster said. "You'd better not move yet. We were almost too late."

Cleevy felt the ship lift and knew that they were leaving the surface of 3-M-22. He staggered to the port and looked at the green land below him.

"It was close," the postmaster said, standing beside Cleevy and looking down. "We got the ship's sprinkler system going just in time. You were standing in the center of the damnedest grass fire I've ever seen." Looking down at the unscarred green land, the postmaster seemed to have a moment of doubt. He looked again, and his expression reminded Cleevy of the panther he had tricked.

"Say—how come you weren't burned?"

THE NECESSARY THING

Richard Gregor was seated at his desk in the dusty offices of the AAA Ace Interplanetary Decontamination Service, staring wearily at a list. The list included some 2,305 separate items. Gregor was trying to remember what, if anything, he had left out.

Antiradiation salve? Vacuum flares? Water-purification kit? Yes, they were all there.

He yawned and glanced at his watch. Arnold, his partner, should have been back by now. Arnold had gone to order the 2,305 items and see them stowed safely aboard the spaceship. In a few hours, AAA Ace was scheduled to blast off on another job.

But had he listed everything important? A spaceship is an island unto itself, self-sufficient, self-sustaining. If you run out of beans on Dementia II, there is no store where you could buy more. No Coast Guard hurries out to replace the burned-out lining on your main drive. You have to have another lining on board, and the tools to replace it with, and the manuals telling you how. Space is just too big to permit much in the way of rescue operations.

Oxygen extractor? Extra cigarettes? It was like attaching jets to a department store, Gregor thought.

He pushed the list aside, found a pack of tattered cards, and laid out a hopeless solitaire of his own devising.

Minutes later, Arnold stepped jauntily in.

Gregor looked at his partner with suspicion. When the little chemist walked with that peculiar bouncing step, his round face beaming happily, it usually meant trouble for AAA Ace.

"Did you get the stuff?" Gregor asked.

"I did better than that," Arnold said proudly.

"We're supposed to blast off—"

"And blast we will," Arnold said. He sat down on the edge of his desk. "I have just saved us a considerable sum of money."

"Oh, no," Gregor sighed. "What have you done?"

"Consider," Arnold said impressively, "just consider the sheer waste in equipping the average expedition. We pack 2,305 items, just on the offchance we may need one. Our payload is diminished, our living space is cramped, and the stuff never gets used."

"Except for once or twice," Gregor said, "when it saves our lives."

"I took that into account," Arnold said. "I gave the whole problem careful study. And I was able to cut down the list considerably. Through a bit of luck, I found the one thing an expedition really needs. The necessary thing."

Gregor arose and towered over his partner. Visions of mayhem danced through his brain, but he controlled himself with an effort. "Arnold," he said, "I don't know what you've done. But you'd better get those 2,305 items on board and get them fast."

"Can't do it," Arnold said, with a nervous little laugh. "The money's gone. This thing will pay for itself, though."

"What thing?"

"The one really necessary thing. Come out to the ship and I'll show you."

Gregor couldn't get another word out of him. Arnold smiled mysteriously to himself on the long drive to Kennedy Spaceport. Their ship was already in a blast pit, scheduled for takeoff in a few hours.

Arnold swung the port open with a flourish. "There!" he cried. "Behold the answer to an expedition's prayers."

Gregor stepped inside. He saw a large and fantastic-looking machine with dials, lights, and indicators scattered haphazardly over it.

"What is it?" Gregor asked.

"Isn't it a beauty?" Arnold patted the machine affectionately. "Joe the Interstellar Junkman happened to have it tucked away. I conned it out of him for a song."

That settled it, as far as Gregor was concerned. He had dealt with Joe the Interstellar Junkman before and had always come out on the disastrously short end of the deal.

Joe's gadgets worked; but when, and how often, and with what kind of an attitude was something else again.

Gregor said sternly, "No gadget of Joe's is going into space with me again. Maybe we can sell it for scrap metal." He began to hunt around for a wrecking bar.

"Wait," Arnold begged. "Let me show you. Consider. We are in deep space. The main drive falters and fails. Upon examination, we find that a durraloy nut has worked its way off the number three pinion. We can't find the nut. What do we do?"

"We take a new nut from the two thousand three hundred and five items we've packed for emergencies just like this," Gregor said.

"Ah! But you didn't include any quarter-inch durraloy nuts!" Arnold said triumphantly. "I checked the list. What then?"

"I don't know," Gregor said. "You tell me."

Arnold stepped up to the machine and punched a button. In a loud, clear voice he said, "Durraloy nut, quarter-inch diameter."

The machine murmured and hummed. Lights flashed. A panel slid back, revealing a bright, freshly machined durraloy nut.

"That's what we do," Arnold said.

"Hmm," Gregor said, not particularly impressed. "So it manufactures nuts. What else does it do?"

Arnold pressed the button again. "A pound of fresh shrimp."

When he slid back the panel, the shrimp were there.

"I should have told it to peel them," Arnold said. "Oh well." He pressed the button. "A graphite rod, four feet long with a diameter of two inches."

The panel opened wider this time to let the rod come through.

"What else can it do?" Gregor asked.

"What else would you like?" Arnold said. "A small tiger cub? A model-A downdraft carburetor? A 25-watt light bulb or a stick of chewing gum?"

"Do you mean it'll turn out *anything?*" Gregor asked.

"Anything at all. It's a Configurator. Try it yourself."

Gregor tried and produced, in rapid succession, a pint of fresh water, a wristwatch, and a jar of cocktail sauce.

"Hmm," he said.

"See what I mean? Isn't this better than packing 2,305 items? Isn't it simpler and more logical to produce what you need when you need it?"

"It *seems* good," Gregor said. "But . . ."

"But what?"

Gregor shook his head. What indeed? He had no idea. It had simply been his experience that gadgets are never so useful, reliable, or consistent as they seem at first glance.

He thought deeply, then punched the button. "A transistor, series GE 1324E."

The machine hummed and the panel opened. There was the tiny transistor.

"Seems pretty good," Gregor admitted. "What are you doing?"

"Peeling the shrimp," Arnold said.

After enjoying a tasty shrimp cocktail, the partners received their clearance from the tower. In an hour, the ship was in space.

They were bound for Dennett IV, an average-sized planet in the Sycophax cluster. Dennett was a hot, steamy, fertile world, suffering from only one major difficulty: too much rain. It rained on Dennett a good nine tenths of the time, and when it wasn't raining, it was threatening rain.

This made it an easy job. The principles of climate control were well known, for many worlds suffered from similar difficulties. It would take only a few days for AAA Ace to interrupt and alter the pattern.

After an uneventful trip, Dennett came into view. Arnold relieved the automatic pilot and brought the ship down through thick cloud banks. They dropped through miles of pale gossamer mist. At last, mountaintops began to appear, and they found a level, barren gray plain.

"Odd color for a landscape," Gregor said.

Arnold nodded. With practiced ease he spiraled, leveled out, came down neatly above the plain, and, with his forces balanced, cut the drive.

"Wonder why there's no vegetation," Gregor mused.

In a moment they found out. The ship hung for a second, then dropped through the plain and fell another eight feet to the ground.

The plain, it seemed, was fog of a density only Dennett could produce.

Hastily they unbuckled themselves and tested various teeth, bones, and ligatures. Upon finding that nothing personal was broken, they checked their ship.

The impact had done the poor old spacecraft no good. The radio and automatic pilot were a complete loss. Ten stern plates had buckled, and, worst of all, some delicate components in the turn-drive control were shattered.

"We were lucky at that," Arnold said.

"Yes," Gregor said, peering through the blanketing fog. "But next time we use instruments."

"In a way I'm glad it happened," Arnold said. "Now you'll see what a lifesaver the Configurator is. Let's go to work."

They listed all the damaged parts. Arnold stepped up to the Configurator, pressed the button, and said, "A drive plate, five inches square, half inch in diameter, steel alloy 342."

The machine quickly turned it out.

"We need ten of them," Gregor said.

"I know." Again Arnold pushed the button. "Another one."

The machine did nothing.

"Probably have to give the whole command," Arnold said. He punched the button again and said, "Drive plate, five inches square, half inch in diameter, steel alloy 342."

The machine was silent.

"That's odd," Arnold said.

"Isn't it, though," Gregor said, with an odd sinking sensation in the pit of his stomach.

Arnold tried again, with no success. He thought deeply, then punched the button and said, "A plastic teacup."

The machine turned out a teacup of bright blue plastic.

"Another one," Arnold said. When the Configurator did nothing, Arnold asked for a wax crayon. The machine gave it to him. "Another wax crayon," Arnold said. The machine did nothing.

"That's interesting," Arnold said. "I suppose I should have thought of the possibility."

"What possibility?"

"Apparently the Configurator will turn out anything,"

Arnold said. "But only once." He experimented again, making the machine produce a number two pencil. It would do it once, but only once.

"That's fine," Gregor said. "We need nine more plates. And the turn-drive needs four identical parts. What are we going to do?"

"We'll think of something," Arnold said cheerfully.

"I hope so," Gregor said.

Outside the rain began. The partners settled down to think.

"Only one explanation," Arnold said, several hours later. "Pleasure principle."

"Huh?" Gregor said. He had been dozing, lulled by the soft patter of rain against the dented side of the spaceship.

"This machine must have some form of intelligence," Arnold said. "After all, it receives stimuli, translates it into action commands, and fabricates a product from a mental blueprint."

"Sure it does," Gregor said. "But only once."

"Yes. But *why* only once? That's the key to our difficulties. I think it must be a self-imposed limit, linked to a pleasure drive. Or perhaps a quasi-pleasure drive."

"I don't follow you," Gregor said.

"Look. The builders wouldn't have limited their machine in this way. The only possible explanation is this: When a machine is constructed on this order of complexity, it takes on quasi-human characteristics. It derives a quasi-humanoform pleasure from producing a new thing. But a thing is only new once. After that, the Configurator wants to produce something else."

Gregor slumped back into his apathetic half-slumber. Arnold went on talking. "Fulfillment of potential, that's what a machine wants. The Configurator's ultimate desire is to create everything possible. From its point of view, repetition would be a waste of time."

"That's the most suspect line of reasoning I've ever heard," Gregor said. "But assuming you're right, what can we do about it?"

"I don't know," Arnold said.

"That's what I thought."

For dinner that evening, the Configurator turned out a

very creditable roast beef. They finished with apple pie *à la machine,* with sharp cheese on the side. Their morale was improved considerably.

"Substitutions," Gregor said later, smoking a cigar *ex machina.* "That's what we'll have to try. Alloy 342 isn't the only thing we can use for the plates. There are plenty of materials that'll last until we get back to Earth."

The Configurator couldn't be tricked into producing a plate of iron or any of the ferrous alloys. They asked for and got a plate of bronze. But then the machine wouldn't give them copper or tin. Aluminum was acceptable, as was cadmium, platinum, gold and silver. A tungsten plate was an interesting rarity; Arnold wished he knew how the machine had cast it. Gregor vetoed plutonium, and they were running short of suitable metals. Arnold hit upon an extra-tough ceramic as a good substitute. And the final plate was pure zinc.

The noble metals would tend to melt in the heat of space, of course; but with proper refrigeration, they might last as far as Earth. All in all it was a good night's work, and the partners toasted each other in an excellent, though somewhat oily, dry sherry.

The next day they bolted in the plates and surveyed their handiwork. The rear of the ship looked like a patchwork quilt.

"I think it's quite pretty," Arnold said.

"I just hope it'll hold up," Gregor said. "Now for the turn-drive components."

But that was a problem of a different nature. Four identical parts were missing: delicate, precisely engineered affairs of glass and wire. No substitutions were possible.

The machine turned out the first without hesitation. But that was all. By noon, both men were disgusted.

"Any ideas?" Gregor asked.

"Not at the moment. Let's take a break for lunch."

They decided that lobster salad would be pleasant, and ordered it on the machine. The Configurator hummed for a moment, but produced nothing.

"What's wrong now?" Gregor asked.

"I was afraid of this," Arnold said.

"Afraid of what? We haven't asked for lobster before."

"No," Arnold said, "but we did ask for shrimp. Both are

shellfish. I'm afraid the Configurator is beginning to make decisions according to classes."

"You'd better break open a few cans then," Gregor said.

Arnold smiled feebly. "Well," he said, "after I bought the Configurator, I didn't think we'd have to bother— I mean—"

"No cans?"

"No."

They returned to the machine and asked for salmon, trout, and tuna, with no results. Then they tried roast pork, leg of lamb, and veal. Nothing.

"It seems to consider our roast beef last night as representative of all mammals," Arnold said. "This is interesting. We might be able to evolve a new theory of classes—"

"While starving to death," Gregor said. He tried roast chicken, and this time the Configurator came through without hesitation.

"Eureka!" Arnold cried.

"Damn!" Gregor said. "I should have asked for turkey."

The rain continued to fall on Dennett, and mist swirled around the spaceship's gaudy patchwork stern. Arnold began a long series of slide-rule calculations. Gregor finished off the dry sherry, tried unsuccessfully to order a case of Scotch, and started playing solitaire.

They ate a frugal supper on the remains of the chicken, and Arnold completed his calculations.

"It might work," he said.

"What might work?"

"The pleasure principle." He stood up and began to pace the cabin. "This machine has quasi-human characteristics. Certainly it possesses learning potential. I think we can teach it to derive pleasure from producing the same thing many times. Namely, the turn-drive components."

"It's worth a try," Gregor said.

Late into the night they talked to the machine. Arnold murmured persuasively about the joys of repetition. Gregor spoke highly of the esthetic values inherent in producing an artistic object like a turn-drive component, not once, but many times, each item an exact and perfect twin. Arnold murmured lyrically to the machine about the thrill, the supreme thrill of fabricating endlessly parts without end. Again and again, the same parts, produced of the same material, turned out at the same rate. Ecstasy! And, Gregor put in, so beautiful a concept philosophically, and so completely suited to the peculiar makeup and capabilities of a machine. As a conceptual system, he continued, Repetition (as opposed to mere Creation) closely approached the status of entropy, which, mechanically, was perfection.

By clicks and flashes, the Configurator showed that it was listening. And when Dennett's damp and pallid dawn was in the sky, Arnold pushed the button and gave the command for a turn-drive component.

The machine hesitated. Lights flickered uncertainly, indicators turned in a momentary hunting process. Uncertainty was manifest in every tube.

There was a click. The panel slid back. And there was another turn-drive component!

"Success!" Gregor shouted, and slapped Arnold on the back. Quickly he gave the order again. But this time the Configurator emitted a loud and emphatic buzz.

And produced nothing.

Gregor tried again. But there was no more hesitation from the machine, and no more components.

"What's wrong now?" Gregor asked.

"It's obvious," Arnold said sadly. "It decided to give repetition a try, just in case it had missed something. But after trying it, the Configurator decided it didn't like it."

"A machine that doesn't like repetition!" Gregor groaned. "It's inhuman!"

"On the contrary," Arnold said unhappily. "It's all too human."

It was suppertime, and the partners had to hunt for foods the Configurator would produce. A vegetable plate was easy enough, but not too filling. The machine allowed them one loaf of bread, but no cake. Milk products were out, as they had had cheese the other day. Finally, after an hour of trial and error, the Configurator gave them a pound of whale steak, apparently uncertain of its category.

Gregor went back to work, crooning the joys of repetition into the machine's receptors. A steady hum and occasional flashes of light showed that the Configurator was still listening.

Arnold took out several reference books and embarked on a project of his own. Several hours later he looked up with a shout of triumph.

"I knew I'd find it!"

Gregor looked up quickly. "What?"

"A substitute turn-drive control!" He pushed the book under Gregor's nose. "Look there. A scientist on Vednier II perfected this 50 years ago. It's clumsy, by modern standards, but it'll work. And it'll fit into our ship."

"But what's it made of?" Gregor asked.

"That's the best part of it. We can't miss! It's made of rubber!"

Quickly he punched the Configurator's button and read the description of the turn-drive control.

Nothing happened.

"You have to turn out the Vednier control!" Arnold shouted at the machine. "If you don't, you're violating your own principles!" He punched the button again and, enunciating with painful clarity, read the description again.

Nothing happened.

Gregor had a sudden terrible suspicion. He walked to the back of the Configurator, found what he had feared, and pointed it out to Arnold.

There was a manufacturer's plate bolted there. It read: *Class 3 Configurator. Made by Vednier Laboratories, Vednier II.*

"So they've already used it for that," Arnold said.

Gregor said nothing. There just didn't seem to be anything to say.

Mildew was beginning to form inside the spaceship, and rust had appeared on the steel plate in the stern. The machine still listened to the partners' hymn to repetition, but did nothing about it.

The problem of another meal came up. Fruit was out because of the apple pie, as were all meats, fish, milk products, and cereals. At last they dined sparsely on frog's legs, baked grasshoppers (from an old Chinese recipe), and filet of iguana. But now with lizards, insects, and amphibians used up, they knew that their machine-made meals were at an end.

Both men were showing signs of strain. Gregor's long face was bonier than ever. Arnold found traces of mildew in his hair. Outside, the rain poured ceaselessly, dripped past the portholes and into the moist earth. The spaceship began to settle, burying itself under its own weight.

For the next meal they could think of nothing.

Then Gregor conceived a final idea.

He thought it over carefully. Another failure would shatter their badly bent morale. But, slim though the chance of success might be, he had to try it.

Slowly he approached the Configurator. Arnold looked up, frightened by the wild light gleaming in his eyes.

"Gregor! What are you going to do?"

"I'm going to give this thing one last command," Gregor said hoarsely. With a trembling hand he punched the button and whispered his request.

For a moment, nothing happened. Then Arnold shouted, "Get back!"

The machine was quivering and shaking, dials twitching, lights flickering. Heat and energy indicators flashed through red into purple.

"What did you tell it to produce?" Arnold asked.

"I didn't tell it to produce anything," Gregor said. "I told it to reproduce!"

The Configurator gave a convulsive shudder and emitted a cloud of black smoke. The partners coughed and gasped for air.

When the smoke cleared away the Configurator was still there, its paint chipped, and several indicators bent out of shape. And beside it, glistening with black machine oil, was a duplicate Configurator.

"You've done it!" Arnold cried. "You've saved us!"

"I've done more than that," Gregor said, with weary satisfaction. "I've made our fortunes." He turned to the duplicate Configurator, pressed its button and cried, "Reproduce yourself!"

Within a week, Arnold, Gregor and three Configurators were back in Kennedy Spaceport, their work on Dennett completed. As soon as they landed, Arnold left the ship and caught a taxi. He went first to Canal Street, then to midtown New York. His business didn't take long, and within a few hours he was back at the ship.

"Yes, it's all right," he called to Gregor. "I contacted several different jewelers. We can dispose of about 20 big stones without depressing the market. After that, I think we should have the Configurators concentrate on platinum for a while, and then—what's wrong?"

Gregor looked at him sourly. "Notice anything different?"

"Huh?" Arnold stared around the cabin, at Gregor, and at the Configurators. Then he noticed it.

There were four Configurators in the cabin, where there had been only three.

"You had them reproduce another?" Arnold said. "Nothing wrong with that. Just tell them to turn out a diamond apiece—"

"You still don't get it," Gregor said sadly. "Watch."

He pressed the button on the nearest Configurator and said, "A diamond."

The Configurator began to quiver.

"You and your damned pleasure principle," Gregor said. "Repetition! These damned machines are sex mad."

The machine shook all over, and produced—

Another Configurator.

REDFERN'S LABYRINTH

•

Charles Angier Redfern received two curious letters in his mail on an otherwise undistinguished morning. One letter was in a plain white envelope, and for a moment Redfern thought he recognized the handwriting. He opened the envelope and took out a letter with no salutation or signature. He puzzled for a while over the strange yet familiar handwriting, then recognized it as an imitation of his own. Mildly intrigued, but with a faint anticipation of boredom, he read the following:

Most of the propositions in Redfern's ineptly titled *Labyrinth* will doubtless go unchallenged, as no one could possibly care one way or another. Redfern's *Labyrinth* fails to evoke anything except Redfern's own baffled impotence. One senses that Redfern has failed to overcome his own meek and hateful slavishness, his boundless desire to comply.

Because of this resonant failure, the reader's first sensation is apt to be pointedly inconsequential: a concern with the humble brevity of the *Labyrinth*, and a spiteful wish that it were shorter still.

But this quickly passes, and the reader discovers that his predominant mood is a muted reluctance to feel anything at all. With gratitude he discovers himself to be indifferent. And, although he surely does not wish to remember the *Labyrinth*, he does not even care enough to forget it.

Thus the reader meets Redfern's boredom with an even more devastating boredom of his own; he imitates Redfern's hostility, and easily surpasses it. He refuses even to acknowledge Redfern's existence; and to that end, he has the absentminded sensation of never having experienced the *Labyrinth* at all. (He is right, of course; no number of reencounters would ever correct that eminently logical conclusion.)

This *Labyrinth*, it seems, could be used as an exemplary monument to tedium, were it not marred (how typical of Redfern!) by a single provocative idea.

This occurs in Proposition 113, which states: "All men know that the Maze rules its haphazard victims with an iron law; but very few realize the logical consequences of this: namely, that the Maze itself must be one of these victims, and must therefore be equally subject to the rule of an irksome law."

Redfern does not state the "law," a lapse which we might have anticipated. But it can easily be inferred from his otherwise meaningless Proposition 282: "Providence, despite all outward appearances, is inevitably merciful."

Therefore, following Redfern: The Maze rules men, but Providence rules the Maze. How can we know this? By the law to which the Maze (in common with all things except Providence) is subject. What is this law? That the Maze is under a mandate to *make itself known.* Our proof of this? The fact that Redfern, the meekest and most imitative of men, knows it.

But now we wish to know exactly what this law is that governs the Maze. *How* must the Maze make itself known? Without a description of this, we have nothing; and Redfern is useless to us in this quest. He cannot tell us, he probably would not even if he could. Therefore, for the description of the law which circumscribes the Maze, its particular manner and form, together with several homely hints to aid in its recognition, we turn to the otherwise undistinguished Charles Angier Redfern.

Redfern put down the letter. Its forced ambiguities had bored him. Its specious and arbitrary manner and its generally meretricious effect had given him the curiously comforting sensation that one gets by discovering as a falsehood what one had suspected as truth. He turned to the second letter.

The envelope was unnaturally long and narrow, and colored a tedious aqua; it retained a faint but unmistakable odor of kelp. His name, printed in a faded, machine-simulated hand, was correctly spelled; but his address was incorrectly given as 132 Bruckner Boulevard. That had been crossed out, and a printed imitation of a post-office stamp read: "Return to Sender." (There was no return address on the envelope.) That, in turn, had been slashed with a black crayon, and someone had written: "Try 137 W. 12th Street," which was his true address.

Redfern realized that these details were superfluous; they seemed to be in imitation of the letter within. He opened the envelope and extracted the letter, which was written gratuitously on a torn piece of brown wrapping paper. It read:

> HI THERE!!!
>
> You have been selected as one of those few truly modern and discerning people for whom novelty outweighs apprehension, and whose desire for the unusual is metered only by his innate good taste and sense of style. Above all we believe that YOU are the sort of uninhibited free-swinger with whom we would like to be friends.
>
> Therefore we take this opportunity of inviting you to the GRAND OPENING of our LABYRINTH!!!!!
>
> This Labyrinth (the only one of its kind on the Eastern Seaboard) is, needless to say, replete with KICKS. There are no squares on our curves! ! ! This Labyrinth beggars the description and infantilizes the desires.
>
> Please call us and we'll arrange a time and place of Entrance to suit your convenience. Our charges are merely life, liberty, and the pursuit of happiness.
>
> Call us soon, hear? AND THANKS A LOT, FELLA! ! ! !

Instead of a signature there was a telephone number.

Redfern flicked the letter regretfully in his hand. It was obviously the work of an overeager English major—tediously hip, drearily cute.

The writer of the letter was obviously trying to perpetrate a hoax; therefore, Redfern decided to hoax the hoaxer through a show of credence. He picked up the telephone and dialed the number he had been given.

The voice of a middle-aged woman, querulous but resigned, said: "Redfern Behavioral Research Institute."

Redfern frowned, cleared his throat, and said, "I am calling to inquire about the Labyrinth."

"About the *what?*" the woman said.

"The Labyrinth."

"What number are you calling?"

Redfern told her. The woman agreed that he had the correct number for the Redfern Institute; but she knew nothing about any Labyrinth. Unless, of course, he was referring to the well-known L Series of mazes, which were used for the testing of rats. The L Series mazes, she went on, were available in various models and were priced according to their square footage. They ranged from the L-1001, a simple forced-choice binary maze of 25 square feet, all the way up to the L-10023, a multiple-choice random-selection model of 900 square feet, suitable for auditorium viewing.

"No," Redfern said, "I'm afraid that wasn't exactly the sort of thing I had in mind."

"Then what exactly did you have in mind?" the woman asked. "We also build custom mazes, as our advertisement in the Yellow Pages points out."

"But I don't want you to *build* a maze for me," Redfern said. "You see, according to the letter I received, this Labyrinth, or maze, is already in existence and seems to be quite extensive in size and to have been designed for humans, that is to say, for people."

"Just exactly what are you talking about?" the woman asked, in tones of deepest suspicion.

Redfern found himself babbling: "It's this letter I received. I've been invited to the grand opening of this Labyrinth, which gave your telephone number for further information—"

"Listen, mister," the woman interrupted in an angry, grating voice, "I don't know if you're some kind of nut or if this is some kind of gag or what, but the Redfern Institute is a respectable business of over 35 years standing, and if you bother me again with this nonsense, I'll have this call traced and you will be prosecuted to the fullest extent of the law!"

She hung up.

Redfern sat back in his chair. He found that his hands were trembling. Having detected the primary hoax, as he had been meant to do, he had tried a counterhoax and had thereby fallen into a second or ancillary hoax. He felt ridiculous.

Then a disturbing thought occurred to him. He opened the Manhattan telephone book and looked up the Redfern Behavioral Research Institute.

There was no such listing.

He dialed information and asked for New Listings, then for regular listings; but as he had foreseen, there was no Redfern Institute. Finally, taking down the Yellow Pages, he looked up Mazes, Labyrinths, Research, Behavior, Scientific Equipment, and Laboratory Equipment. There was no Redfern, and no firm which specialized in the construction of mazes.

He realized that, in penetrating the secondary hoax, he had inevitably fallen for a tertiary hoax; nor did this necessarily end the series.

But of course, too much evidence had accumulated by now to permit him to retain the thought of a hoax. The series had been, in fact, a part of the Labyrinth itself, a small loop, curving quickly back to its original point of departure. Or to a point *closely resembling the original*.

One of the primary aspects of a labyrinth is duplication. That had been faithfully carried out: overtly by the use of Redfern's name in both letters and the imitation of his handwriting; implicitly by the monotonous contradiction of every statement.

The description of the law of the maze (which, it was asserted, he had known but also had not known) was simple enough now. It could be a description only of his own emotions concerning the maze: its forced ambiguities had bored him. Its specious and arbitrary manner and its generally meretricious effect had given him the curiously comforting sensation that one gets by discovering as a falsehood what one had suspected as truth.

Following this, he saw, the first letter was actually the Labyrinth—that slavish, endlessly duplicating monument to tedium whose perfection was marred by one significant detail: its own existence. The second letter was the obligatory duplication of the first, thus fulfilling the requirements for a labyrinth.

Other viewpoints were also possible; but at this point, it occurred to Redfern that he might have thought all of this before.

PROOF OF THE PUDDING

His arms were very tired, but he lifted the chisel and mallet again. He was almost through; only a few more letters and the inscription, cut deeply into the tough granite, would be finished. He rounded out the last period and straightened up, dropping his tools carelessly to the floor of the cave. Proudly he wiped the perspiration from his dirty stubbled face and read what he had written.

> I ROSE FROM THE SLIME OF THE PLANET. NAKED AND DEFENSELESS, I FASHIONED TOOLS. I BUILT AND DEMOLISHED, CREATED AND DESTROYED. I CREATED A THING GREATER THAN MYSELF THAT DESTROYED ME.
> MY NAME IS MAN AND THIS IS MY LAST WORK.

He smiled. What he had written was good. Not literary enough, perhaps, but a fitting tribute to the human race, written by the last man. He glanced at the tools at his feet. Having no further use for them, he dissolved them, and, hungry from his long work, squatted in the rubble of the cave and created a dinner. He stared at the food for a moment, wondering what was lacking; then, sheepishly, created a table and chair, utensils and plates. He was embarrassed. He had forgotten them again.

Although there was no need to rush, he ate hurriedly, noting the odd fact that when he didn't think of anything specific, he always created hamburger, mashed potatoes, peas, bread, and ice cream. Habit, he decided. Finished, he made the remnants of the meal disappear, and with them the plates, utensils, and table. The chair he retained. Sitting on it, he stared thoughtfully at the inscription. It's fine, he thought, but no human other than myself will ever read it.

It was fairly certain that he was the last man alive on Earth. The war had been thorough. Thorough as only man, a meticulous animal, could make it. There had been no neutrals in this war, no middle-of-the-road policy. You were on one side or the other. Bacteria, gas, and radiations had covered Earth like a vast cloud. In the first days of that war, invincible secret weapon had succeeded secret weapon with almost monotonous regularity. And after the last hand had pushed the last button, the bombs, automatically guided and impelled, had continued to rain down. Unhappy Earth was a huge junkyard, without a living thing, plant or animal, from pole to pole.

He had watched a good part of it. He had waited until he was fairly sure the last bomb had been dropped; then he had come down.

Very clever of you, he thought bitterly, looking out the mouth of the cave at the lava plain his ship rested on and at the twisted mountains behind it.

You're a traitor—but who cares?

He had been a captain in the Western Hemisphere Defense. Within two days of warfare, he had known what the end would be. Filling a cruiser with canned air, food, and water, he had fled. In the confusion and destruction, he knew that he would never be missed; after a few days there was no one left to miss him. He had raced the big ship to the dark side of the moon and waited. It was a 12-day-war—he had guessed it would last 14—but he had to wait nearly six months before the automatic missiles stopped falling. Then he had come down.

To find himself the only survivor . . .

He had expected others to recognize the futility of it, load ships, and flock to the dark side of the moon, also. Evidently there had been no time, even if there had been the desire. He had thought that there would be scattered groups of survivors, but he hadn't found any. The war had been too thorough.

Landing on Earth should have killed him, for the air itself was poisoned. He hadn't cared—and he had lived. He seemed to be immune to the various kinds of germs and radiations, or perhaps that was part of his new power. He certainly had encountered enough of both, skipping around the world in his ship, from the ruins of one city to another, across blasted valleys and plains, scorched mountains. He had found no life, but he did discover something.

He could create. He realized the power on his third day on Earth. Wistfully, he had wished for a tree in the midst of the melted rock and metal; a tree had appeared. The rest of the day he experimented and found that he could create anything that he had ever seen or heard about.

Things he knew best, he could create best. Things he knew just from books or conversation—palaces, for example—tended to be lopsided and uncertain, although he could make them nearly perfect by laboring mentally over the details. Everything he created was three-dimensional. Even food tasted like food and seemed to nourish him. He could forget all about one of his creations, go to sleep, and it would still be there when he awakened. He could also uncreate. A single concentrated thought and the thing he had made would vanish. The larger the thing, the longer it took to uncreate.

Things he *hadn't* made—valleys and mountains—he could uncreate, too, but it took longer. It seemed as though matter was easier to handle once he had shaped it. He could make birds and small animals, or things that looked like birds and small animals.

He had never tried to make a human being.

He wasn't a scientist; he had been a space pilot. He had a vague concept of atomic theory and practically no idea of genetics. He thought that some change must have taken place in his germ plasm, or in his brain, or perhaps in Earth. The why of it all didn't expecially bother him. It was a fact and he accepted it.

He stared at the monument again. Something about it bothered him.

Of course, he could have created it, but he didn't know if the things he made would endure after his death. They seemed stable enough, but they might dissolve with his own dissolution. Therefore he compromised. He created a chisel and mallet, but selected a granite wall that he hadn't made. He cut the letters into the inside of the wall of the cave so they would be safe from the elements, working many hours at a stretch, sleeping and eating beside the wall.

From the mouth of the cave, he could see his ship, perched on a level plain of scorched ground. He was in no rush to get back to it. In six days the inscription was done, cut deeply and eternally into the rock.

The thought that had been bothering him as he stared at the gray granite finally came to the surface. The only people who would come to read it would be visitors from the stars. How would they decipher it? He stared at the inscription angrily. He should have written it in symbols. But what kind of symbols? Mathematics? Of course, but what would that tell them about Man? And what made him think *they* would discover the cave anyway? There was no use for an inscription when Man's entire history was written over the face of the planet, scorched into the crust for anyone to see. He cursed his stupidity for wasting six days working at the useless inscription. He was about to uncreate it when he turned his head, hearing footsteps at the mouth of the cave.

He almost fell off the chair getting to his feet.

A girl was standing there. He blinked rapidly, and she was still there, a tall, dark-haired girl dressed in a torn, dirty one-piece cover all.

"Hi," she said, and walked into the cave. "I heard your hammer from the valley."

Automatically, he offered her his chair and created another for himself. She tested it gingerly before she sat down.

"I saw you do it," she said, "but I still don't believe it. Mirrors?"

"No," he muttered uncertainly. "I create. That is, I have the power to—wait a minute! How did you get here?" While he was demanding to know, he was considering and rejecting possibilities. Hidden in a cave? On a mountaintop? No, there would be only one possible way. . . .

"I was in your ship, pal." She leaned back in the chair and clasped her hands around one knee. "When you loaded up that crusier, I figured you were going to beat it. I was getting tired of setting fuses 18 hours a day, so I stowed away. Anybody else alive?"

"No. Why didn't I see you, then?" He stared at the ragged, beautiful girl, and a vague thought crossed his mind. He reached out and touched her arm. She didn't draw back, but her pretty face grew annoyed.

"I'm real," she said bluntly. "You must have seen me at the base. Remember?"

He tried to think back to the time when there had been a base—centuries ago, it seemed. There *had* been a dark-haired girl there, one who had never given him a tumble.

"I think I froze to death," she was saying. "Or into coma, anyhow, a few hours after your ship took off. Lousy heating system you have in that crate!" She shivered reminiscently.

"Would have used up too much oxygen," he explained. "Just kept the pilot's compartment heated and aired. Used a suit to drag supplies forward when I needed them."

"I'm glad you didn't see me," she laughed. "I must have looked like the devil, all covered with frost and killed, I bet. Some sleeping beauty I probably made! Well, I froze. When you opened all the compartments, I revived. That's the whole story. Guess it took a few days. How come you didn't see me?"

"I suppose I never looked back there," he admitted. "Quick enough, I found I didn't need supplies. Funny, I thought I opened all the compartments, but I don't really remember—"

She looked at the inscription on the wall. "What's that?"

"I thought I'd leave a sort of monument—"

"Who's going to read it?" she asked practically.

"No one, probably. It was just a foolish idea." He concentrated on it. In a few moments the granite wall was bare. "I still don't understand how you could be alive now," he said puzzled.

"But I am. I don't see how you do that"—she gestured at the chair and wall—"but I'll accept the fact that you can. Why don't you accept the fact that I'm alive?"

"Don't get me wrong," the man said. "I want company very much, especially female company. It's just—turn your back."

She complied with a questioning look. Quickly he destroyed the stubble on his face and created a clean pair of pressed pants and a shirt. Stepping out of his tattered uniform, he put on the new clothes, destroyed the rags, and, on an afterthought, created a comb and straightened his tangled brown hair.

"All right," he said. "You can turn back now."

"Not bad," she smiled, looking him over. "Let me use that comb—and would you please make me a dress? Size 12, but see that the weight goes in the right places."

On the third attempt he had the thing right—he had never realized how deceptive the shapes of women could be—and then he made a pair of gold sandals with high heels for her.

"A little tight," she said, putting them on, "and not too practical without sidewalks. But thanks much. This trick of yours really solves the Christmas-present problem, doesn't it?" Her dark hair was shiny in the noon sun, and she looked very lovely and warm and human.

"See if *you* can create," he urged, anxious to share his startling new ability with her.

"I've already tried," she said. "No go. Still a man's world."

He frowned. "How can I be absolutely sure you're real?"

"That again? Do you remember creating me, master?" she asked mockingly, bending to loosen the strap on one shoe.

"I had been thinking—about women," he said grimly. "I might have created you while I was asleep. Why shouldn't my subconscious mind have as much power as my conscious mind? I would have equipped you with a memory, given you a background. You would have been extremely plausible. And if my subconscious mind did create you, then it would make certain that my conscious mind would never know."

"You're ridiculous!"

"Because if my conscious mind knew," he went on relentlessly, "it would reject your existence. Your entire function, as a creation of my subconscious, would be to keep me from knowing. To prove, by any means in your power, by any logic, that you were—"

"Let's see you make a woman, then, if your mind is so good!" She crossed her arms and leaned back in the chair, giving a single sharp nod.

"All right." He stared at the cave wall and a woman started to appear. It took shape sloppily, one arm too short, legs too long. Concentrating harder, he was able to make its proportions fairly true. But its eyes were set at an odd angle; its shoulders and back were sloped and twisted. He had created a shell without brains or internal organs, an automaton. He commanded it to speak, but only gulps came from the shapeless mouth; he hadn't given it any vocal apparatus. Shuddering, he destroyed the nightmare figure.

"I'm not a sculptor," he said. "Nor am I God."

"I'm glad you finally realize that."

"That still doesn't prove," he continued stubbornly, "that *you're* real. I don't know what my subconscious mind is capable of."

"Make something for me," she said abruptly. "I'm tired of listening to this nonsense."

I've hurt her feelings, he thought. The only other human on Earth and I've hurt her. He nodded, took her by the hand, and led her out of the cave. On the flat plain below he created a city. He had experimented with it a few days back, and it was much easier this time. Patterned after pictures and childhood dreams of the *Thousand and One Nights*, it towered black and white and rose. The walls were gleaming ruby, and the gates were of silver-stained ebony. The towers were red gold, and sapphires glittered in them. A great staircase of milky ivory climbed to the highest opal spire, set with thousands of steps of veined marble. There were lagoons of blue water, and little birds fluttered above them, and silver and goldfish darted through the still depths.

They walked through the city, and he created roses for her, white and yellow and red, and gardens of strange blossoms. Between two domed and spired buildings he created a vast pool of water; on it he put a purple-canopied pleasure barge, loading it with every kind of food and drink he could remember.

They floated across the lagoon, fanned by the soft breeze he had created.

"And all this is false," he reminded her after a little while.

She smiled. "No, it's not. You can touch it. It's real."

"Will it be here after I die?"

"Who cares? Besides, if you can do all this, you can cure any sickness. Perhaps you can even cure old age and death." She plucked a blossom from an overhanging bough and sniffed its fragrance. "You could keep this from fading and dying. You could probably do the same for us, so where's the problem?"

"Would you like to go away?" he said, puffing on a newly created cigarette. "Would you like to find a new planet, untouched by war? Would you like to start over?"

"Start over? You mean . . . Later perhaps. Now I don't even want to go near the ship. It reminds me of the war."

They floated on a little way.

"Are you sure now that I'm real?" she asked.

"If you want me to be honest, no," he replied. "But I want very much to believe it."

"Then listen to me," she said, leaning toward him. "I'm real." She slipped her arms around his neck. "I've always been real. I always will be real. You want proof? Well, I know I'm real. So do you. What more can you ask?"

He stared at her for a long moment, felt her warm arms around his neck, listened to her breathing. He could smell the fragrance of her skin and hair, the unique essence of an individual.

Slowly he said, "I believe you. I love you. What—what is your name?"

She thought for a moment. "Joan."

"Strange," he said. "I always dreamed of a girl named Joan. What's your last name?"

She kissed him.

Overhead, the swallows he had created—*his* swallows— wheeled in wide circles above the lagoon, his fish darted aimlessly to and fro, and his city stretched, proud and beautiful, to the edge of the twisted lava mountains.

"You didn't tell me your last name," he said.

"Oh, that. A girl's maiden name never matters—she always takes her husband's."

"That's an evasion!"

She smiled. "It is, isn't it?"

THE LAXIAN KEY

Richard Gregor was at his desk in the dusty office of the AAA Ace Interplanetary Decontamination Service. It was almost noon, but Arnold, his partner, hadn't showed up yet. Gregor was just laying out an unusually complicated game of solitaire. Then he heard a loud crash in the hall.

The door of AAA Ace opened, and Arnold stuck his head in.

"Banker's hours?" Gregor asked.

"I have just made our fortunes," Arnold said. He threw the door fully open and beckoned dramatically. "Bring it in, boys."

Four sweating workmen lugged in a square black machine the size of a baby elephant.

"There it is," Arnold said proudly. He paid the workmen, and stood, hands clasped behind his back, eyes half shut, surveying the machine.

Gregor put his cards away with the slow, weary motions of a man who has seen everything. He stood up and walked around the machine. "All right, I give up. What is it?"

"It's a million bucks, right in our fists," Arnold said.

"Of course. But *what* is it?"

"It's a Free Producer," Arnold said. He smiled proudly. "I was walking past Joe's Interstellar Junkyard this morning, and there it was, sitting in the window. I picked it up for next to nothing. Joe didn't even know what it was."

"I don't either," Gregor said. "Do you?"

Arnold was on his hands and knees, trying to read the instructions engraved on the front of the machine. Without looking up, he said, "You've heard of the planet Meldge, haven't you?"

Gregor nodded. Meldge was a third-rate little planet on the northern periphery of the galaxy, some distance from the trade routes. At one time, Meldge had possessed an extremely advanced civilization, made possible by the so-called Meldgen Old Science. The Old Science techniques had been lost ages ago, although an occasional artifact still turned up here and there.

"And this is a product of the Old Science?" Gregor asked.

"Right. It's a Meldgen Free Producer. I doubt if there are more than four or five of them in the entire universe. They're unduplicatable."

"What does it produce?" Gregor asked.

"How should I know?" Arnold said. "Hand me the Meldge-English dictionary, will you?"

Keeping a stern rein on his patience, Gregor walked to the bookshelf. "You don't know what it produces—"

"Dictionary. Thank you. What does it matter what it produces? It's *free!* This machine grabs energy out of the air, out of space, the sun, anywhere. You don't have to plug it in, fuel or service it. It runs indefinitely."

Arnold opened the dictionary and started to look up the words on the front of the Producer.

"Free energy—"

"Those scientists were no fools," Arnold said, jotting down his translation on a pocket pad. "The Producer just grabs energy out of the air. So it really doesn't matter what it turns out. We can always sell it, and anything we get will be pure profit."

Gregor stared at his dapper little partner, and his long, unhappy face became sadder than ever.

"Arnold," he said, "I'd like to remind you of something. First of all, you are a chemist. I am an ecologist. We know nothing about machinery and less than nothing about complicated alien machinery."

Arnold nodded absently and turned a dial. The Producer gave a dry gurgle.

"What's more," Gregor said, retreating a few steps, "we are planetary decontaminationists. Remember? We have no reason to—"

The Producer began to cough unevenly.

"Got it now," Arnold said. "It says, 'The Meldge Free Producer, another triumph of Glotten Laboratories. This Producer is Warranted Indestructible, Unbreakable, and

Free of All Defects. No Power Hookup Is Required. To
Start, Press Button One. To Stop, Use Laxian Key. Your
Meldge Free Producer comes with an Eternal Guarantee
against Malfunction. If Defective in Any Way, Please Return at Once to Glotten Laboratories.' "

"Perhaps I didn't make myself clear," Gregor said. "We
are planetary—"

"Don't be stodgy," Arnold said. "Once we get this thing
working, we can retire. Here's Button One."

The machine began to clank ominously, then shifted to a
steady purr. For long minutes, nothing happened.

"Needs warming up," Arnold said anxiously.

Then, out of an opening at the base of the machine, a
gray powder began to pour.

"Probably a waste product," Gregor muttered. But the
powder continued to stream over the floor for 15 minutes.

"Success!" Arnold shouted.

"What is it?" Gregor asked.

"I haven't the faintest idea. I'll have to run some tests."
Grinning triumphantly, Arnold scooped some powder into
a test tube and hurried over to his desk.

Gregor stood in front of the Producer, watching the
gray powder stream out. Finally he said, "Shouldn't we
turn it off until we find out what it is?"

"Of course not," Arnold said. "Whatever it is, it must be
worth money." He lighted his bunsen burner, filled a test
tube with distilled water, and went to work.

Gregor shrugged his shoulders. He was used to Arnold's
harebrained schemes. Ever since they had formed AAA
Ace, Arnold had been looking for a quick road to wealth.
His shortcuts usually resulted in more work than plain old-
fashioned labor, but Arnold was quick to forget that.

Well, Gregor thought, at least it kept things lively. He
sat down at his desk and dealt out a complex solitaire.

There was silence in the office for the next few hours.
Arnold worked steadily, adding chemicals, pouring off
precipitates, checking the results in several large books he
kept on his desk. Gregor brought in sandwiches and coffee.
After eating, he paced up and down and watched the gray
powder tumble steadily out of the machine.

The purr of the Producer grew steadily louder, and the
powder flowed in a thick stream.

An hour after lunch Arnold stood up. "We are in!" he stated.

"What is that stuff?" Gregor asked, wondering if, for once, Arnold had hit upon something.

"That stuff," Arnold said, "is Tangreese." He looked expectantly at Gregor.

"Tangreese, eh?"

"Absolutely."

"Then would you kindly tell me what Tangreese is?" Gregor shouted.

"I thought you knew. Tangreese is the basic food of the Meldgen people. An adult Meldgen consumes several tons a year."

"Food, eh?" Gregor looked at the thick gray powder with new respect. A machine which turned out food steadily, 24 hours a day, might be a very good moneymaker. Especially if the machine never needed servicing, and cost nothing to run.

Arnold already had the telephone book open. "Here we are." He dialed a number. "Hello, Interstellar Food Corporation? Let me speak to the president. What? He isn't? The vice-president, then. This is important. . . . Channels, eh? All right, here's the story. I am in a position to supply you with an almost unlimited quantity of Tangreese, the basic food of the Meldgen people. That's right. I knew you'd be interested. Yes, of course I'll hold on."

He turned to Gregor. "These corporations think they can push—yes? . . . Yes sir, that's right, sir. You *do* handle Tangreese, eh? . . . Fine, splendid!"

Gregor moved closer, trying to hear what was being said on the other end. Arnold pushed him away.

"Price? Well, what is the fair market price? . . . Oh. Well, five dollars a ton isn't much, but I suppose—what? Five *cents* a ton? You're kidding! Let's be serious now."

Gregor walked away from the telephone and sank wearily into a chair. Apathetically he listened to Arnold saying, "Yes, yes. Well, I didn't know that. . . . I see. Thank you."

Arnold hung up. "It seems," he said, "there's not much demand for Tangreese on Earth. There are only about 50 Meldgens here, and the cost of transporting it to the northern periphery is prohibitively high."

Gregor raised both eyebrows and looked at the Producer. Apparently it had hit its stride, for Tangreese was pouring out like water from a high-pressure hose. There was gray powder over everything in the room. It was half a foot deep in front of the machine.

"Never mind," Arnold said. "It must be used for something else." He returned to his desk and opened several more large books.

"Shouldn't we turn it off in the meantime?" Gregor asked.

"Certainly not," Arnold said. "It's *free,* don't you understand? It's making money for us."

He plunged into his books. Gregor began to pace the floor, but found it difficult wading through the ankle-deep Tangreese. He slumped into his chair, wondering why he hadn't gone into landscape gardening.

By early evening, gray dust filled the room to a depth of several feet. Several pens, pencils, a briefcase and a small filing cabinet were already lost in it, and Gregor was beginning to wonder if the floor would hold the weight. He had to shovel a path to the door, using a wastepaper basket as an improvised spade.

Arnold finally closed his books with a look of weary satisfaction. "There *is* another use."

"What?"

"Tangreese is used as a building material. After a few weeks' exposure to the air, it hardens like granite, you know."

"No, I didn't."

"Get a construction company on the telephone. We'll take care of this right now."

Gregor called the Toledo-Mars Construction Company and told a Mr. O'Toole that they were prepared to supply them with an almost unlimited quantity of Tangreese.

"Tangreese, eh?" O'Toole said. "Not too popular as a building material these days. Doesn't hold paint, you know."

"No, I didn't," Gregor said.

"Fact. Tell you what. Tangreese can be eaten by some crazy race. Why don't you—"

"We prefer to sell it as a building material," Gregor said.

"Well, I suppose we can buy it. Always some cheap construction going on. Give you 15 a ton for it."

"Dollars?"

"Cents."

"I'll let you know," Gregor said.

His partner nodded sagely when he heard the offer. "That's all right. Say this machine of our produces ten tons a day, every day, year after year. Let's see . . ." He did some quick figuring with his slide rule. "That's almost 550 dollars a year. Won't make us rich, but it'll help pay the rent."

"But we can't leave it here," Gregor said, looking with alarm at the ever-increasing pile of Tangreese.

"Of course not. We'll find a vacant lot in the country and turn it loose. They can haul the stuff away any time they like."

Gregor called O'Toole and said they would be happy to do business.

"All right," O'Toole said. "You know where our plant is. Just truck the stuff in any old time."

"Us truck it in? I thought you—"

"At 15 cents a ton? No, we're doing you a favor just taking it off your hands. *You* truck it in."

"That's bad," Arnold said, after Gregor had hung up. "The cost of transporting it—"

"Would be far more than 15 cents a ton," Gregor said. "You'd better shut that thing off until we decide what to do."

Arnold waded up to the Producer. "Let me see," he said. "To turn it off I use the Laxian Key." He studied the front of the machine.

"Go ahead, turn it off," Gregor said.

"Just a moment."

"Are you going to turn it off or not?"

Arnold straightened up and gave an embarrassed little laugh. "It's not that easy."

"Why not?"

"We need a Laxian Key to turn it off. And we don't seem to have one."

The next few hours were spent in frantic telephone calls around the country. Gregor and Arnold contacted museums, research institutions, the archeological departments of colleges, and anyone else they could think of. No one had ever seen a Laxian Key or heard of one being found.

In desperation, Arnold called Joe, the Interstellar Junkman, at his downtown penthouse.

"No, I ain't got no Laxian Key," Joe said. "Why you think I sold you the gadget so cheap?"

They put down the telephone and stared at each other. The Meldgen Free Producer was cheerfully blasting out its stream of worthless powder. Two chairs and a radiator had disappeared into it, and the gray Tangreese was approaching desk-top level.

"Nice little wage earner," Gregor said.

"We'll think of something."

"We?"

Arnold returned to his books and spent the rest of the night searching for another use for Tangreese. Gregor had to shovel the gray powder into the hall, to keep their office from becoming completely submerged.

The morning came, and the sun gleamed gaily on their windows through a film of gray dust. Arnold stood up and yawned.

"No luck?" Gregor asked.

"I'm afraid not."

Gregor waded out for coffee. When he returned, the building superintendent and two large red-faced policemen were shouting at Arnold.

"You gotta get every bit of that sand outa my hall!" the super screamed.

"Yes, and there's an ordinance against operating a factory in a business district," one of the red-faced policemen said.

"This isn't a factory," Gregor explained. "This is a Meldgen Free—"

"I say it's a factory," the policeman said. "And I say you gotta cease operation at once."

"That's our problem," Arnold said. "We can't seem to turn it off."

"Can't turn it off?" The policeman glared at them suspiciously. "You trying to kid me? I say you *gotta* turn it off."

"Officer, I swear to you—"

"Listen, wise guy, I'll be back in an hour. You get that thing turned off and this mess out of here, or I'm giving you a summons." The three men marched out.

Gregor and Arnold looked at each other, then at the Free Producer. The Tangreese was at desk-top level now, and coming steadily.

"Damn it all," Arnold said, with a touch of hysteria, "there *must* be a way of working it out. There must be a market? It's free, I tell you. Every bit of this powder is free, free, free!"

"Steady," Gregor said, wearily scratching sand out of his hair.

"Don't you understand? When you get something free, in unlimited quantities, there has to be an application for it. And all this is free—"

The door opened, and a tall, thin man in a dark business suit walked in, holding a complex little gadget in his hand.

"So *here* it is," the man said.

Gregor was struck by a sudden wild thought. "Is that a Laxian Key?" he asked.

"A what key? No, I don't suppose it is," the man said. "It is a drainometer."

"Oh," Gregor said.

"And it seems to have brought me to the source of the trouble," the man said. "I'm Mr. Garstairs." He cleared sand from Gregor's desk, took a last reading on his drainometer and started to fill out a printed form.

"What's all this about?" Arnold asked.

"I'm from the Metropolitan Power Company," Garstairs said. "Starting around noon yesterday, we observed a sudden enormous drain on our facilities."

"And it's coming from here?" Gregor asked.

"From that machine of yours," Garstairs said. He completed his form, folded it and put it in his pocket. "Thanks for your cooperation. You will be billed for this, of course." With some difficulty he opened the door, then turned and took another look at the Free Producer.

"It must be making something extremely valuable," he said, "to justify the expenditure of so much power. What is it? Platinum dust?"

He smiled, nodded pleasantly and left.

Gregor turned to Arnold. "Free power, eh?"

"Well," Arnold said, "I guess it just grabs it from the nearest power source."

"So I see. Draws power out of the air, out of space, out of the sun. And out of the power company's lines, if they're handy."

"So it seems. But the basic principle—"

"To hell with the basic principle!" Gregor shouted. "We can't turn this damned thing off without a Laxian Key, no one's got a Laxian Key, we're submerged in worthless dust which we can't even afford to truck out, and we're probably burning up power like a sun gone nova!"

"There must be a solution," Arnold said sullenly.

"Yeah? Suppose you find it."

Arnold sat down where his desk had been and covered his eyes. There was a loud knock on the door, and angry voices outside.

"Lock the door," Arnold said.

Gregor locked it. Arnold thought for a few moments longer, then stood up.

"All is not lost," he said. "Our fortunes will still be made from this machine."

"Let's just destroy it," Gregor said. "Drop it in an ocean or something."

"No! I've got it now! Come on, let's get the spaceship warmed up."

The next few days were hectic ones for AAA Ace. They had to hire men, at exorbitant rates, to clear the building of Tangreese. Then came the problem of getting the machine, still spouting gray dust, into their spaceship. But at last, everything was done. The Free Producer sat in the hold, rapidly filling it with Tangreese, and their ship was out of the system and moving fast on overdrive.

"It's only logical," Arnold explained later. "Naturally there's no market for Tangreese on Earth. Therefore there's no use trying to sell it on Earth. But on the planet Meldge—"

"I don't like it," Gregor said.

"It can't fail. It costs too much to transport Tangreese to Meldge. But we're moving our entire factory there. We can pour out a constant stream of the stuff."

"Suppose the market is low?" Gregor asked.

"How low can it get? This stuff is like bread to the Meldgens. It's their basic diet. How can we miss?"

After two weeks in space, Meldge hove in sight on their starboard bow. It came none too soon. Tangreese had completely filled the hold. They had sealed it off, but the increasing pressure threatened to burst the sides of the ship. They had to dump tons of it every day, but dumping took time, and there was a loss of heat and air in the process.

So they spiraled into Meldge with every inch of their ship crammed with Tangreese, low on oxygen and extremely cold.

As soon as they had landed, a large orange-skinned customs official came on board.

"Welcome," he said. "Seldom do visitors come to our unimportant little planet. Do you expect to stay long?"

"Probably," Arnold said. "We're going to set up a business."

"Excellent!" the official said, smiling happily. "Our planet needs new blood, new enterprise. Might I enquire what business?"

"We're going to sell Tangreese, the basic food of—"

The official's face darkened. "You're going to sell what?"

"Tangreese. We have a Free Producer, and—"

The official pressed a button on a wrist dial. "I am sorry, you must leave at once."

"But we've got passports, clearance papers—"

"And we have laws. You must blast off immediately and take your Free Producer with you."

"Now look here," Gregor said, "there's supposed to be free enterprise on this planet."

"Not in the production of Tangreese there isn't."

Outside, a dozen army tanks rumbled onto the landing field and ringed themselves around the ship. The official backed out the port and started down the ladder.

"Wait!" Gregor cried in desperation. "I suppose you're afraid of unfair competition. Well, take the Free Producer as our gift."

"No!" Arnold shouted.

"Yes! Just dig it out and take it. Feed your poor with it. Just raise a statue to us sometime."

A second row of army tanks appeared. Overhead, antiquated jet planes dipped low over the field.

"Get off this planet!" the official shouted. "Do you really think you can sell Tangreese on Meldge? Look around!"

They looked. The landing field was gray and powdery, and the buildings were the same unpainted gray. Beyond them stretched dull gray fields, to a range of low gray mountains.

On all sides, as far as they could see, everything was Tangreese gray.

"Do you mean," Gregor asked, "that the whole planet—"

"Figure it out for yourself," the official said, backing down the ladder. "The Old Science originated here, and there are always fools who have to tamper with its artifacts. Now get going. But if you ever find a Laxian Key, come back and name your price."

THE LAST WEAPON

Edsel was in a murderous mood. He, Parke, and Faxon had spent three weeks in this part of the deadlands, breaking into every mound they came across, not finding anything, and moving on to the next. The swift Martian summer was passing, and each day became a little colder. Each day Edsel's nerves, uncertain at the best of times, had frayed a little more. Little Faxon was cheerful, dreaming of all the money they would make when they found the weapons, and Parke plodded silently along, apparently made of iron, not saying a word unless he was spoken to.

But Edsel had reached his limit. They had broken into another mound, and again there had been no sign of the lost Martian weapons. The watery sun seemed to be glaring at him, and the stars were visible in an impossibly blue sky. The afternoon cold seeped into Edsel's insulated suit, stiffening his joints, knotting his big muscles.

Quite suddenly, Edsel decided to kill Parke. He had disliked the silent man since they had formed the partnership on Earth. He disliked him even more than he despised Faxon.

Edsel stopped.

"Do you know where we're going?" he asked Parke, his voice ominously low.

Parke shrugged his slender shoulders negligently. His pale, hollow face showed no trace of expression.

"Do you?" Edsel asked.

Parke shrugged again.

A bullet in the head, Edsel decided, reaching for his gun.

"Wait!" Faxon pleaded, coming up between them. "Don't fly off, Edsel. Just think of all the money we can make when we find the weapons!" The little man's eyes glowed at the thought. "They're right around here some-where, Edsel. The next mound, maybe."

Edsel hesitated, glaring at Parke. Right now he wanted to kill more than anything else in the world. If he had known it would be like this, when they formed the com-pany on Earth . . . It had seemed so easy then. He had the plaque, the one which told where a cache of the fabulous lost Martian weapons were. Parke was able to read the Martian script, and Faxon could finance the expedition. So, he had figured all they'd have to do would be to land on Mars and walk up to the mound where the stuff was hidden.

Edsel had never been off Earth before. He hadn't counted on the weeks of freezing, starving on concentrated rations, always dizzy from breathing thin, tired air circulat-ing through a replenisher. He hadn't thought about the sore, aching muscles you get, dragging your way through the thick Martian brush.

All he had thought about was the price a government—any government—would pay for those legendary weapons.

"I'm sorry," Edsel said, making up his mind suddenly. "This place gets me. Sorry I blew up, Parke. Lead on."

Parke nodded, and started again. Faxon breathed a sigh of relief, and followed Parke.

After all, Edsel thought. I can kill them anytime.

They found the correct mound in mid-afternoon, just as Edsel's patience was wearing thin again. It was a strange, massive affair, just as the script had said. Under a few inches of dirt was metal. The men scraped and found a door.

"Here, I'll blast it open," Edsel said, drawing his revolver.

Parke pushed him aside, turned the handle and opened the door.

Inside was a tremendous room. And there, row upon gleaming row, were the legendary lost weapons of Mars, the missing artifacts of Martian civilization.

The three men stood for a moment, just looking. Here was the treasure that men had almost given up looking for. Since man had landed on Mars, the ruins of great cities had been explored. Scattered across the plains were ruined vehicles, art forms, tools, everything indicating the ghost of a titanic civilization, a thousand years beyond Earth's. Patiently deciphered scripts had told of the great wars ravaging the surface of Mars. The scripts stopped too soon, though, because nothing told what had happened to the Martians. There hadn't been an intelligent being on Mars for several thousand years. Somehow, all animal life on the planet had been obliterated.

And, apparently, the Martians had taken their weapons with them.

These lost weapons, Edsel knew, were worth their weight in radium. There just wasn't anything like them.

The men went inside. Edsel picked up the first thing his hand reached. It looked like a .45, but bigger. He went to the door and pointed the weapon at a shrub on the plain.

"Don't fire it," Faxon said, as Edsel took aim. "It might backfire or something. Let the government men fire them, after we sell."

Edsel squeezed the trigger. The shrub, 75 feet away, erupted in a bright red flash.

"Not bad," Edsel said, patting the gun. He put it down and reached for another.

"Please, Edsel," Faxon said, squinting nervously at him. "There's no need to try them out. You might set off an atomic bomb or something."

"Shut up," Edsel said, examining the weapon for a firing stud.

"Don't shoot any more," Faxon pleaded. He looked to Parke for support, but the silent man was watching Edsel. "You know, something in this place might have been responsible for the destruction of the Martian race. You wouldn't want to set if off again, would you?"

Edsel watched a spot on the plain glow with heat as he fired at it.

"Good stuff." He picked up another, rod-shaped instrument. The cold was forgotten. Edsel was perfectly happy now, playing with all the shiny things.

"Let's get started," Faxon said, moving toward the door.

"Started? Where?" Edsel demanded. He picked up another glittering weapon, curved to fit his wrist and hand.

"Back to the port," Faxon said. "Back to sell this stuff,

like we planned. I figure we can ask just about any price, any price at all. A government would give billions for weapons like these."

"I've changed my mind," Edsel said. Out of the corner of his eye he was watching Parke. The slender man was walking between the stacks of weapons, but so far he hadn't touched any.

"Now listen," Faxon said, glaring at Edsel. "I financed this expedition. We planned on selling the stuff. I have a right to—well, perhaps not."

The untried weapon was pointed squarely at his stomach.

"What are you going to do?" he asked, trying not to look at the gun.

"To hell with selling it," Edsel said, leaning against the cave wall where he could also watch Parke. "I figure I can use this stuff myself." He grinned broadly, still watching both men.

"I can outfit some of the boys back home. With the stuff that's here, we can knock over one of those little governments in Central America easy. I figure we could hold it forever."

"Well," Faxon said, watching the gun, "I don't want to be a party to that sort of thing. Just count me out."

"All right," Edsel said.

"Don't worry about me talking," Faxon said quickly. "I won't. I just don't want to be in on any shooting or killing. So I think I'll go back."

"Sure," Edsel said. Parke was standing to one side, examining his fingernails.

"If you get that kingdom set up, I'll come down," Faxon said, grinning weakly. "Maybe you can make me a duke or something."

"I think I can arrange that."

"Swell. Good luck." Faxon waved his hand and started to walk away. Edsel let him get 20 feet, then aimed the new weapon and pressed the stud.

The gun didn't make any noise; there was no flash, but Faxon's arm was neatly severed. Quickly, Edsel pressed the stud again and swung the gun down on Faxon. The little man was chopped in half, and the ground on either side of him was slashed, also.

Edsel turned, realizing that he had left his back exposed to Parke. All the man had to do was pick up the nearest gun and blaze away. But Parke was just standing there, his arms folded over his chest.

"That beam will probably cut through anything," Parke said. "Very useful."

Edsel had a wonderful half hour, running back and forth to the door with different weapons. Parke made no move to touch anything, but watched with interest. The ancient Martian arms were as good as new, apparently unaffected by their thousands of years of disuse. There were many blasting weapons, of various designs and capabilities. Then heat and radiation guns, marvelously compact things. There were weapons which would freeze and weapons which would burn; others which would crumble, cut, coagulate, paralyze, and do any of the other things to snuff out life.

"Let's try this one," Parke said. Edsel, who had been on the verge of testing an interesting-looking three-barreled rifle, stopped.

"I'm busy," he said.

"Stop playing with those toys. Let's have a look at some real stuff."

Parke was standing near a squat black machine on wheels. Together they tugged it outside. Parke watched while Edsel moved the controls. A faint hum started deep in the machine. Then a blue haze formed around it. The haze spread as Edsel manipulated the controls until it surrounded the two men.

"Try a blaster on it," Parke said. Edsel picked up one of the explosive pistols and fired. The charge was absorbed by the haze. Quickly he tested three others. They couldn't pierce the blue glow.

"I believe," Parke said softly, "this will stop an atomic bomb. This is a force field."

Edsel turned it off and they went back inside. It was growing dark in the cave as the sun neared the horizon.

"You know," Edsel said, "you're a pretty good guy, Parke. You're OK."

"Thanks," Parke said, looking over the mass of weapons.

"You don't mind my cutting down Faxon, do you? He was going straight to the government."

"On the contrary, I approve."

"Swell. I figure you must be OK. You could have killed me when I was killing Faxon." Edsel didn't add that it was what he would have done.

Parke shrugged his shoulders.

"How would you like to work on this kingdom deal with me?" Edsel asked, grinning. "I think we could swing it. Get ourselves a nice place, plenty of girls, lots of laughs. What do you think?"

"Sure," Parke said. "Count me in." Edsel slapped him on the shoulder, and they went through the ranks of weapons.

"All these are pretty obvious," Parke said as they reached the end of the room. "Variations on the others."

At the end of the room was a door. There were letters in Martian script engraved on it.

"What's that stuff say?" Edsel asked.

"Something about 'final weapons,'" Parke told him, squinting at the delicate tracery. "A warning to stay out." He opened the door. Both men started to step inside, then recoiled suddenly.

Inside was a chamber fully three times the size of the room they had just left. And filling the great room, as far as they could see, were soldiers. Gorgeously dressed, fully armed, the soldiers were motionless, statuelike.

They were not alive.

There was a table by the door, and on it were three things. First, there was a sphere about the size of a man's fist, with a calibrated dial set in it. Beside that was a shining helmet. And next was a small, black box with Martian script on it.

"Is it a burial place?" Edsel whispered, looking with awe at the strong unearthly faces of the Martian soldiery. Parke, behind him, didn't answer.

Edsel walked to the table and picked up the sphere. Carefully he turned the dial a single notch.

"What do you think it's supposed to do?" he asked Parke. "Do you think—" Both men gasped, and moved back.

The lines of fighting men had moved. Men in ranks

swayed, then came to attention. But they no longer held the rigid posture of death. The ancient fighting men were alive.

One of them, in an amazing uniform of purple and silver, came forward and bowed to Edsel.

"Sir, your troops are ready." Edsel was too amazed to speak.

"How can you live after thousands of years?" Parke answered. "Are you Martians?"

"We are the servants of the Martians," the soldier said. Parke noticed that the soldier's lips hadn't moved. The man was telepathic. "Sir, we are Synthetics."

"Whom do you obey?" Parke asked.

"The Activator, sir." The Synthetic was speaking directly to Edsel, looking at the sphere in his hand. "We require no food or sleep, sir. Our only desire is to serve you and to fight." The soldiers in the ranks nodded approvingly.

"Lead us into battle, sir!"

"I sure will!" Edsel said, finally regaining his senses. "I'll show you boys some fighting, you can bank on that!"

The soldiers cheered him, solemnly, three times. Edsel grinned, looking at Parke.

"What do the rest of these numbers do?" Edsel asked. But the soldier was silent. The question was evidently beyond his built-in knowledge.

"It might activate other Synthetics," Parke said. "There are probably more chambers underground."

"Brother!" Edsel shouted. "*Will* I lead you into battle!" Again the soldiers cheered, three solemn cheers.

"Put them to sleep and let's make some plans," Parke said. Dazed, Edsel turned the switch back. The soldiers froze again into immobility.

"Come on outside."

"Right."

"And bring that stuff with you." Edsel picked up the shining helmet and the black box and followed Parke outside. The sun had almost disappeared now, and there were black shadows over the red land. It was bitterly cold, but neither man noticed.

"Did you hear what they said, Parke? Did you hear it? They said I was their leader! With men like those—" He laughed at the sky. With those soldiers, those weapons, nothing could stop him. He'd really stock his land—prettiest girls in the world, and would he have a time!

"I'm a general!" Edsel shouted, and slipped the helmet over his head. "How do I look, Parke? Don't I look like a—" He stopped. He was hearing a voice in his ears, whispering, muttering. What was it saying?

". . . *damned idiot, with his little dream of a kingdom. Power like this is for a man of genius, a man who can remake history. Myself!*"

"Who's talking? That's you, isn't it Parke?" Edsel realized suddenly that the helmet allowed him to listen in on thoughts. He didn't have time to consider what a weapon this would be for a ruler.

Parke shot him neatly through the back with a gun he had been holding all the time.

"What an idiot," Parke told himself, slipping the helmet on his head. "A kingdom! All the power in the world, and he dreamed of a little kingdom!" He glanced back at the cave.

"With those troops—the force field—and the weapons— I can take over the world." He said it coldly, knowing it was a fact. He turned to go back to the cave to activate the Synthetics, but stopped first to pick up the little black box Edsel had carried.

Engraved on it, in flowing Martian script, was, "The Last Weapon."

I wonder what it could be, Parke asked himself. He had let Edsel live long enough to try out all the others; no use chancing a misfire himself. It was too bad he hadn't lived long enough to try out this one, too.

Of course, I really don't need it, he told himself. He had plenty. But this might make the job a lot easier, a lot safer. Whatever it was, it was bound to be good.

Well, he told himself, let's see what the Martians considered their last weapon. He opened the box.

A vapor drifted out, and Parke threw the box from him, thinking about poison gas.

The vapor mounted, drifted haphazardly for a while, then began to coalesce. It spread, grew and took shape.

In a few seconds, it was complete, hovering over the box. It glimmered white in the dying light, and Parke saw that it was just a tremendous mouth, topped by a pair of unblinking eyes.

"Ho ho," the mouth said. "Protoplasm!" It drifted to the body of Edsel. Parke lifted a blaster and took careful aim.

"Quiet protoplasm," the thing said, nuzzling Edsel's body. "I like quiet protoplasm." It took down the body in a single gulp.

Parke fired, blasting a ten-foot hole in the ground. The giant mouth drifted out of it, chuckling.

"It's been so long," it said.

Parke was clenching his nerves in a forged grip. He refused to let himself become panicked. Calmly he activated the force field, forming a blue sphere around himself.

Still chuckling, the thing drifted through the blue haze.

Parke picked up the weapon Edsel had used on Faxon, feeling the well-balanced piece swing up in his hand. He backed to one side of the force field as the thing approached, and turned on the beam.

The thing kept coming.

"Die, die!" Parke screamed, his nerves breaking.

But the thing came on, grinning broadly.

"I like *quiet* protoplasm," the thing said as its gigantic mouth converged on Parke.

"But I also like *lively* protoplasm."

It gulped once, then drifted out the other side of the field, looking anxiously around for the millions of units of protoplasm, as there had been in the old days.

FISHING SEASON

They had been living in the housing project only a week, and this was their first invitation. They arrived on the dot of eight-thirty. The Carmichaels were obviously prepared for them, for the porch light was on, the front door partially open, and the living room a blaze of light.

"Do I look all right?" Phyllis asked at the door. "Seams straight, hair curly?"

"You're a vision in a red hat," her husband assured her. "Just don't spoil the effect by leading aces." She made a small face at him and rang the doorbell. Soft chimes sounded inside.

Mallen straightened his tie while they waited. He pulled out his breast handkerchief a microscopic fraction farther.

"They must be making gin in the subcellar," he told his wife. "Shall I ring again?"

"No—wait a moment." They waited, and he rang again. Again the chimes sounded.

"That's very strange," Phyllis said a few minutes later. "It was tonight, wasn't it?" Her husband nodded. The Carmichaels had left their windows open to the warm spring weather. Through the Venetian blinds they could see a table set for bridge, chairs drawn up, candy dishes out, everything in readiness. But no one answered the door.

"Could they have stepped out?" Phyllis Mallen asked. Her husband walked quickly across the lawn to the driveway.

"Their car's in." He came back and pushed the front door open further.

"Jimmy—don't go in."

"I'm not." He put his head in the door. "Hello! Anybody home?"

Silence in the house.

"Hello!" he shouted, and listened intently. He could hear Friday-night noises next door—people talking, laughing. A car passed in the street. He listened. A board creaked somewhere in the house, then silence again.

"They wouldn't go away and leave their house open like this," he told Phyllis. "Something might have happened." He stepped inside. She followed, but stood uncertainly in the living room while he went into the kitchen. She heard him open the cellar door, call out, "Anyone home!" And close it again. He came back to the living room, frowned and went upstairs.

In a little while Mallen came down with a puzzled expression on his face. "There's no one there," he said.

"Let's get out of here," Phyllis said, suddenly nervous in the bright, empty house. They debated leaving a note, decided against it and started down the walk.

"Shouldn't we close the front door?" Jim Mallen asked, stopping.

"What good will it do? All the windows are open."

"Still—" He went back and closed it. They walked home slowly, looking back over their shoulders at the house. Mallen half-expected the Carmichaels to come running after them, shouting, "Surprise!"

But the house remained silent.

Their home was only a block away, a brick bungalow just like two hundred others in the development. Inside, Mr. Carter was making artificial trout flies on the card-table. Working slowly and surely, his deft fingers guided the colored threads with loving care. He was so intent on his work that he didn't hear the Mallens enter.

"We're home, dad," Phyllis said.

"Ah," Mr. Carter murmured. "Look at this beauty." He held up a finished fly. It was an almost exact replica of a hornet. The hook was cleverly concealed by overhanging yellow and black threads.

"The Carmichaels were out—we think," Mallen said, hanging up his jacket.

"I'm going to try Old Creek in the morning," Mr. Carter said. "Something tells me the elusive trout may be there." Mallen grinned to himself. It was difficult talking with Phyllis' father. Nowadays he never discussed anything except fishing. The old man had retired from a highly successful business on his seventieth birthday to devote himself wholeheartedly to his favorite sport.

Now, nearing eighty, Mr. Carter looked wonderful. It was amazing, Mallen thought. His skin was rosy, his eyes clear and untroubled, his pure white hair neatly combed back. He was in full possession of his senses, too—as long as you talked about fishing.

"Let's have a snack," Phyllis said. Regretfully she took off the red hat, smoothed out the veil and put it down on a coffee table. Mr. Carter added another thread to his trout fly, examined it closely, then put it down and followed them into the kitchen.

While Phyllis made coffee, Mallen told the old man what had happened. Mr. Carter's answer was typical.

"Try some fishing tomorrow and get it off your mind. Fishing, Jim, is more than a sport. Fishing is a way of life, and a philosophy as well. I like to find a quiet pool and sit on the banks of it. I figure, if there's fish anywhere, they might as well be there."

Phyllis smiled, watching Jim twist uncomfortably on his chair. There was no stopping her father once he got started. And anything would start him.

"Consider," Mr. Carter went on, "a young executive. Someone like yourself, Jim—dashing through a hall. Common enough? But at the end of the last long corridor is a trout stream. Consider a politician. You certainly see enough of them in Albany. Briefcase in hand, worried—"

"That's strange," Phyllis said, stopping her father in midflight. She was holding an unopened bottle of milk in her hand.

"Look." Their milk came from Stannerton Dairies. The green label on this bottle read: "Stanneron Daries."

"And look." She pointed. Under that, it read: "lisensed by the neW yoRk Bord of healthh." It looked like a clumsy imitation of the legitimate label.

"Where did you get this?" Mallen asked.

"Why, I suppose from Mr. Elger's store. Could it be an advertising stunt?"

"I despise the man who would fish with a worm," Mr. Carter intoned gravely. "A fly—a fly is a work of art. But the man who'd use a worm would rob orphans and burn churches."

"Don't drink it," Mallen said. "Let's look over the rest of the food."

There were three more counterfeited items. A candy bar which purported to be a Mello-Bite had an orange label instead of the familiar crimson. There was a jar of Ammerican ChEEse, almost a third larger than the usual jars of that brand, and a bottle of SPArkling Watr.

"That's very odd," Mallen said, rubbing his jaw.

"I always throw the little one back," Mr. Carter said. "It's not sporting to keep them, and that's part of a fisherman's code. Let them grow, let them ripen, let them gain experience. It's the old, crafty ones I want, the ones who skulk under logs, who dart away at the first sight of the angler. Those are the lads who put up a fight!"

"I'm going to take this stuff back to Elger," Mallen said, putting the items into a paper bag. "If you see anything else like it, save it."

"Old Creek is the place," Mr. Carter said. "That's where they hide out."

Saturday morning was bright and beautiful. Mr. Carter ate an early breakfast and left for Old Creek, stepping lightly as a boy, his battered fly-decked hat set at a jaunty angle. Jim Mallen finished coffee and went over to the Carmichael house.

The car was still in the garage. The windows were still open, the bridge table set, and every light was on, exactly as it had been the night before. It reminded Mallen of a story he had read once about a ship under full sail, with everything in order—but not a soul on board.

"I wonder if there's anyone we can call?" Phyllis asked when he returned home. "I'm sure there's something wrong."

"Sure. But who?" They were strangers in the project. They had a nodding acquaintance with three or four families, but no idea who might know the Carmichaels.

The problem was settled by the ringing of the telephone.

"If it's anyone from around here," Jim said as Phyllis answered it, "ask them."

"Hello?"

"Hello. I don't believe you know me. I'm Marian Carpenter, from down the block. I was just wondering—has my husband dropped over there?" The metallic telephone voice managed to convey worry, fear.

"Why no. No one's been in this morning."

"I see." The thin voice hesitated.

"Is there anything I can do?" Phyllis asked.

"I don't understand it," Mrs. Carpenter said. "George— my husband—had breakfast with me this morning. Then he went upstairs for his jacket. That was the last I saw of him."

"Oh—"

"I'm sure he didn't come back downstairs. I went up to see what was holding him—we were going for a drive— and he wasn't there. I searched the whole house. I thought he might be playing a practical joke, although George never joked in his life—so I looked under beds and in the closets. Then I looked in the cellar, and I asked next door, but no one's seen him. I thought he might have visited you—he was speaking about it—"

Phyllis explained to her about the Carmichaels' disappearance. They talked for a few seconds longer, then hung up.

"Jim," Phyllis said, "I don't like it. You'd better tell the police about the Carmichaels."

"We'll look pretty foolish when they turn up visiting friends in Albany."

"We'll have to chance it."

Jim found the number and dialed, but the line was busy.

"I'll go down."

"And take this stuff with you." She handed him the paper bag.

Police Captain Lesner was a patient, ruddy-faced man who had been listening to an unending stream of complaints all night and most of the morning. His patrolmen were tired, his sergeants were tired, and he was the tiredest of all. Nevertheless, he ushered Mr. Mallen into his office and listened to his story.

"I want you to write down everything you've told me," Lesner said when he was through. "We got a call on the Carmichaels from a neighbor late last night. Been trying to locate them. Counting Mrs. Carpenter's husband, that makes ten in two days."

"Ten what?"

"Disappearances."

"My Lord," Mallen breathed softly. He shifted the paper bag. "All from this town?"

"Every one," Captain Lesner said harshly, "from the Vainsville housing project in this town. As a matter of fact, from four square blocks in that project." He named the streets.

"I live in there," Mallen said.

"So do I."

"Have you any idea who the—the kidnapper could be?" Mallen asked.

"We don't think it's a kidnapper," Lesner said, lighting his twentieth cigarette for the day. "No ransom notes. No selection. A good many of the missing persons wouldn't be worth a nickel to a kidnapper. And wholesale like that— not a chance!"

"A maniac then?"

"Sure. But how has he grabbed whole families? Or grown men, big as you? And where has he hidden them, or their bodies?" Lesner ground out the cigarette viciously. "I've got men searching every inch of this town. Every cop within 20 miles of here is looking. The state police are stopping cars. And we haven't found a thing."

"Oh, and here's something else." Mallen showed him the counterfeited items.

"Again, I don't know," Captain Lesner confessed sourly. "I haven't had much time for this stuff. We've had other complaints—" The telephone rang, but Lesner ignored it.

"It looks like a black-market scheme. I've sent some stuff like it to Albany for analysis. I'm trying to trace outlets. Might be foreign. As a matter of fact, the F.B.I. might— damn that 'phone!"

He yanked it out of its cradle.

"Lesner speaking. Yes. . . . yes. You're sure? Of course, Mary. I'll be right over." He hung up. His red face was suddenly drained of color.

"That was my wife's sister," he announced. "My wife's missing!"

Mallen drove home at breakneck speed. He slammed on the brakes, almost cracking his head against the windshield, and ran into the house.

"Phyllis!" he shouted. Where was she? Oh, God, he thought. If she's gone—

"Anything wrong?" Phyllis asked, coming out of the kitchen.

"I thought—" He grabbed her and hugged until she squealed.

"Really," she said, smiling. "We're not newlyweds. Why, we've been married a whole year and a half—"

He told her what he'd found out in the police station.

Phyllis looked around the living room. It had seemed so warm and cheerful a week ago. Now, a shadow under the couch frightened her; an open closet door was something to shudder at. She knew it would never be the same.

There was a knock at the door.

"Don't go," Phyllis said.

"Who's there?" Mallen asked.

"Joe Dutton, from down the block. I suppose you've heard the news?"

"Yes," Mallen said, standing beside the closed door.

"We're barricading the streets," Dutton said. "Going to look over anyone going in or out. We're going to put a stop to this, even if the police can't. Want to join us?"

"You bet," Mallen said, and opened the door. The short, swarthy man on the other side was wearing an old army jacket. He was gripping a two-foot chunk of wood.

"We're going to cover these blocks like a blanket," Dutton said. "If anyone else is grabbed, it'll have to be underground." Mallen kissed his wife and joined him.

That afternoon there was a mass meeting in the school auditorium. Everyone from the affected blocks was there, and as many of the townspeople as could crowded in. The first thing they found out was that, in spite of the blockades, three more people were missing from the Vainsville project.

Captain Lesner spoke and told them that he had called

Albany for help. Special officers were on their way down, and the F.B.I. was coming in on it, too. He stated frankly that he didn't know what or who was doing it, or why. He couldn't even figure out why all the missing were from one part of the Vainsville project.

He had gotten word from Albany about the counterfeited food that seemed to be scattered all over the project. The examining chemists could detect no trace of any toxic agent. That seemed to explode a recent theory that the food had been used to drug people, making them walk out of their homes to whatever was taking them. However, he cautioned everyone not to eat it. You could never tell.

The companies whose labels had been impersonated had disclaimed any knowledge. They were prepared to bring suit against anyone infringing on their copyrights.

The mayor spoke, in a series of well-intentioned platitudes, counselling them to be of good heart; the civic authorities were taking the whole situation in hand.

Of course, the mayor didn't live in the Vainsville project.

The meeting broke up, and the men returned to the barricades. They started looking for firewood for the evening, but it was unnecessary. Help arrived from Albany, a cavalcade of men and equipment. The four blocks were surrounded by armed guards. Portable searchlights were set up and the area declared under an eight-o'clock curfew.

Mr. Carter missed all the excitement. He had been fishing all day. At sunset he returned, empty-handed but happy. The guards let him through, and he walked into the house.

"A beautiful fishing day," he declared.

The Mallens spent a terrible night, fully clothed, dozing in snatches, looking at the searchlights playing against their windows and hearing the tramp of armed guards.

Eight o'clock Sunday morning—two more people missing. Gone from four blocks more closely guarded than a concentration camp.

At ten o'clock Mr. Carter, brushing aside the objections of the Mallens, shouldered his fishing kit and left. He hadn't missed a day since April thirtieth and wasn't planning on missing one all season.

Sunday noon—another person gone, bringing the total up to sixteen.

Sunday, one o'clock—all the missing children were found!

A police car found them on a road near the outskirts of town, eight of them, including the Carmichael boy, walking dazedly toward their homes. They were rushed to a hospital.

There was no trace of the missing adults, though.

Word of mouth spread the news faster than the newspapers or radio could. The children were completely unharmed. Under examination by psychiatrists it was found that they didn't remember where they had been or how they had been taken there. All the psychiatrists could piece together was a sensation of flying, accompanied by a sickness in the stomach. The children were kept in the hospital for safety, under guard.

But between noon and evening, another child disappeared from Vainsville.

Just before sunset, Mr. Carter came home. In his knapsack were two big rainbow trout. He greeted the Mallens gaily and went to the garage to clean his fish.

Jim Mallen stepped into the backyard and started to the garage after him, frowning. He wanted to ask the old man about something he had said a day or two ago. He couldn't quite remember what it was, but it seemed important.

His next-door neighbor, whose name he couldn't remember, greeted him.

"Mallen," he said. "I think I know."

"What?" Mallen asked.

"Have you examined the theories?" the neighbor asked.

"Of course." His neighbor was a skinny fellow in shirtsleeves and vest. His bald head glistened red in the sunset.

"Then listen. It can't be a kidnapper. No sense in their methods. Right?"

"Yes, I suppose so."

"And a maniac is out. How could he snatch 15, 16 people? And return the children? Even a gang of maniacs couldn't do that, not with the number of cops we've got watching. Right?"

"Go on." Out of the corner of his eye Mallen saw his neighbor's fat wife come down the back steps. She walked over to them and listened.

"The same goes for a gang of criminals, or even Martians. Impossible to do it, and no reason even if they could. We've got to look for something *illogical*—and that leaves just one logical answer."

Mallen waited, and glanced at the woman. She was looking at him, arms folded across her aproned chest. In fact, she was glaring at him. Can she be angry at me? Mallen thought. What have I done?

"The only answer," his neighbor said slowly, "is that there is a hole somewhere around here. A hole in the space-time continuum."

"What!" blurted Mallen. "I don't quite follow that."

"A hole in time," the bald neighbor explained, "or a hole in space. Or in both. Don't ask me how it got there; it's there. What happens is, a person steps into that hole, and bingo! He's somewhere else. Or in some other time. Or both. This hole can't be seen, of course—it's fourth dimensional—but it's there. The way I see it, if you traced the movements of these people, you'd find every one of them passed through a certain spot—and vanished."

"Hmmm." Mallen thought it over. "That sounds interesting—but we know that lots of people vanished right out of their own homes."

"Yeah," the neighbor agreed. "Let me think—I know! The hole in space-time isn't fixed. It drifts, moves around. First it's in Carpenter's house, then it moves on aimlessly—"

"Why doesn't it move out of these four blocks?" Mallen asked, wondering why the man's wife was still glaring at him, her lips tightly compressed.

"Well," the neighbor said, "it has to have some limitations."

"And why were the children returned?"

"Oh, for heaven's sake. Mallen, you can't ask me to figure out every little thing, can you? It's a good working theory. We'll have to have more facts before we can work out the whole thing."

"Hello there!" Mr. Carter called, emerging from the garage. He held up two beautiful trout, neatly cleaned and washed.

"The trout is a gamey fighter and makes magnificent eating as well. The most excellent of sports, and the most excellent of foods!" He walked unhurriedly into the house.

"I've got a better theory," the neighbor's wife said, unfolding her arms and placing her hands on her ample hips.

Both men turned to look at her.

"Who is the only person around here who isn't the least bit worried about what's going on? Who goes walking all over with a bag he *says* has *fish* in it? Who *says* he spends all his time fishing?"

"Oh, no," Mallen said. "Not Dad Carter. He has a whole philosophy about fishing—"

"I don't care about philosophy!" the woman shrieked. "He fools you, but he doesn't fool me! I only know he's the only man in this neighborhood who isn't the least bit worried and he's around and gone every day and lynching would probably be too good for him!" With that she spun and went waddling into her house.

"Look, Mallen," the bald neighbor said. "I'm sorry. You know how women are. She's upset, even if Danny is safe in the hospital."

"Sure," Mallen said.

"She doesn't understand the space-time continuum," he went on earnestly. "But I'll explain it to her tonight. She'll apologize in the morning. You'll see."

The men shook hands and returned to their respective homes.

Darkness came swiftly, and searchlights went on all over town. Beams of light knifed down streets, into backyards, reflected from closed windows. The inhabitants of Vainsville settled down to wait for more disappearances.

Jim Mallen wished he could put his hands on whatever was doing it. Just for a second—that was all he'd need. But to have to sit and wait. He felt so helpless. His wife's lips were pale and cracked, and her eyes were tired. But Mr. Carter was cheerful, as usual. He fried the trout over a gas burner, serving both of them.

"I found a beautiful quiet pool today," Mr. Carter announced. "It is near the mouth of Old Creek, up a little tributary. I fished there all day, leaning back against the grassy bank and watching the clouds. Fantastic things, clouds! I shall go there tomorrow and fish in it one more day. Then I will move on. A wise fisherman does not fish out a stream. Moderation is the code of the fisherman. Take a little, leave a little. I have often thought—"

"Oh Dad, please!" Phyllis screamed, and burst into tears. Mr. Carter shook his head sadly, smiled an understanding smile and finished his trout. Then he went into the living room to work on a new fly.

Exhausted, the Mallens went to bed. . . .

Mallen awoke and sat upright. He looked over and saw his wife asleep beside him. The luminous dial of his watch read four-fifty-eight. Almost morning, he thought.

He got out of bed, slipped on a bathrobe and padded softly downstairs. The searchlights were flashing against the living-room window, and he could see a guard outside.

That was a reassuring sight, he thought, and went into the kitchen. Moving quietly, he poured a glass of milk. There was fresh cake on top of the refrigerator, and he cut himself a slice.

Kidnappers, he thought. Maniacs. Men from Mars. Holes in space. Or any combination thereof. No, that was wrong. He wished he could remember what he wanted to ask Mr. Carter. It was important.

He rinsed out the glass, put the cake back on the refrigerator and walked to the living room. Suddenly he was thrown violently to one side.

Something had hold of him! He flailed out, but there was nothing to hit. Something was gripping him like an iron hand, dragging him off his feet. He threw himself to one side, scrambling for a footing. His feet left the floor and he hung for a moment, kicking and squirming. The grip around his ribs was so tight he couldn't breathe, couldn't make a sound. Inexorably, he was being lifted.

Hole in space, he thought, and tried to scream. His wildly flailing arms caught a corner of the couch and he seized it. The couch was lifted with him. He yanked, and the grip relaxed for a moment, letting him drop to the floor.

He scrambled across the floor toward the door. The grip caught him again, but he was near a radiator. He wrapped both arms around it, trying to resist the pull. He yanked again and managed to get one leg around, then the other.

The radiator creaked horribly as the pull increased. Mallen felt as though his waist would part, but he held on, every muscle stretched to the breaking point. Suddenly the grip relaxed completely.

He collapsed to the floor.

When he came to, it was broad daylight. Phyllis was splashing water in his face, her lower lip caught between her teeth. He blinked, and wondered for a moment where he was.

"Am I still here?" he asked.

"Are you all right?" Phyllis demanded. "What happened? Oh, darling! Let's get out of this place—"

"Where's your father?" Mallen asked groggily, getting to his feet.

"Fishing. Now please sit down. I'm going to call a doctor."

"No. Wait." Mallen went into the kitchen. On the refrigerator was the cake box. It read "Johnson's Cake Shop. Vainsville, New YorK." A capital K in New York. Really a very small error.

And Mr. Carter? Was the answer there? Mallen raced upstairs and dressed. He crumpled the cakebox and thrust it into his pocket, and hurried out the door.

"Don't touch anything until I get back!" he shouted at Phyllis. She watched him get into the car and race down the street. Trying hard to keep from crying, she walked into the kitchen.

Mallen was at Old Creek in 15 minutes. He parked the car and started walking up the stream.

"Mr. Carter!" he shouted as he went. "Mr. Carter!"

He walked and shouted for half an hour, into deeper and deeper woods. The trees overhung the stream now, and he had to wade to make any speed at all. He increased his pace, splashing, slipping on stones, trying to run.

"Mr. Carter!"

"Hello!" He heard the old man's voice. He followed the sound, up a branch of the stream. There was Mr. Carter, sitting on the steep bank of a little pool, holding his long bamboo pole. Mallen scrambled up beside him.

"Take it easy, son," Mr. Carter said. "Glad you took my advice about fishing."

"No," Mallen panted. "I want you to tell me something."

"Gladly," the old man said. "What would you like to know?"

"A fisherman wouldn't fish out a pool completely, would he?"

"I wouldn't. But some might."

"And bait. Any good fisherman would use artificial bait?"

"I pride myself on my flies," Mr. Carter said. "I try to approximate the real thing. Here, for example, is a beautiful replica of a hornet." He plucked a yellow hook from his hat. "And here is a lovely mosquito."

Suddenly his line stirred. Easily, surely, the old man brought it in. He caught the gasping trout in his hand and showed him to Mallen.

"A little fellow—I won't keep him." He removed the hook gently, easing it out of the gasping gill, and placed the fish back in water.

"When you throw him back—do you think he knows? Does he tell the others?"

"Oh, no," Mr. Carter said. "The experience doesn't teach him anything. I've had the same young fish bite my line two or three times. They have to grow up a bit before they know."

"I thought so." Mallen looked at the old man. Mr. Carter was unaware of the world around him, untouched by the terror that had struck Vainsville.

Fishermen live in a world of their own, thought Mallen.

"But you should have been here an hour ago," Mr. Carter said. "I hooked a beauty. A magnificent fellow, two pounds if he was an ounce. What a battle for an old warhorse like me! And he got away. But there'll come another—hey, where are you going?"

"Back!" Mallen shouted, splashing into the stream. He knew now what he had been looking for in Mr. Carter. A parallel. And now it was clear.

Harmless Mr. Carter, pulling up his trout, just like that other, greater fisherman, pulling up his—

"Back to warn the other fish!" Mallen shouted over his shoulder, stumbling along the stream bed. If only Phyllis hadn't touched any food! He pulled the cake box out of his pocket and threw it from him as hard as he could. The hateful lure!

While the fishermen, each in his respective sphere, smiled and dropped their lines into the water again.

DREAMWORLD

Infinite worlds exist in the infinite in every cycle—AETII DE PLACITIS RELIQUAE.

Lanigan dreamed the dream again and managed to wake himself with a hoarse cry. He sat upright in bed and glared around him into the violet darkness. His teeth were clenched and his lips were pulled back into a spastic grin. Beside him he felt his wife, Estelle, stir and sit up. Lanigan didn't look at her. Still caught in his dream, he waited for tangible proofs of the world.

A chair slowly drifted across his field of vision and fetched up against the wall with a quiet thump. Lanigan's face relaxed slightly. Then Estelle's hand was on his arm—a touch meant to be soothing, but which burned like lye.

"Here," she said. "Drink this."

"No," Lanigan said. "I'm all right now."

"Drink it anyhow."

"No, really. I really am all right."

For now he was completely out of the grip of the nightmare. He was himself again, and the world was its habitual self. That was very precious to Lanigan; he didn't want to let go of it just now, not even for the soothing release of a sedative.

"Was it the same dream?" Estelle asked him.

"Yes, just the same. . . . I don't want to talk about it."

"All right," Estelle said. (She is humoring me, Lanigan thought. I frighten her. I frighten myself.)

She asked, "Hon, what time is it?"

Lanigan looked at his watch. "Six-fifteen." But as he said it, the hour hand jumped forward convulsively. "No, it's five to seven."

"Can you get back to sleep?"

"I don't think so," Lanigan said. "I think I'll stay up."

"Fine, dear," Estelle said. She yawned, closed her eyes, opened them again and asked, "Hon, don't you think it might be a good idea if you called—"

"I have an appointment with him for twelve-ten," Lanigan said.

"That's fine," Estelle said. She closed her eyes again. Sleep came over her while Lanigan watched. Her auburn hair turned a faint blue and she sighed once, heavily.

Lanigan got out of bed and dressed. He was, for the most part, a large man, unusually easy to recognize. His features were curiously distinct. He had a rash on his neck. He was in no other way outstanding, except that he had a recurring dream which was driving him insane.

He spent the next few hours on his front porch watching stars go nova in the dawn sky.

Later, he went out for a stroll. As luck would have it, he ran into George Torstein just two blocks from his home. Several months ago, in an incautious moment, he had told Torstein about his dream. Torstein was a bluff, hearty fellow, a great believer in self-help, discipline, practicality, common sense, and other, even duller virtues. His hardheaded no-nonsense attitude had come as a momentary relief to Lanigan. But now it acted as an abrasive. Men like Torstein were undoubtedly the salt of the earth and the backbone of the country; but for Lanigan, wrestling with the impalpable (and losing), Torstein had grown from a nuisance into a horror.

"Well, Tom, how's the boy?" Torstein greeted him.

"Fine," Lanigan said, "just fine." He nodded pleasantly and began to walk on under a melting green sky. But one did not escape from Torstein so easily.

"Tom, boy, I've been thinking about your problem," Torstein said. "I've been quite disturbed about you."

"Well, that's very nice of you," Lanigan said. "But really, you shouldn't concern yourself—"

"I do it because I want to," Torstein said, speaking the simple, deplorable truth. "I take an interest in people, Tom. Always have, ever since I was a kid. And you and I've been friends and neighbors for a long time."

"That's true enough," Lanigan said numbly. (The worst thing about needing help was having to accept it.)

"Well, Tom, I think what would help you would be a little vacation."

Torstein had a simple prescription for everything. As he practiced soul-doctoring without a license, he was always careful to prescribe a drug you could buy over the counter.

"I really can't afford a vacation this month," Lanigan said. (The sky was ochre and pink now; three pines had withered; an oak had turned into a cactus.)

Torstein laughed heartily. "Boy, you can't afford not to take a vacation just now! Did you ever consider that?"

"No, I guess not."

"Well, *consider* it! You're tired, tense, all keyed-up. You've been working too hard."

"I've been on leave of absence all week," Lanigan said. He glanced at his watch. The gold case had turned to lead, but the time seemed accurate enough. Nearly two hours had passed since he had begun this conversation.

"It isn't good enough," Torstein was saying. "You've stayed right here in town, right close to your work. You need to get in touch with nature. Tom, when was the last time you went camping?"

"Camping? I don't think I've ever gone camping."

"There, you see! Boy, you've got to put yourself back in touch with real things. Not streets and buildings, but mountains and rivers."

Lanigan looked at his watch again and was relieved to see it turn back to gold. He was glad; he had paid 60 dollars for that case.

"Trees and lakes," Torstein was rhapsodizing. "The feel of grass growing under your feet, the sight of tall black mountains marching across a golden sky—"

Lanigan shook his head. "I've been in the country, George. It doesn't do anything for me."

Torstein was obstinate. "You must get away from artificialities."

"It all seems equally artificial," Lanigan said. "Trees or buildings—what's the difference?"

"Men make buildings," Torstein intoned. "But God makes trees."

Lanigan had his doubts about both propositions, but he

wasn't going to tell them to Torstein. "You might have something there. I'll think about it."

"You do that," Torstein said. "It happens I know the perfect place. It's in Maine, Tom, and it's right near this little lake—"

Torstein was a master of the interminable description. Luckily for Lanigan, there was a diversion. Across the street, a house burst into flames.

"Hey, whose house is that?" Lanigan asked.

"Makelby's," Torstein said. "That's his second fire this month."

"Maybe we ought to give the alarm."

"You're right. I'll do it myself," Torstein said. "Remember what I told you about that place in Maine, Tom."

Torstein turned to go, and something rather humorous happened. As he stepped over the pavement, the concrete liquified under his left foot. Caught unawares, Torstein went in ankle-deep. His forward motion pitched him head-first into the street.

Tom hurried to help him out before the concrete hardened again. "Are you all right?" he asked.

"Twisted my damned ankle," Torstein muttered. "It's OK, I can walk."

He limped off to report the fire. Lanigan stayed and watched. He judged the fire had been caused by spontaneous combustion. In a few minutes, as he expected, it put itself out by spontaneous decombustion.

One shouldn't be pleased by another man's misfortunes; but Lanigan couldn't help chuckling about Torstein's twisted ankle. Not even the sudden appearance of flood waters on Main Street could mar his good spirits.

Then he remembered his dream, and the panic began again. He walked quickly to the doctor's office.

Dr. Sampson's office was small and dark this week. The old gray sofa was gone; in its place were two Louis Quinze chairs and a hammock. The worn carpet had rewoven itself, and there was a cigarette burn on the puce ceiling. But the portrait of Andretti was in its usual place on the wall, and the big free-form ashtray was scrupulously clean.

The inner door opened and Dr. Sampson's head popped

out. "Hi," he said. "Won't be a minute." His head popped back in again.

Sampson was as good as his word. It took him exactly three seconds by Lanigan's watch to do whatever he had to do. One second later Lanigan was stretched out on the leather couch with a fresh paper doily under his head. And Dr. Sampson was saying, "Well, Tom, how have things been going?"

"The same," Lanigan said. "Worse."

"The dream?"

Lanigan nodded.

"Let's just run through it again."

"I'd rather not," Lanigan said.

"Afraid?"

"More afraid than ever."

"Even now?"

"Yes. Especially now."

There was a moment of therapeutic silence. Then Dr. Sampson said, "You've spoken before of your fear of this dream; but you've never told me *why* you fear it so."

"Well. . . . It sounds so silly."

Sampson's face was serious, quiet, composed; the face of a man who found nothing silly, who was constitutionally incapable of finding anything silly. It was a pose, perhaps, but one which Lanigan found reassuring.

"All right, I'll tell you," Lanigan said abruptly. Then he stopped.

"Go on," Dr. Sampson said.

"Well, it's because I believe that somehow, in some way I don't understand . . ."

"Yes, go on," Sampson said.

"Well, that somehow the world of my dream is becoming the real world." He stopped again, then went on with a rush. "And someday I am going to wake up and find myself *in* that world. And then that world will have become the real one and this world will be the dream."

He turned to see how this mad revelation had affected Sampson. If the doctor was disturbed, he didn't show it. He was quietly lighting his pipe with the smoldering tip of his left forefinger. He blew out his forefinger and said, "Yes, please go on."

"Go on? But that's it, that's the whole thing!"

A spot the size of a quarter appeared on Sampson's mauve carpet. It darkened, thickened, grew into a small fruit tree. Sampson picked one of the purple pods, sniffed it, then set it down on his desk. He looked at Lanigan sternly, sadly.

"You've told me about your dreamworld before, Tom." Lanigan nodded.

"We have discussed it, traced its origins, explored its meaning for you. In past months we have discovered, I believe, why you *need* to cripple yourself with this nightmare fear."

Lanigan nodded unhappily.

"Yet you refuse the insights," Sampson said. "You forget each time that your dreamworld is a *dream,* nothing but a dream, operated by arbitrary dream laws which you have invented to satisfy your psychic needs."

"I wish I could believe that," Lanigan said. "The trouble is, my dreamworld is so damnably reasonable."

"Not at all," Sampson said. "It is just that your delusion is hermetic, self-enclosed and self-sustaining. A man's actions are based upon certain assumptions about the nature of the world. Grant his assumptions and his behavior is entirely reasonable. But to change those assumptions, those fundamental axioms, is nearly impossible. For example, how do you prove to a man that he is not being controlled by a secret radio which only he can hear?"

"I see the problem," Lanigan muttered. "And that's me?"

"Yes, Tom; that, in effect, is you. You want me to prove to you that this world is real, and that the world of your dream is false. You propose to give up your fantasy if I supply you with those necessary proofs."

"Yes, exactly!" Lanigan cried.

"But you see, I can't supply them," Sampson said. "The nature of the world is apparent, but unprovable."

Lanigan thought for a while. Then he said, "Look, Doc, I'm not as sick as the guy with the secret radio, am I?"

"No, you're not. You're more reasonable, more rational. You have doubts about the reality of the world; but luckily, you also have doubts about the validity of your delusion."

"Then give it a try," Lanigan said. "I understand your

problem; but I swear to you, I'll accept anything I can possibly bring myself to accept."

"It's not my field, really," Sampson said. "This sort of thing calls for a metaphysician. I don't think I'd be very skilled at it. . . ."

"Give it a try," Lanigan pleaded.

"All right, here goes." Sampson's forehead wrinkled as he concentrated. Then he said, "It seems to me that we inspect the world through our senses, and therefore we must in the final analysis accept the testimony of those senses."

Lanigan nodded, and the doctor went on.

"So, we know that a thing exists because our senses tell us it exists. How do we check the accuracy of our observations? By comparing them with the sensory impressions of other men. We know that our senses don't lie when other men's senses agree upon the existence of the thing in question."

Lanigan thought about this, then said, "Therefore, the real world is simply what most men think it is."

Sampson twisted his mouth and said, "I told you that metaphysics was not my forte. Still, I think it is an acceptable demonstration."

"Yes. . . . But, Doc, suppose *all* of those observers are wrong? For example, suppose there are many worlds and many realities, not just one? Suppose this is simply one arbitrary existence out of an infinity of existences? Or suppose that the nature of reality itself is capable of change, and that somehow I am able to perceive that change?"

Sampson sighed, found a little green bat fluttering inside his jacket and absentmindedly crushed it with a ruler.

"There you are," he said. "I can't disprove a single one of your suppositions. I think, Tom, that we had better run through the entire dream."

Lanigan grimaced. "I really would rather not. I have a feeling . . ."

"I know you do," Sampson said, smiling faintly. "But this will prove or disprove it once and for all, won't it?"

"I guess so," Lanigan said. He took courage—unwisely—and said, "Well, the way it begins, the way my dream starts—"

Even as he spoke the horror came over him. He felt dizzy, sick, terrified. He tried to rise from the couch. The doctor's face ballooned over him. He saw the glint of metal, heard Sampson saying, "Just try to relax . . . brief seizure . . . try to think of something pleasant."

Then either Lanigan or the world or both passed out.

Lanigan and/or the world came back to consciousness. Time may or may not have passed. Anything might or might not have happened. Lanigan sat up and looked at Sampson.

"How do you feel now?" Sampson asked.

"I'm all right," Lanigan said. "What happened?"

"You had a bad moment. Take it easy for a bit."

Lanigan leaned back and tried to calm himself. The doctor was sitting at his desk, writing notes. Lanigan counted to 20 with his eyes closed, then opened them cautiously. Sampson was still writing notes.

Lanigan looked around the room, counted the five pictures on the wall, recounted them, looked at the green carpet, frowned at it, closed his eyes again. This time he counted to 50.

"Well, care to talk about it?" Sampson asked, closing a notebook.

"No, not just now," Lanigan said. (Five paintings, green carpet.)

"Just as you please," the doctor said. "I think our time is just about up. But if you'd like to lie down in the anteroom . . ."

"No thanks, I'll go home," Lanigan said.

He stood up, walked across the green carpet to the door, looked back at the five paintings and at the doctor, who smiled at him encouragingly. Then Lanigan went through the door and into the anteroom, through the anteroom to the outer door, and through that and down the corridor to the stairs and down the stairs to the street.

He walked and looked at the trees, on which green leaves moved faintly and predictably in a faint breeze. There was traffic, which moved soberly down one side of the street and up the other. The sky was an unchanging blue and had obviously been so for quite some time.

Dream? He pinched himself; a dream pinch? He did not awaken. He shouted; an imaginary shout? He did not waken.

He was in the familiar territory of his nightmare. But it had lasted far longer than any of the others. Ergo, it was no longer a dream. (A dream is the shorter life, a life is the longer dream.) Lanigan had made the transition; or the transition had made Lanigan. The impossible had happened by the simple expedient of happening.

The pavement never once yielded beneath his feet. Over there was the First National City Bank; it had been there yesterday, it would be there tomorrow. Grotesquely devoid of possibilities, it would never become a tomb, an airplane, or the bones of a prehistoric monster. Sullenly it would remain, a building of concrete and steel, madly persisting in its fixity until men with tools came and tediously tore it down.

Lanigan walked through this petrified world, under a blue sky that oozed a coy white around the edges, promising something it could never deliver. Traffic moved to the right, people crossed at crossings, clocks were within minutes of agreement.

Somewhere beyond the town lay the countryside; but Lanigan knew that the grass did not grow under one's feet; it simply lay there, growing no doubt, but imperceptibly, unusable to the senses. And the mountains were still black and tall, but they were giants stopped in midstride, destined never to march against a golden (or purple or green) sky.

This was the frozen world. This was the slow-motion world of preordination, routine, habituation. This was the world in which the eerie quality of *boredom* was not only possible; it was inevitable. This was the world in which change, that quicksilver substance, had been reduced to a sluggish and reluctant glue.

Because of this, the magic of the phenomenal world was no longer possible. And without magic, no one could live.

Lanigan screamed. He screamed while people gathered around and looked at him (but didn't do anything or become anything), and then a policeman came, as he was supposed to (but the sun didn't change shape once), and then an ambulance rushed down the invariable street (but without trumpets, minus strumpets, on four wheels instead of a pleasing three or 25) and the ambulance men took him to a building which was exactly where they expected to find it, and there was a great deal of talk by people who stood, untransformed and untransformable, asking him questions in a room with relentlessly white walls.

They prescribed rest, quiet, sedation. This, horribly enough, was the very poison which Lanigan had been trying to throw out of his system. Naturally they gave him an overdose.

He didn't die; it wasn't that good a poison. Instead, he became completely insane. He was discharged three weeks later, a model patient and a model cure.

Now he walks around and believes that change is impossible. He has become a masochist; he revels in the insolent regularity of things. He has become a sadist; he preaches to others the divine mechanical order of things.

He has completely assimilated his insanity or the world's, in all ways except one. He is not happy. Order and happiness are contradictions which the universe has not succeeded in reconciling as yet.

DIPLOMATIC IMMUNITY

"Come right in, gentlemen," the Ambassador waved them into the very special suite the State Department had given him. "Please be seated."

Colonel Cercy accepted a chair, trying to size up the individual who had all Washington chewing its fingernails. The Ambassador hardly looked like a menace. He was of medium height and slight build, dressed in a conservative brown tweed suit that the State Department had given him. His face was intelligent, finely molded and aloof.

As human as a human, Cercy thought, studying the alien with bleak, impersonal eyes.

"How may I serve you?" the Ambassador asked, smiling.

"The President has put me in charge of your case," Cercy said. "I've studied Professor Darrig's reports"—he nodded at the scientist beside him—"but I'd like to hear the whole thing for myself."

"Of course," the alien said, lighting a cigarette. He seemed genuinely pleased to be asked; which was interesting, Cercy thought. In the week since he had landed, every important scientist in the country had been at him.

But in a pinch they call the Army, Cercy reminded himself. He settled back in his chair, both hands jammed carelessly into his pockets. His right hand was resting on the butt of a .45, the safety off.

"I have come," the alien said, "as an ambassador-at-large, representing an empire that stretches halfway across the Galaxy. I wish to extend the welcome of my people and to invite you to join our organization."

"I see," Cercy replied. "Some of the scientists got the impression that participation was compulsory."

"You will join," the Ambassador said, blowing smoke through his nostrils.

Cercy could see Darrig stiffen in his chair and bite his lip. Cercy moved the automatic to a position where he could draw it easily. "How did you find us?" he asked.

"We ambassadors-at-large are each assigned an unexplored section of space," the alien said. "We examine each star system in that region for planets, and each planet for intelligent life. Intelligent life is rare in the Galaxy, you know."

Cercy nodded, although he hadn't been aware of the fact.

"When we find such a planet, we land, as I did, and prepare the inhabitants for their part in our organization."

"How will your people know that you have found intelligent life?" Cercy asked.

"There is a sending mechanism that is part of our structure," the Ambassador answered. "It is triggered when we reach an inhabited planet. This signal is beamed continually into space, to an effective range of several thousand light-years. Followup crews are continually sweeping through the limits of the reception area of each ambassador, listening for such messages. Detecting one, a colonizing team follows it to the planet."

He tapped his cigarette delicately on the edge of an ashtray. "This method has definite advantages over sending combined colonization and exploration teams obviously. It avoids the necessity of equipping large forces for what may be decades of searching."

"Sure." Cercy's face was expressionless. "Would you tell me more about this message?"

"There isn't much more you need know. The beam is not detectable by your methods and, therefore, cannot be jammed. The message continues as long as I am alive."

Darrig drew in his breath sharply, glancing at Cercy.

"If you stopped broadcasting," Cercy said casually, "our planet would never be found."

"Not until this section of space was resurveyed," the diplomat agreed.

"Very well. As a duly appointed representative of the President of the United States, I ask you to stop transmitting. We don't choose to become part of your empire."

"I'm sorry," the Ambassador said. He shrugged his shoulders easily. Cercy wondered how many times he had played this scene on how many other planets.

"There really is nothing I can do." He stood up.

"Then you won't stop?"

"I can't. I have no control over the sending once it's activated." The diplomat turned and walked to the window. "However, I have prepared a philosophy for you. It is my duty, as your ambassador, to ease the shock of transition as much as possible. This philosophy will make it instantly apparent that—"

As the Ambassador reached the window, Cercy's gun was out of his pocket and roaring. He squeezed six rounds in almost a single explosion, aiming at the Ambassador's head and back. Then an uncontrollable shudder ran through him.

The Ambassador was no longer there!

Cercy and Darrig stared at each other. Darrig muttered something about ghosts. Then, just as suddenly, the Ambassador was back.

"You didn't think," he said, "that it would be as easy as all that, did you? We ambassadors have, necessarily, a certain diplomatic immunity." He fingered one of the bullet holes in the wall. "In case you don't understand, let me put it this way. It is not in your power to kill me. You couldn't even understand the nature of my defense."

He looked at them, and in that moment Cercy felt the Ambassador's complete alienness.

"Good day, gentlemen," he said.

Darrig and Cercy walked silently back to the control room. Neither had really expected that the Ambassador would be killed so easily, but it had still been a shock when the slugs had failed.

"I suppose you saw it all, Malley?" Cercy asked when he reached the control room.

The thin, balding psychiatrist nodded sadly. "Got it on film, too."

"I wonder what his philosophy is," Darrig mused, half to himself.

"It was illogical to expect it would work. No race would

send an ambassador with a message like that and expect him to live through it. Unless—"

"Unless what?"

"Unless he had a pretty effective defense," the psychiatrist finished unhappily.

Cercy walked across the room and looked at the video panel. The Ambassador's suite was very special. It had been hurriedly constructed two days after he had landed and delivered his message. The suite was steel-and-lead-lined, filled with video and movie cameras, recorders and a variety of other things.

It was the last word in elaborate death cells.

In the screen, Cercy could see the Ambassador sitting at a table. He was typing on a little portable the Government had given him.

"Hey, Harrison!" Cercy called. "Might as well go ahead with Plan Two."

Harrison came out of a side room where he had been examining the circuits leading to the Ambassador's suite. Methodically he checked his pressure gauges, set the controls and looked at Cercy. "Now?" he asked.

"Now." Cercy watched the screen. The Ambassador was still typing.

Suddenly, as Harrison sent home the switch, the room was engulfed in flames. Fire blasted out of concealed holes in the walls, poured from the ceiling and floor.

In a moment, the room was like the inside of a blast furnace.

Cercy let it burn for two minutes, then motioned Harrison to cut the switch. They stared at the roasted room.

They were looking, hopefully, for a charred corpse.

But the Ambassador reappeared beside his desk, looking ruefully at the charred typewriter. He was completely unsinged.

"Could you get me another typewriter?" he asked, looking directly at one of the hidden projectors. "I'm setting down a philosophy for you ungrateful wretches."

He seated himself in the wreckage of an armchair. In a moment, he was apparently asleep.

"All right, everyone grab a seat," Cercy said. "Time for a council of war."

Malley straddled a chair backward. Harrison lighted a pipe as he sat down, slowly puffing it into life.

"Now then," Cercy said. "The Government has dropped this squarely in our laps. We have to kill the Ambassador —obviously. I've been put in charge." Cercy grinned with regret. "Probably because no one higher up wants the responsibility of failure. And I've selected you three as my staff. We can have anything we want, any assistance or advice we need. All right. Any ideas?"

"How about Plan Three?" Harrison asked.

"We'll get to that," Cercy said. "But I don't believe it's going to work."

"I don't either," Darrig agreed. "We don't even know the nature of his defense."

"That's the first order of business. Malley, take all our data so far, and get someone to feed it into the Derichman Analyzer. You know the stuff we want. What properties has X, if X can do thus and thus?"

"Right," Malley said. He left, muttering something about the ascendancy of the physical sciences.

"Harrison," Cercy asked, "is Plan Three set up?"

"Sure."

"Give it a try."

While Harrison was making his last adjustments, Cercy watched Darrig. The plump little physicist was staring thoughtfully into space, muttering to himself. Cercy hoped he would come up with something. He was expecting great things of Darrig.

Knowing the impossibility of working with great numbers of people, Cercy had picked his staff with care. Quality was what he wanted.

With that in mind, he had chosen Harrison first. The stocky, sour-faced engineer had a reputation for being able to build anything, given half an idea of how it worked.

Cercy had selected Malley, the psychiatrist, because he wasn't sure that killing the Ambassador was going to be a purely physical problem.

Darrig was a mathematical physicist, but his restless, curious mind had come up with some interesting theories in other fields. He was the only one of the four who was really interested in the Ambassador as an intellectual problem.

"He's like Metal Old Man," Darrig said finally.

"What's that?"

"Haven't you ever heard the story of Metal Old Man? Well, he was a monster covered with black metal armor. He was met by Monster-Slayer, an Apache culture hero. Monster-Slayer, after many attempts, finally killed Metal Old Man."

"How did he do it?"

"Shot him in the armpit. He didn't have any armor there."

"Fine," Cercy grinned. "Ask our Ambassador to raise his arm."

"All set!" Harrison called.

"Fine. Go."

In the Ambassador's room, an invisible spray of gamma rays silently began to flood the room with deadly radiation.

But there was no Ambassador to receive them.

"That's enough," Cercy said after a while. "That would kill a herd of elephants."

But the Ambassador stayed invisible for five hours, until some of the radioactivity had abated. Then he appeared again.

"I'm still waiting for that typewriter," he said.

"Here's the Analyzer's report." Malley handed Cercy a sheaf of papers. "This is the final formulation, boiled down."

Cercy read it aloud: "The simplest defense against any and all weapons is to *become* each particular weapon."

"Great," Harrison said. "What does it mean?"

"It means," Darrig explained, "that when we attack the Ambassador with fire, he turns into fire. Shoot at him, and he turns into a bullet—until the menace is gone, and then he changes back again." He took the papers out of Cercy's hand and riffled through them.

"Hmmm. Wonder if there's any historical parallel? Don't suppose so." He raised his head. "Although this isn't conclusive, it seems logical enough. Any other defense would involve recognition of the weapon first, then an appraisal, then a countermove predicated on the potentialities of the weapon. The Ambassador's defense would be a lot faster and safer. He wouldn't have to recognize the weapon. I suppose his body simply *identifies*, in some way, with the menace at hand."

"Did the Analyzer say there was any way of breaking this defense?" Cercy asked.

"The Analyzer stated definitely that there was no way, if the premise were true," Malley answered gloomily.

"We can discard that judgment," Darrig said. "The machine is limited."

"But we still haven't got any way of stopping him," Malley pointed out. "And he's still broadcasting that beam."

Cercy thought for a moment. "Call in every expert you can find. We're going to throw the book at the Ambassador. I know," he said, looking at Darrig's dubious expression, "but we have to try."

During the next few days, every combination and permutation of death was thrown at the Ambassador. He was showered with weapons, ranging from Stone Age axes to modern high-powered rifles, peppered with hand grenades, drowned in acid, suffocated in poison gas.

He kept shrugging his shoulders philosophically and continued to work on the new typewriter they had given him.

Bacteria was piped in, first the known germ diseases, then mutated species.

The diplomat didn't even sneeze.

He was showered with electricity, radiation, wooden weapons, iron weapons, copper weapons, brass weapons, uranium weapons—anything and everything, just to cover all possibilities.

He didn't suffer a scratch, but his room looked as though a barroom brawl had been going on in it continually for 50 years.

Malley was working on an idea of his own, as was Darrig. The physicist interrupted himself long enough to remind Cercy of the Baldur myth. Baldur had been showered with every kind of weapon and remained unscathed, because everything on Earth had promised to love him. Everything except the mistletoe. When a little twig of it was shot at him, he died.

Cercy turned away impatiently, but had an order of mistletoe sent up, just in case.

It was, at least, no less effective than the explosive shells or the bow and arrow. It did nothing except lend an oddly festive air to the battered room.

After a week of this, they moved the unprotesting Ambassador into a newer, bigger, stronger death cell. They were unable to venture into his old one because of the radioactivity and microorganisms.

The Ambassador went back to work at his typewriter. All his previous attempts had been burned, torn or eaten away.

"Let's go talk to him," Darrig suggested after another day had passed. Cercy agreed. For the moment, they were out of ideas.

"Come right in, gentlemen," the Ambassador said so cheerfully that Cercy felt sick. "I'm sorry I can't offer you anything. Through an oversight, I haven't been given any food or water for about ten days. Not that it matters, of course."

"Glad to hear it," Cercy said. The Ambassador hardly looked as if he had been facing all the violence Earth had to offer. On the contrary, Cercy and his men looked as though *they* had been under bombardment.

"You've got quite a defense there," Malley said conversationally.

"Glad you like it."

"Would you mind telling us how it works?" Darrig asked innocently.

"Don't you know?"

"We think so. You become what is attacking you. Is that right?"

"Certainly," the Ambassador said. "You see, I have no secrets from you."

"Is there anything we can give you," Cercy asked, "to get you to turn off that signal?"

"A bribe?"

"Sure," Cercy said. "Anything you—?"

"Nothing," the Ambassador replied.

"Look, be reasonable," Harrison said. "You don't want

to cause a war, do you? Earth is united now. We're arming—"

"With what?"

"Atom bombs," Malley answered him. "Hydrogen bombs. We're—"

"Drop one on me," the Ambassador said. "It wouldn't kill me. What makes you think it will have any effect on my people?"

The four men were silent. Somehow, they hadn't thought of that.

"A people's ability to make war," the Ambassador stated, "is a measure of the status of their civilization. Stage one is the use of simple physical extensions. Stage two is control at the molecular level. You are on the threshold of stage three, although still far from mastery of atomic and subatomic forces." He smiled ingratiatingly. "My people are reaching the limits of stage five."

"What would that be?" Darrig asked.

"You'll find out," the Ambassador said. "But perhaps you've wondered if my powers are typical? I don't mind telling you that they're not. In order for me to do my job and nothing more, I have certain built-in restrictions, making me capable only of passive action."

"Why?" Darrig asked.

"For obvious reasons. If I were to take positive action in a moment of anger, I might destroy your entire planet."

"Do you expect us to believe that?" Cercy asked.

"Why not? Is it so hard to understand? Can't you believe that there are forces you know nothing about? And there is another reason for my passiveness. Certainly by this time you've deduced it?"

"To break our spirit, I suppose," Cercy said.

"Exactly. My telling you won't make any difference, either. The pattern is always the same. An Ambassador lands and delivers his message to a high-spirited, wild young race like yours. There is frenzied resistance against him, spasmodic attempts to kill him. After all these fail, the people are usually quite crestfallen. When the colonization team arrives, their indoctrination goes along just that much faster." He paused, then said, "Most planets are more interested in the philosophy I have to offer. I assure you, it will make the transition far easier."

He held out a sheaf of typewritten pages. "Won't you at least look through it?"

Darrig accepted the papers and put them in his pocket. "When I get time."

"I suggest you give it a try," the Ambassador said. "You must be near the crisis point now. Why not give it up?"

"Not yet," Cercy replied tonelessly.

"Don't forget to read the philosophy," the Ambassador urged them.

The men hurried from the room.

"Now look," Malley said once they were back in the control room, "there are a few things we haven't tried. How about utilizing psychology?"

"Anything you like," Cercy agreed, "including black magic. What did you have in mind?"

"The way I see it," Malley answered, "the Ambassador is geared to respond instantaneously to any threat. He must have an all-or-nothing defensive reflex. I suggest first we try something that won't trigger that reflex."

"Like what?" Cercy asked.

"Hypnotism. Perhaps we can find out something."

"Sure," Cercy said. "Try it. Try anything."

Cercy, Malley and Darrig gathered around the video screen as an infinitesimal amount of a light hypnotic gas was admitted into the Ambassador's room. At the same time, a bolt of electricity lashed into the chair where the Ambassador was sitting.

"That was to distract him," Malley explained. The Ambassador vanished before the electricity struck him, and then appeared again, curled up in his armchair.

"That's enough," Malley whispered, and shut the valve. They watched. After a while, the Ambassador put down his book and stared into the distance.

"How strange," he said. "Alfern dead. Good friend . . . just a freak accident. He ran into it out there. Didn't have a chance. But it doesn't happen often."

"He's thinking out loud," Malley whispered, although there was no possibility of the Ambassador's hearing them. "Vocalizing his thoughts. His friend must have been on his mind for some time."

"Of course," the Ambassador went on, "Alfern had to die sometime. No immortality—yet. But that way—no defense. Out there in space they just pop up. Always there, underneath, just waiting for a chance to boil out."

"His body isn't reacting to the hypnotic as a menace yet," Cercy whispered.

"Well," the Ambassador told himself, "the regularizing principle has been doing pretty well, keeping it all down, smoothing out the inconsistencies—"

Suddenly he leaped to his feet, his face pale for a moment, as he obviously tried to remember what he had said. Then he laughed.

"Clever. That's the first time that particular trick has been played on me, and the last time. But, gentlemen, it didn't do you any good. I don't know, myself, how to go about killing me." He laughed at the blank walls.

"Besides," he continued, "the colonizing team must have the direction now. They'll find you with or without me."

He sat down again, smiling.

"That does it!" Darrig cried. "He's not invulnerable. Something killed his friend Alfern."

"Something out in space," Cercy reminded him. "I wonder what it was."

"Let me see," Darrig reflected aloud. "The regularizing principle. That must be a natural law we knew nothing about. And underneath—what would be underneath?"

"He said the colonization team would find us anyhow," Malley reminded them.

"First things first," Cercy said. "He might have been bluffing us . . . no, I don't suppose so. We still have to get the Ambassador out of the way."

"I think I know what is underneath!" Darrig exclaimed. "This is wonderful. A new cosmology, perhaps."

"What is it?" Cercy asked. "Anything we can use?"

"I think so. But let me work it out. I think I'll go back to my hotel. I have some books there I want to check, and I don't want to be disturbed for a few hours."

"All right," Cercy agreed. "But what—?"

"No, no, I could be wrong," Darrig said. "Let me work it out."

He hurried from the room.

"What do you think he's driving at?" Malley asked.

"Beats me," Cercy shrugged. "Come on, let's try some more of that psychological stuff."

First they filled the Ambassador's room with several feet of water. Not enough to drown him, just enough to make him good and uncomfortable.

To this, they added the lights. For eight hours, lights flashed in the Ambassador's room—bright lights to pry under his eyelids; dull, clashing ones to disturb him.

Sound came next—screeches and screams and shrill, grating noises; the sound of a man's fingernails being dragged across slate, amplified a thousand times: and strange, sucking noises, and shouts and whispers.

Then the smells. Then, everything else they could think of that could drive a man insane.

The Ambassador slept peacefully through it all.

"Now look," Cercy said, the following day, "let's start using our damned heads." His voice was hoarse and rough. Although the psychological torture hadn't bothered the Ambassador, it seemed to have backfired on Cercy and his men.

"Where in hell is Darrig?"

"Still working on that idea of his," Malley said, rubbing his stubbled chin. "Says he's just about got it."

"We'll work on the assumption that he can't produce," Cercy said. "Start thinking. For example, if the Ambassador can turn into anything, what is there he can't turn into?"

"Good question," Harrison grunted.

"It's the payoff question," Cercy said. "No use throwing a spear at a man who can turn into one."

"How about this?" Malley asked. "Taking it for granted he can turn into anything, how about putting him in a situation where he'll be attacked even *after* he alters?"

"I'm listening," Cercy said.

"Say he's in danger. He turns into the thing threatening him. What if *that thing* were itself being threatened? And, in turn, was in the act of threatening something else? What would he do then?"

"How are you going to put that into action?" Cercy asked.

"Like this." Malley picked up the telephone. "Hello? Give me the Washington Zoo. This is urgent."

The Ambassador turned as the door opened. An unwilling, angry, hungry tiger was propelled in. The door slammed shut.

The tiger looked at the Ambassador. The Ambassador looked at the tiger.

"Most ingenious," the Ambassador said.

At the sound of his voice, the tiger came unglued. He sprang like a steel spring uncoiled, landing on the floor where the Ambassador had been.

The door opened again. Another tiger was pushed in. He snarled angrily and leaped at the first. They smashed together in midair.

The Ambassador appeared a few feet off, watching. He moved back when a lion entered the door, head up and alert. The lion sprang at him, almost going over on his head when he struck nothing. Not finding any human, the lion leaped on one of the tigers.

The Ambassador reappeared in his chair, where he sat smoking and watching the beasts kill each other.

In ten minutes the room looked like an abattoir.

But by then the Ambassador had tired of the spectacle and was reclining on his bed, reading.

"I give up," Malley said. "That was my last bright idea."

Cercy stared at the floor, not answering. Harrison was seated in the corner, getting quietly drunk.

The telephone rang.

"Yeah?" Cercy said.

"I've got it!" Darrig's voice shouted over the line. "I really think this is it. Look, I'm taking a cab right down. Tell Harrison to find some helpers."

"What is it?" Cercy asked.

"The chaos underneath!" Darrig replied, and hung up.

They paced the floor, waiting for him to show up. Half an hour passed, then an hour. Finally, three hours after he had called, Darrig strolled in.

"Hello," he said casually.

"Hello, hell!" Cercy growled. "What kept you?"

"On the way over," Darrig said, "I read the Ambassador's philosophy. It's quite a work."

"Is that what took you so long?"

"Yes. I had the driver take me around the park a few times while I was reading it."

"Skip it. How about—"

"I can't skip it," Darrig said in a strange, tight voice. "I'm afraid we were wrong. About the aliens, I mean. It's perfectly right and proper that they should rule us. As a matter of fact, I wish they'd hurry up and get here."

But Darrig didn't look certain. His voice shook and perspiration poured from his face. He twisted his hands together, as though in agony.

"It's hard to explain," he said. "Everything became clear as soon as I started reading it. I saw how stupid we were, trying to be independent in this interdependent Universe. I saw—oh, look, Cercy. Let's stop all this foolishness and accept the Ambassador as our friend."

"Calm down!" Cercy shouted at the perfectly calm physicist. "You don't know what you're saying."

"It's strange," Darrig said. "I know how I felt—I just don't feel that way any more. I think. Anyhow, I know *your* trouble. You haven't read the philosophy. You'll see what I mean once you've read it." He handed Cercy the pile of papers. Cercy promptly ignited them with his cigarette lighter.

"It doesn't matter," Darrig said. "I've got it memorized. Just listen. Axiom one. All peoples—"

Cercy hit him, a short, clean blow, and Darrig slumped to the floor.

"Those words must be semantically keyed," Malley said. "They're designed to set off certain reactions in us, I suppose. All the Ambassador does is alter the philosophy to suit the peoples he's dealing with."

"Look, Malley," Cercy said. "This is your job now. Darrig knows, or thought he knew, the answer. You have to get that out of him."

"That won't be easy," Malley said. "He'd feel that he was betraying everything he believes in if he were to tell us."

"I don't care how you get it," Cercy said. "Just get it."

"Even if it kills him?" Malley asked.

"Even if it kills you."

"Help me get him to my lab," Malley said.

That night Cercy and Harrison kept watch on the Ambassador from the control room. Cercy found his thoughts were racing in circles.

What had killed Alfern in space? Could it be duplicated on Earth? What was the regularizing principle? What was the "chaos underneath"?

What in hell am I doing here? he asked himself. But he couldn't start that sort of thing.

"What do you figure the Ambassador is?" he asked Harrison. "Is he a man?"

"Looks like one," Harrison said drowsily.

"But he doesn't act like one. I wonder if this is his true shape?"

Harrison shook his head, and lighted his pipe.

"What is there of him?" Cercy asked. "He looks like a man, but he can change into anything else. You can't attack him; he adapts. He's like water, taking the shape of any vessel he's poured into."

"You can boil water," Harrison yawned.

"Sure. Water hasn't any shape, has it? Or has it? What's basic?"

With an effort, Harrison tried to focus on Cercy's words. "Molecular pattern? The matrix?"

"Matrix," Cercy repeated, yawning himself. "Pattern. Must be something like that. A pattern is abstract, isn't it?"

"Sure. A pattern can be impressed on anything. What did I say?"

"Let's see," Cercy said. "Pattern. Matrix. Everything about the Ambassador is capable of change. There must be some unifying force that retains his personality. Something that *doesn't* change, no matter what contortions he goes through."

"Like a piece of string," Harrison murmured with his eyes closed.

"Sure. Tie it in knots, weave a rope out of it, wind it around your finger; it's still string."

"Yeah."

"But how do you attack a pattern?" Cercy asked. And why couldn't he get some sleep? To hell with the Ambassador and his hordes of colonists, he was going to close his eyes for a moment. . . .

"Wake up, Colonel!"

Cercy pried his eyes open and looked up at Malley. Beside him, Harrison was snoring deeply. "Did you get anything?"

"Not a thing," Malley confessed. "The philosophy must've had quite an effect on him. But it didn't work all the way. Darrig knew that he *had wanted* to kill the Ambassador, and for good and sufficient reasons. Although he felt differently now, he still had the feeling that he was betraying us. On the one hand, he couldn't hurt the Ambassador; on the other, he wouldn't hurt us."

"Won't he tell anything?"

"I'm afraid it's not that simple," Malley said. "You know, if you have an insurmountable obstacle that *must* be surmounted . . . and also, I think the philosophy had an injurious effect on his mind."

"What are you trying to say?" Cercy got to his feet.

"I'm sorry," Malley apologized, "there wasn't a damned thing I could do. Darrig fought the whole thing out in his mind, and when he couldn't fight any longer, he—retreated. I'm afraid he's hopelessly insane."

"Let's see him."

They walked down the corridor to Malley's laboratory. Darrig was relaxed on a couch, his eyes glazed and staring.

"Is there any way of curing him?" Cercy asked.

"Shock therapy, maybe." Malley was dubious. "It'll take a long time. And he'll probably block out everything that had to do with producing this."

Cercy turned away, feeling sick. Even if Darrig could be cured, it would be too late. The aliens must have picked up the Ambassador's message by now and were undoubtedly heading for Earth.

"What's this?" Cercy asked, picking up a piece of paper that lay by Darrig's hand.

"Oh, he was doodling," Malley said. "Is there anything written on it?"

Cercy read aloud: " 'Upon further consideration, I can see that Chaos and the Gorgon Medusa are closely related.' "

"What does that mean?" Malley asked.

"I don't know," Cercy puzzled. "He was always interested in folklore."

"Sounds schizophrenic," the psychiatrist said.

Cercy read it again. " 'Upon further consideration, I can see that Chaos and the Gorgon Medusa are closely related.' " He stared at it. "Isn't it possible," he asked Malley, "that he was trying to give us a clue? Trying to trick himself into giving and not giving at the same time?"

"It's possible," Malley agreed. "An unsuccessful compromise—but what could it mean?"

"Chaos." Cercy remembered Darrig's mentioning that word in his telephone call. "That was the original state of the Universe in Greek myth, wasn't it? The formlessness out of which everything came?"

"Something like that," Malley said. "And Medusa was one of those three sisters with the horrible faces."

Cercy stood for a moment, staring at the paper. Chaos . . . Medusa . . . and the organizing principle! Of course!

"I think—" He turned and ran from the room. Malley looked at him; then loaded a hypodermic and followed.

In the control room, Cercy shouted Harrison into consciousness.

"Listen," he said, "I want you to build something, quick. Do you hear me?"

"Sure." Harrison blinked and sat up. "What's the rush?"

"I know what Darrig wanted to tell us," Cercy said. "Come on, I'll tell you what I want. And Malley, put down that hypodermic. I haven't cracked. I want you to get me a book on Greek mythology. And hurry it up."

Finding a Greek mythology isn't an easy task at two o'clock in the morning. With the aid of F.B.I. men, Malley routed a book dealer out of bed. He got his book and hurried back.

Cercy was red-eyed and excited, and Harrison and his helpers were working away at three crazy-looking rigs. Cercy snatched the book from Malley, looked up one item, and put it down.

"Great work," he said. "We're all set now. Finished, Harrison?"

"Just about." Harrison and ten helpers were screwing in the last parts. "Will you tell me what this is?"

"Me, too," Malley put in.

"I don't mean to be secretive," Cercy said. "I'm just in a hurry. I'll explain as we go along." He stood up. "OK, let's wake up the Ambassador."

They watched the screen as a bolt of electricity leaped from the ceiling to the Ambassador's bed. Immediately, the Ambassador vanished.

"Now he's a part of that stream of electrons, right?" Cercy asked.

"That's what he told us," Malley said.

"But still keeping his pattern within the stream," Cercy continued. "He has to, in order to get back into his own shape. Now we start the first disrupter."

Harrison hooked the machine into circuit and sent his helpers away.

"Here's a running graph of the electron stream," Cercy said. "See the difference?" On the graph there was an irregular series of peaks and valleys, constantly shifting and leveling. "Do you remember when you hypnotized the Ambassador? He talked about his friend who'd been killed in space."

"That's right," Malley nodded. "His friend had been killed by something that had just popped up."

"He said something else," Cercy went on. "He told us that the basic organizing force of the Universe usually stopped things like that. What does that mean to you?"

"The organizing force," Malley repeated slowly. "Didn't Darrig say that that was a new natural law?"

"He did. But think of the implications, as Darrig did. If an organizing principle is engaged in some work, there must be something that opposes it. That which opposes organization is—"

"Chaos!"

"That's what Darrig thought and what we should have seen. The chaos is underlying, and out of it there arose an organizing principle. This principle, if I've got it right, sought to suppress the fundamental chaos, to make all things regular.

"But the chaos still boils out in spots, as Alfern found out. Perhaps the organizational pattern is weaker in space. Anyhow, those spots are dangerous, until the organizing principle gets to work on them."

He turned to the panel. "Okay, Harrison. Throw in the second disrupter." The peaks and valleys altered on the graph. They started to mount in crazy, meaningless configurations.

"Take Darrig's message in the light of that. Chaos, we know, is underlying. Everything was formed out of it. The Gorgon Medusa was something that *couldn't be looked upon*. She turned men into stone, you recall, destroyed them. So, Darrig found a relationship between chaos and that which can't be looked upon. All with regard to the Ambassador, of course."

"The Ambassador can't look upon chaos!" Malley cried.

"That's it. The Ambassador is capable of an infinite number of alterations and permutations. *But something*—the matrix—can't change, because then there would be nothing left. To destroy something as abstract as a pattern, we need a state in which no pattern is possible. A state of chaos."

The third disrupter was thrown into circuit. The graph looked as if a drunken caterpillar had been sketching on it.

"Those disrupters are Harrison's idea," Cercy said. "I told him I wanted an electrical current with absolutely no coherent pattern. The disrupters are an extension of radio jamming. The first alters the electrical pattern. That's its purpose: to produce a state of patternlessness. The second tries to destroy the pattern left by the first; the third tries to destroy the pattern made by the first two. They're fed back then, and any remaining pattern is systematically destroyed in circuit—I hope."

"This is supposed to produce a state of chaos?" Malley asked, looking into the screen.

For a while there was only the whining of the machines and the crazy doodling of the graph. Then, in the middle of the Ambassador's room, a spot appeared. It wavered, shrank, expanded.

What happened was indescribable. All they knew was that everything within the spot had disappeared.

"Switch it off!" Cercy shouted. Harrison cut the switch.

The spot continued to grow.

"How is it we're able to look at it?" Malley asked, staring at the screen.

"The shield of Perseus, remember?" Cercy said. "Using it as a mirror, he could look at Medusa."

"It's still growing!" Malley shouted.

"There was a calculated risk in all this," Cercy said. "There's always the possibility that the chaos may go on, unchecked. If that happens, it won't matter much what—"

The spot stopped growing. Its edges wavered and rippled, and then it started to shrink.

"The organizing principle," Cercy said, and collapsed into a chair.

"Any sign of the Ambassador?" he asked in a few minutes.

The spot was still wavering. Then it was gone. Instantly there was an explosion. The steel walls buckled inward, but held. The screen went dead.

"The spot removed all the air from the room," Cercy explained, "as well as the furniture and the Ambassador."

"He couldn't take it," Malley said. "No pattern can cohere, in a state of patternlessness. He's gone to join Alfern."

Malley started to giggle. Cercy felt like joining him, but pulled himself together.

"Take it easy," he said. "We're not through yet."

"Sure we are! The Ambassador—"

"Is out of the way. But there's still an alien fleet homing in on this region of space. A fleet so strong we couldn't scratch it with an H-bomb. They'll be looking for us."

He stood up.

"Go home and get some sleep. Something tells me that tomorrow we're going to have to start figuring out some way of camouflaging a planet."

GHOST V

"He's reading our sign now," Gregor said, his long bony face pressed against the peephole in the office door.

"Let me see," Arnold said.

Gregor pushed him back. "He's going to knock—no, he's changed his mind. He's leaving."

Arnold returned to his desk and laid out another game of solitaire. Gregor kept watch at the peephole.

They had constructed the peephole out of sheer boredom three months after forming their partnership and renting the office. During that time, the AAA Ace Planet Decontamination Service had had no business—in spite of being first in the telephone book. Planetary decontamination was an old, established line, completely monopolized by two large outfits. It was discouraging for a small new firm run by two young men with big ideas and a lot of unpaid-for equipment.

"He's coming back," Gregor called. "*Quick*—look busy and important!"

Arnold swept his cards into a drawer and just finished buttoning his lab gown when the knock came.

Their visitor was a short, bald, tired-looking man. He stared at them dubiously.

"You decontaminate planets?"

"That is correct, sir," Gregor said, pushing away a pile of papers and shaking the man's moist hand. "I am Richard Gregor. This is my partner, Doctor Frank Arnold."

Arnold, impressively garbed in a white lab gown and black horn-rimmed glasses, nodded absently and resumed his examination of a row of ancient, crusted test tubes.

"Kindly be seated, Mister—"

"Ferngraum."

"Mr. Ferngraum. I think we can handle just about anything you require," Gregor said heartily. "Flora or fauna control, cleansing atmosphere, purifying water supply, sterilizing soil, stability testing, volcano and earthquake control—anything you need to make a planet fit for human habitation."

Ferngraum still looked dubious. "I'm going to level with you. I've got a problem planet on my hands."

Gregor nodded confidently. "Problems are our business."

"I'm a freelance real-estate broker," Ferngraum said. "You know how it works—buy a planet, sell a planet, everyone makes a living. Usually I stick with the scrub worlds and let my buyers do their decontaminating. But a few months ago I had a chance to buy a real quality planet— took it right out from under the noses of the big operators."

Ferngraum mopped his forehead unhappily.

"It's a beautiful place," he continued with no enthusiasm whatsoever. "Average temperature of 71 degrees. Mountainous, but fertile. Waterfalls, rainbows, all that sort of thing. And no fauna at all."

"Sounds perfect," Gregor said. "Microorganisms?"

"Nothing dangerous."

"Then what's wrong with the place?"

Ferngraum looked embarrassed. "Maybe you heard about it. The government catalogue number is RJC-5. But everyone else calls it 'Ghost V.' "

Gregor raised an eyebrow. "Ghost" was an odd nickname for a planet, but he had heard odder. After all, you had to call them something. There were thousands of planet-bearing suns within spaceship range, many of them inhabitable or potentially inhabitable. And there were plenty of people from the civilized worlds who wanted to colonize them. Religious sects, political minorities, philosophic groups—or just plain pioneers, out to make a fresh start.

"I don't believe I've heard of it," Gregor said.

Ferngraum squirmed uncomfortably in his chair. "I should have listened to my wife. But no—I was gonna be a big operator. Paid ten times my usual price for Ghost V and now I'm stuck with it."

"But what's *wrong* with it?" Gregor asked.

"It seems to be haunted," Ferngraum said in despair.

Ferngraum had radar-checked his planet, then leased it to

a combine of farmers from Dijon VI. The eight-man advance guard landed and, within a day, began to broadcast garbled reports about demons, ghouls, vampires, dinosaurs and other inimical fauna.

When a relief ship came for them, all were dead. An autopsy report stated that the gashes, cuts and marks on their bodies could indeed have been made by almost anything, even demons, ghouls, vampires or dinosaurs, if such existed.

Ferngraum was fined for improper decontamination. The farmers dropped their lease. But he managed to lease it to a group of sun worshipers from Opal II.

The sun worshipers were cautious. They sent their equipment, but only three men accompanied it, to scout out trouble. The men set up camp, unpacked and declared the place a paradise. They radioed the home group to come at once—then, suddenly, there was a wild scream and radio silence.

A patrol ship went to Ghost V, buried the three mangled bodies and departed in five minutes flat.

"And that did it," Ferngraum said. "Now no one will touch it at any price. Space crews refuse to land on it. And I still don't know what happened."

He sighed deeply and looked at Gregor. "It's your baby, if you want it."

Gregor and Arnold excused themselves and went into the anteroom.

Arnold whooped at once, "We've got a job!"

"Yeah," Gregor said, "but what a job."

"We wanted the tough ones," Arnold pointed out. "If we lick this, we're established—to say nothing of the profit we'll make on a percentage basis."

"You seem to forget," Gregor said, "I'm the one who has to actually land on the planet. All you do is sit here and interpret my data."

"That's the way we set it up," Arnold reminded him. "I'm the research department—you're the troubleshooter. Remember?"

Gregor remembered. Ever since childhood, he had been sticking his neck out while Arnold stayed home and told him why he was sticking his neck out.

"I don't like it," he said.

"You don't believe in ghosts, do you?"

"No, of course not."

"Well, we can handle anything else. Faint heart ne'er won fair profit."

Gregor shrugged his shoulders. They went back to Ferngraum.

In half an hour, they had worked out their terms—a large percentage of future development profits if they succeeded, a forfeiture clause if they failed.

Gregor walked to the door with Ferngraum. "By the way, sir," he asked, "how did you happen to come to us?"

"No one else would handle it," Ferngraum said, looking extremely pleased with himself. "Good luck."

Three days later, Gregor was aboard a rickety space freighter, bound for Ghost V. He spent his time studying reports on the two colonization attempts and reading survey after survey on supernatural phenomena.

They didn't help at all. No trace of animal life had been found on Ghost V. And no proof of the existence of supernatural creatures had been discovered anywhere in the Galaxy.

Gregor pondered this, then checked his weapons as the freighter spiraled into the region of Ghost V. He was carrying an arsenal large enough to start a small war and win it.

If he could find something to shoot at . . .

The captain of the freighter brought his ship to within several thousand feet of the smiling green surface of the planet, but no closer. Gregor parachuted his equipment to the site of the last two camps, shook hands with the captain and 'chuted himself down.

He landed safely and looked up. The freighter was streaking into space as though the furies were after it.

He was alone on Ghost V.

After checking his equipment for breakage, he radioed Arnold that he had landed safely. Then, with drawn blaster, he inspected the sun worshipers' camp.

They had set themselves up at the base of a mountain, beside a small, crystal-clear lake. The prefabs were in perfect condition.

No storms had ever damaged them, because Ghost V

was blessed with a beautifully even climate. But they looked pathetically lonely.

Gregor made a careful check of one. Clothes were still neatly packed in cabinets, pictures were hung on the wall and there was even a curtain on one window. In a corner of the room, a case of toys had been opened for the arrival of the main party's children.

A water pistol, a top and a bag of marbles had spilled onto the floor.

Evening was coming, so Gregor dragged his equipment into the prefab and made his preparations. He rigged an alarm system and adjusted it so finely that even a roach would set if off. He put up a radar alarm to scan the immediate area. He unpacked his arsenal, laying the heavy rifles within easy reach, but keeping a hand-blaster in his belt. Then, satisfied, he ate a leisurely supper.

Outside, the evening drifted into night. The warm and dreamy land grew dark. A gentle breeze ruffled the surface of the lake and rustled silkily in the tall grass.

It was all very peaceful.

The settlers must have been hysterical types, he decided. They had probably panicked and killed each other.

After checking his alarm system one last time, Gregor threw his clothes onto a chair, turned off the lights and climbed into bed. The room was illuminated by starlight, stronger than moonlight on Earth. His blaster was under his pillow. All was well with the world.

He had just begun to doze off when he became aware that he was not alone in the room.

That was impossible. His alarm system hadn't gone off. The radar was still humming peacefully.

Yet every nerve in his body was shrieking alarm. He eased the blaster out and looked around.

A man was standing in a corner of the room.

There was no time to consider how he had come. Gregor aimed the blaster and said, "Okay, raise your hands," in a quiet, resolute voice.

The figure didn't move.

Gregor's finger tightened on the trigger, then suddenly relaxed. He recognized the man. It was his own clothing, heaped on a chair, distorted by the starlight and his own imagination.

He grinned and lowered the blaster. The pile of clothing began to stir faintly. Gregor felt a faint breeze from the window and continued to grin.

Then the pile of clothing stood up, stretched itself and began to walk toward him purposefully.

Frozen to his bed, he watched the disembodied clothing, assembled roughly in manlike form, advance on him.

When it was halfway across the room and its empty sleeves were reaching for him, he began to blast.

And kept on blasting, for the rags and remnants slithered toward him as if filled with a life of their own. Flaming bits of cloth crowded toward his face and a belt tried to coil around his legs. He had to burn everything to ashes before the attack stopped.

When it was over, Gregor turned on every light he could find. He brewed a pot of coffee and poured in most of a bottle of brandy. Somehow, he resisted an urge to kick his useless alarm system to pieces. Instead, he radioed his partner.

"That's very interesting," Arnold said, after Gregor had brought him up to date. "Animation! Very interesting indeed."

"I hoped it would amuse you," Gregor answered bitterly. After several shots of brandy, he was beginning to feel abandoned and abused.

"Did anything else happen?"

"Not yet."

"Well, take care. I've got a theory. Have to do some research on it. By the way, some crazy bookie is laying five to one against you."

"Really?"

"Yeah. I took a piece of it."

"Did you bet for me or against me?" Gregor asked, worried.

"For you, of course," Arnold said indignantly. "We're partners, aren't we?"

They signed off and Gregor brewed another pot of coffee. He was not planning on any more sleep that night. It was comforting to know that Arnold had bet on him. But, then, Arnold was a notoriously bad gambler.

By daylight, Gregor was able to get a few hours of fitful

sleep. In the early afternoon he awoke, found some clothes and began to explore the sun worshipers' camp.

Toward evening, he found something. On the wall of a prefab, the word *"Tgasklit"* had been hastily scratched. *Tgasklit.* It meant nothing to him, but he relayed it to Arnold at once.

He then searched his prefab carefully, set up more lights, tested the alarm system and recharged his blaster.

Everything seemed in order. With regret, he watched the sun go down, hoping he would live to see it rise again. Then he settled himself in a comfortable chair and tried to do some constructive thinking.

There was no animal life here—nor were there any walking plants, intelligent rocks or giant brains dwelling in the planet's core. Ghost V hadn't even a moon for someone to hide on.

And he couldn't believe in ghosts or demons. He knew that supernatural happenings tended to break down, under detailed examination, into eminently natural events. The ones that didn't break down—stopped. Ghosts just wouldn't stand still and let a non-believer examine them. The phantom of the castle was invariably on vacation when a scientist showed up with cameras and tape recorders.

That left another possibility. Suppose someone wanted this planet, but wasn't prepared to pay Ferngraum's price? Couldn't this someone hide here, frighten the settlers, kill them if necessary in order to drive down the price?

That seemed logical. You could even explain the behavior of his clothes that way. Static electricity, correctly used, could—

Something was standing in front of him. His alarm system, as before, hadn't gone off.

Gregor looked up slowly. The thing in front of him was about ten feet tall and roughly human in shape, except for its crocodile head. It was colored a bright crimson and had purple stripes running lengthwise on its body. In one claw, it was carrying a large brown can.

"Hello," it said.

"Hello," Gregor gulped. His blaster was on a table only two feet away. He wondered, would the thing attack if he reached for it?

"What's your name?" Gregor asked, with the calmness of deep shock.

"I'm the Purple-striped Grabber," the thing said. "I grab things."

"How interesting." Gregor's hand began to creep toward the blaster.

"I grab things named Richard Gregor," the Grabber told him in its bright, ingenuous voice. "And I usually eat them in chocolate sauce." It held up the brown can and Gregor saw that it was labeled "Smig's Chocolate—An Ideal Sauce to Use with Gregors, Arnolds and Flynns."

Gregor's fingers touched the butt of the blaster. He asked, "Were you planning to eat me?"

"Oh, yes," the Grabber said.

Gregor had the gun now. He flipped off the safety catch and fired. The radiant blast cascaded off the Grabber's chest and singed the floor, the walls and Gregor's eyebrows.

"That won't hurt me," the Grabber explained. "I'm too tall."

The blaster dropped from Gregor's fingers. The Grabber leaned forward.

"I'm not going to eat you now," the Grabber said.

"No?" Gregor managed to enunciate.

"No. I can only eat you tomorrow, on May first. Those are the rules. I just came to ask a favor."

"What is it?"

The Grabber smiled winningly. "Would you be a good sport and eat a few apples? They flavor the flesh so wonderfully."

And, with that, the striped monster vanished.

With shaking hands, Gregor worked the radio and told Arnold everything that had happened.

"Hmm," Arnold said. "Purple-striped Grabber, eh? I think that clinches it. Everything fits."

"What fits? What is it?"

"First, do as I say. I want to make sure."

Obeying Arnold's instructions, Gregor unpacked his chemical equipment and laid out a number of test tubes, retorts and chemicals. He stirred, mixed, added and subtracted as directed and finally put the mixture on the stove to heat.

"Now," Gregor said, coming back to the radio, "Tell me what's going on."

"Certainly. I looked up the word '*Tgasklit.*' It's Opalian. It means 'many-toothed ghost.' The sun worshipers were from Opal. What does that suggest to you?"

"They were killed by a home-town ghost," Gregor replied nastily. "It must have stowed away on their ship. Maybe there was a curse and—"

"Calm down," Arnold said. "There aren't any ghosts in this. Is the solution boiling yet?"

"No."

"Tell me when it does. Now let's take your animated clothing. Does it remind you of anything?"

Gregor thought. "Well," he said, "when I was a kid— no, that's ridiculous."

"Out with it," Arnold insisted.

"When I was a kid, I never left clothing on a chair. In the dark, it always looked like a man or a dragon or something. I guess everyone's had that experience. But it doesn't explain—"

"Sure it does! Remember the Purple-striped Grabber now?"

"No. Why should I?"

"Because you invented him! Remember? We must have been eight or nine, you and me and Jimmy Flynn. We invented the most horrible monster you could think of—he was our own personal monster and he only wanted to eat you or me or Jimmy—flavored with chocolate sauce. But only on the first of every month, when the report cards were due. You had to use the magic word to get rid of him."

Then Gregor remembered and wondered how he could ever have forgotten. How many nights had he stayed up in fearful expectation of the Grabber? It had made bad report cards seem very unimportant.

"Is the solution boiling?" Arnold asked.

"Yes," said Gregor, glancing obediently at the stove.

"What color is it?"

"A sort of greenish blue. No, it's more blue than—"

"Right. You can pour it out. I want to run a few more tests, but I think we've got it licked."

"Got *what* licked? Would you do a little explaining?"

"It's obvious. The planet has no animal life. There are no ghosts or at least none solid enough to kill off a party of armed men. Hallucination was the answer, so I looked for something that would produce it. I found plenty. Aside from all the drugs on Earth, there are about a dozen hallucination-forming gases in the *Catalogue of Alien Trace Elements*. There are depressants, stimulants, stuff that'll make you feel like a genius or an earthworm or an eagle. This particular one corresponds to Longstead 42 in the catalogue. It's a heavy, transparent, odorless gas, not harmful physically. It's an imagination stimulant."

"You mean I was just having hallucinations? I tell you—"

"Not quite that simple," Arnold cut in. "Longstead 42 works directly on the subconscious. It releases your strongest subconscious fears, the childhood terrors you've been suppressing. It animates them. And that's what you've been seeing."

"Then there's actually nothing here?" Gregor asked.

"Nothing physical. But the hallucinations are real enough to whoever is having them."

Gregor reached over for another bottle of brandy. This called for a celebration.

"It won't be hard to decontaminate Ghost V," Arnold went on confidently. "We can cancel the Longstead 42 with no difficulty. And then—we'll be rich, partner!"

Gregor suggested a toast, then thought of something disturbing. "If they're just hallucinations, what happened to the settlers?"

Arnold was silent for a moment. "Well," he said finally, "Longstead may have a tendency to stimulate the mortido—the death instinct. The settlers must have gone crazy. Killed each other."

"And no survivors?"

"Sure, why not? The last ones alive committed suicide or died of wounds. Don't worry about it. I'm chartering a ship immediately and coming out to run those tests. Relax. I'll pick you up in a day or two."

Gregor signed off. He allowed himself the rest of the bottle of brandy that night. It seemed only fair. The mystery of Ghost V was solved and they were going to be rich. Soon *he* would be able to hire a man to land on strange planets for him while *he* sat home and gave instructions over a radio.

He awoke late the next day with a hangover. Arnold's ship hadn't arrived yet, so he packed his equipment and waited. By evening, there was still no ship. He sat in the doorway of the prefab and watched a gaudy sunset, then went inside and made dinner.

The problem of the settlers still bothered him, but he determined not to worry about it. Undoubtedly there was a logical answer.

After dinner, he stretched out on a bed. He had barely closed his eyes when he heard someone cough apologetically.

"Hello," said the Purple-striped Grabber.

His own personal hallucination had returned to eat him.

"Hello, old chap," Gregor said cheerfully, without a bit of fear or worry.

"Did you eat the apples?"

"Dreadfully sorry. I forgot."

"Oh, well." The Grabber tried to conceal his disappointment. "I brought the chocolate sauce." He held up the can.

Gregor smiled. "You can leave now," he said. "I know you're just a figment of my imagination. You can't hurt me."

"I'm not going to hurt you," the Grabber said. "I'm just going to eat you."

He walked up to Gregor. Gregor held his ground, smiling, although he wished the Grabber didn't appear so solid and undreamlike. The Grabber leaned over and bit his arm experimentally.

He jumped back and looked at his arm. There were toothmarks on it. Blood was oozing out—real blood—*his* blood.

The colonists had been bitten, gashed, torn and ripped.

At that moment, Gregor remembered an exhibition of hypnotism he had once seen. The hypnotist had told the subject he was putting a lighted cigarette on his arm. Then he had touched the spot with a pencil.

Within seconds, an angry red blister had appeared on

the subject's arm, because he *believed* he had been burned. If your subconscious thinks you're dead, you're dead. If it orders the stigmata of toothmarks, they are there.

He didn't believe in the Grabber.

But his subconscious did.

Gregor tried to run for the door. The Grabber cut him off. It seized him in its claws and bent to reach his neck.

The magic word! What was it?

Gregor shouted, *"Alphoisto?"*

"Wrong word," said the Grabber. "Please don't squirm."

"Regnastikio!"

"Nope. Stop wriggling and it'll be over before you—"

"Voorshpellhappilo!"

The Grabber let out a scream of pain and released him. It bounded high into the air and vanished.

Gregor collapsed into a chair. That had been close. Too close. It would be a particularly stupid way to die—rent by his own death-desiring subconscious, slashed by his own imagination, killed by his own conviction. It was fortunate he had remembered the word. Now if Arnold would only hurry . . .

He heard a low chuckle of amusement.

It came from the blackness of a half-opened closet door, touching off an almost forgotten memory. He was nine years old again, and the Shadower—his Shadower—was a strange, thin, grisly creature who hid in doorways, slept under beds and attacked only in the dark.

"Turn out the lights," the Shadower said.

"Not a chance," Gregor retorted, drawing his blaster. As long as the lights were on, he was safe.

"You'd better turn them off."

"No!"

"Very well. Egan, Megan, Degan!"

Three little creatures scampered into the room. They raced to the nearest light bulb, flung themselves on it and began to gulp hungrily.

The room was growing darker.

Gregor blasted at them each time they approached a light. Glass shattered, but the nimble creatures darted out of the way.

And then Gregor realized what he had done. The creatures couldn't actually eat light. Imagination can't make any impression on inanimate matter. He had *imagined* that the room was growing dark and—

He had shot out his light bulbs! His own destructive subconscious had tricked him.

Now the Shadower stepped out. Leaping from shadow to shadow, he came toward Gregor.

The blaster had no effect. Gregor tried frantically to think of the magic word—and terrifiedly remembered that no magic word banished the Shadower.

He backed away, the Shadower advancing, until he was stopped by a packing case. The Shadower towered over him and Gregor shrank to the floor and closed his eyes.

His hands came in contact with something cold. He was leaning against the packing case of toys for the settlers' children. And he was holding a water pistol.

Gregor brandished it. The Shadower backed away, eying the weapon with apprehension.

Quickly, Gregor ran to the tap and filled the pistol. He directed a deadly stream of water into the creature.

The Shadower howled in agony and vanished.

Gregor smiled tightly and slipped the empty gun into his belt.

A water pistol was the right weapon to use against an imaginary monster.

It was nearly dawn when the ship landed and Arnold stepped out. Without wasting any time, he set up his tests. By midday, it was done and the element definitely established as Longstead 42. He and Gregor packed up immediately and blasted off.

Once they were in space, Gregor told his partner everything that had happened.

"Pretty rough," said Arnold softly, but with deep feeling.

Gregor could smile with modest heroism now that he was safely off Ghost V. "Could have been worse," he said.

"How?"

"Suppose Jimmy Flynn were here. There was a kid who could really dream up monsters. Remember the Grumbler?"

"All I remember is the nightmares it gave me," Arnold said.

They were on their way home. Arnold jotted down some

notes for an article entitled "The Death Instinct on Ghost V: An Examination of Subconscious Stimulation, Hysteria, and Mass Hallucination in Producing Physical Stigmata." Then he went to the control room to set the autopilot.

Gregor threw himself on a couch, determined to get his first decent night's sleep since landing on Ghost V. He had barely dozed off when Arnold hurried in, his face pasty with terror.

"I think there's something in the control room," he said.

Gregor sat up. "There can't be. We're off the—"

There was a low growl from the control room.

"Oh, my God!" Arnold gasped. He concentrated furiously for a few seconds. "I know. I left the airlocks open when I landed. We're still breathing Ghost V air!"

And there, framed in the open doorway, was an immense gray creature with red spots on its hide. It had an amazing number of arms, legs, tentacles, claws and teeth, plus two tiny wings on its back. It walked slowly toward them, mumbling and groaning.

They both recognized it as the Grumbler.

Gregor dashed forward and slammed the door in its face. "We should be safe in here," he panted. "That door is airtight. But how will we pilot the ship?"

"We won't," Arnold said. "We'll have to trust the robot pilot—unless we can figure out some way of getting that thing out of there."

They noticed that a faint smoke was beginning to seep through the sealed edges of the door.

"What's that?" Arnold asked, with a sharp edge of panic in his voice.

Gregor frowned. "You remember, don't you? The Grumbler can get into any room. There's no way of keeping him out."

"I don't remember anything about him," Arnold said. "Does he eat people?"

"No. As I recall, he just mangles them thoroughly."

The smoke was beginning to solidify into the immense gray shape of the Grumbler. They retreated into the next compartment and sealed the door. Within seconds, the thin smoke was leaking through.

"This is ridiculous," Arnold said, biting his lip. "To be

hunted by an imaginary monster—wait! You've still got your water pistol, haven't you?"

"Yes, but—"

"Give it to me!"

Arnold hurried over to a water tank and filled the pistol. The Grumbler had taken form again and was lumbering toward them, groaning unhappily. Arnold raked it with a stream of water.

The Grumbler kept on advancing.

"Now it's all coming back to me," Gregor said. "A water pistol never could stop the Grumbler."

They backed into the next room and slammed the door. Behind them was only the bunkroom, with nothing behind that but the deadly vacuum of space.

Gregor asked, "Isn't there something you can do about the atmosphere?"

Arnold shook his head. "It's dissipating now. But it takes about twenty hours for the effects of Longstead to wear off."

"Haven't you any antidote?"

"No."

Once again the Grumbler was materializing, and neither silently nor pleasantly.

"How can we kill it?" Arnold asked. "There must be a way. Magic words? How about a wooden sword?"

Gregor shook his head. "I remember the Grumbler now," he said unhappily.

"What kills it?"

"It can't be destroyed by water pistols, cap guns, firecrackers, slingshots, stink bombs, or any other childhood weapon. The Grumbler is absolutely unkillable."

"That Flynn and his damned imagination! Why did we have to talk about him? How do you get rid of it then?"

"I told you. You don't. It just has to go away of its own accord."

The Grumbler was full size now. Gregor and Arnold hurried into the tiny bunkroom and slammed their last door.

"*Think*, Gregor," Arnold pleaded. "No kid invents a monster without a defense of some sort. *Think!*"

"The Grumbler cannot be killed," Gregor said.

The red-spotted monster was taking shape again. Gregor

thought back over all the midnight horrors he had ever known. He *must* have done something as a child to neutralize the power of the unknown.

And then—almost too late—he remembered.

Under auto-pilot controls, the ship flashed Earthward with the Grumbler as complete master. He marched up and down the empty corridors and floated through steel partitions into cabins and cargo compartments, moaning, groaning and cursing because he could not get at any victim.

The ship reached the Solar System and took up an automatic orbit around the Moon.

Gregor peered out cautiously, ready to duck back if necessary. There was no sinister shuffling, no moaning or groaning, no hungry mist seeping under the door or through the walls.

"All clear," he called out to Arnold. "The Grumbler's gone."

Safe within the ultimate defense against night horrors— wrapped in the blankets that had covered their heads— they climbed out of their bunks.

"I told you the water pistol wouldn't do any good," Gregor said.

Arnold gave him a sick grin and put the pistol in his pocket. "I'm hanging onto it. If I ever get married and have a kid, it's going to be his first present."

"Not for any of mine," said Gregor. He patted the bunk affectionately. "You can't beat blankets over the head for protection."

How many of these Dell Bestsellers have you read?

ROSEMARY'S BABY by Ira Levin   **95c**

GO TO THE WIDOW-MAKER by James Jones   **$1.25**

CAPABLE OF HONOR by Allen Drury   **$1.25**

THE SECRET OF SANTA VITTORIA by Robert Crichton   **95c**

MADAME SARAH by Cornelia Otis Skinner   **95c**

THE FIXER by Bernard Malamud   **95c**

GAMES PEOPLE PLAY by Dr. Eric Berne   **$1.25**

THE DOCTORS by Martin L. Gross   **$1.25**

TAI-PAN by James Clavell   **95c**

THE PAPER DRAGON by Evan Hunter   **95c**

POOR COW by Nell Dunne   **75c**

THE LEMON EATERS by Jerry Sohl   **95c**

The smash bestseller the whole country is talking about!

Rosemary's Baby

by Ira Levin

SUPPOSE you were a young housewife who moved into an old and elegant apartment house with a strange past. SUPPOSE that only after you became pregnant did you suspect that the building harbored a group of devil worshippers who had mastered the art of black magic. SUPPOSE that this satanic conspiracy set out to claim not only your husband but your baby. Well, this is what happened to Rosemary. *Or did it?*

DON'T REVEAL THE ENDING

"The climax is an icy shock which no one will ever quite forget." —*Providence Journal*

Watch for the Paramount movie starring Mia Farrow

A DELL BOOK   95¢

The solid gold bestseller of the year!

OUR CROWD

by Stephen Birmingham

A novelist who has specialized in creating tales of the rich and well-placed now offers his first full-length work of nonfiction; a fascinating insider's view of one of the richest segments of a rich city, Jewish upper-class life in New York.

"A blend of urbanity, compassion and wit . . . always well told, always engrossing"—*Life Magazine*

A DELL BOOK $1.25

A NOVEL

7ᵀᴴ AVE.

**"A novel of sex and ambition. . . . Everybody is
going to be reading SEVENTH AVENUE"**
—Washington Star

SEVENTH AVENUE
by Norman Bogner

*From showroom to bedroom, a bold novel about
New York's glittering fashion world.*

"Norman Bogner has created characters who are real,
capable of being loved, hated, pitied, and above all, believed. His work is about hunger and passion, sex and love,
hatred and revenge, pity and disgust, dissipation and
nobility. It is life."

—Nashville Banner

"The scorching success of Jay Blackman . . . ripping his
way from a two-bit basement peddling rags to become a
multimillionaire operator . . . enormous, penetrating and
perceptive"

—Portland Sunday Telegram

"A narrative gift . . . a sure hand with character . . . con-
vincing . . . impressive"

—Saturday Review Syndicate

A DELL BOOK 95¢